continued . . .

"*Leah's Choice* is a wonderful, fresh addition to the growing collection of novels about the Amish life. Marta Perry has created characters that I came to care for deeply and a plot that kept me guessing at every turn."

—Deborah Raney, author of *Above All Things* and the Hanover Falls novels

"*Leah's Choice* captured me on the first page— complex characters, unexpected conflicts, and deep emotion. Make the right choice. Savor this special book."

—Lyn Cote, author of the Texas: Star of Destiny series

**Other Pleasant Valley novels
by Marta Perry**

LEAH'S CHOICE
RACHEL'S GARDEN

ANNA'S RETURN

Pleasant Valley

BOOK THREE

MARTA PERRY

Doubleday Large Print
Home Library Edition

B

BERKLEY BOOKS, NEW YORK

This Large Print Edition, prepared especially for Doubleday Large Print Home Library, contains the complete, unabridged text of the original Publisher's Edition.

THE BERKLEY PUBLISHING GROUP
Published by the Penguin Group
Penguin Group (USA) Inc.
375 Hudson Street, New York, New York 10014, USA
Penguin Group (Canada), 90 Eglinton Avenue East,
Suite 700, Toronto, Ontario M4P 2Y3, Canada
(a division of Pearson Penguin Canada Inc.)
Penguin Books Ltd., 80 Strand, London WC2R 0RL, England
Penguin Group Ireland, 25 St. Stephen's Green,
Dublin 2, Ireland (a division of Penguin Books Ltd.)
Penguin Group (Australia), 250 Camberwell Road,
Camberwell, Victoria 3124, Australia
(a division of Pearson Australia Group Pty. Ltd.)
Penguin Books India Pvt. Ltd., 11 Community Centre,
Panchsheel Park, New Delhi—110 017, India
Penguin Group (NZ), 67 Apollo Drive, Rosedale,
North Shore 0632, New Zealand
(a division of Pearson New Zealand Ltd.)
Penguin Books (South Africa) (Pty.) Ltd., 24 Sturdee
Avenue, Rosebank, Johannesburg 2196, South Africa

Penguin Books Ltd., Registered Offices: 80 Strand, London
WC2R 0RL, England

ISBN 978-1-61664-550-2

PRINTED IN THE UNITED STATES OF AMERICA

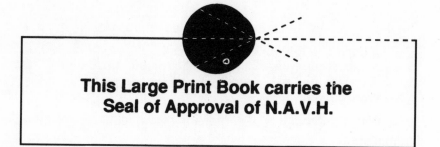

**This Large Print Book carries the
Seal of Approval of N.A.V.H.**

This story is dedicated to the treasured friends whose unfailing encouragement and support helped to make it possible—you know who you are! And, as always, to my husband, Brian, who always believes in me.

ACKNOWLEDGMENTS

I'd like to express my gratitude to those whose expertise, patience, and generosity helped me in the writing of this book: to Erik Wesner, whose *Amish America* newsletters are enormously helpful in visualizing aspects of daily life; to Donald Kraybill and John Hostetler, whose books are the definitive works on Amish life; to Louise Stoltzfus, Lovina Eicher, and numerous others who've shared what it means to be Amish; to the unnamed Plain People whose insights have enriched my life; and most of all to my family, for giving me a rich heritage upon which to draw.

Chapter One

She was beginning to fear that the prodigal daughter wouldn't make it home after all. Anna Beiler pressed on the gas pedal. "Come on, you can do it." The old car responded with nothing more than a shudder.

Daad would probably say that this was what she got for depending on something so English as a car to get her home, and maybe he'd be right. Just the thought of seeing her father made her stomach queasy. How would he, how would any of the family, react to Anna's turning up at her Amish home three years after she'd given up all they believed in to disappear into the English world?

The car gave an ominous sputter. It might be her prized possession, but she didn't know much about its inner workings. Still, that noise and the shaking couldn't be good signs.

She gripped the steering wheel tighter, biting her lip, and faced the truth. She wasn't going to make it to the Beiler farm, the place where she'd been born, the place she'd left in rebellion and disgrace. She'd been almost nineteen then, sure she knew all about the world. Now, at twenty-two, she felt a decade older than the girl she'd been.

But there, just ahead, she spotted the turnoff to Mill Race Road. Two miles down Mill Race was the home of her brother and sister-in-law. Joseph and Myra would welcome her, wouldn't they?

Forced into a decision, she'd have to take that chance. She turned onto the narrow road, earning another protesting groan from the car. Her fingers tensed so much that she'd have to peel them from the steering wheel. Worse, now that she was so close, all the arguments for and against coming here pummeled her mind.

Was this the right choice? Her stomach clenched again. She didn't know. She just knew returning was her only option.

It was strange that things looked the same after three years. Pleasant Valley, Pennsylvania, didn't change, or at least not quickly. Maybe there'd been a little more traffic on the main road, but now that she was off that, not a car was in sight.

The fields on either side of the road overflowed with pumpkins, cabbage, and field corn that had yet to be cut. Neat barns and silos, farmhouse gardens filled with chrysanthemums, sumac topped with the dark red plumes that made them look like flaming torches—this was September in Pennsylvania Dutch country, and she was coming home.

Maybe she should have written, but when had there been time? There'd been no time for anything but to get out of Chicago as quickly as possible. And there was no way she could explain the unexplainable.

She glanced into the backseat, and her heart expanded with love. Gracie slept in her car seat, good as gold, just as she'd been throughout the long trip. At not quite a year old, she could hardly have understood her mother's fear, but she'd cooperated.

The neat white sign for Joseph's machine shop stood where it always had. Anna turned into the narrow gravel lane, determination settling over her. It was far too late to worry if her decision would work. She had to make it work, for Gracie's sake.

Joseph and Myra's place was a hundred-year-old white frame farmhouse, identifiable as Amish only by the fact that no electric lines ran to the house. They owned only a few acres, not enough to farm but plenty for the machine shop that her mechanically minded brother ran.

In the pasture to the right of the lane a bay horse lifted his head, eyeing her curiously, probably wondering what a car was doing here. Tossing his mane, he trotted a few feet beside her along the fence.

If Gracie were awake, she would point out the horsey, something that up until now Gracie had seen only in her picture books. Everything about this place would be strange and new to her.

Not to Anna. For her, it all had an almost heartless familiarity. The very sameness made it seem to her that Pleasant Valley had gotten along quite nicely without her, thank you very much, and could continue to do so.

Joseph's shop was in the large outbuilding at the end of the lane, while off to the left beyond it stood the horse barn. Surely there'd be room in one of them to store the car.

Get it out of sight—that was all she could think. Get the car out of sight, and then they'd be safe.

Maybe she ought to drive straight to the shop. She could park behind it, if nothing else. As if it had read her mind, the car gave one last sputter, a cough, and died, just short of the house.

"No, don't do this," she muttered. She switched the key off and then turned it on again, touching the gas pedal gently.

Nothing. The car seemed to sink down on its wheels, like a horse sagging into clean straw after a hard day's work.

She pounded the steering wheel with the heel of her hand. Still, at least she was here. Joseph would help her, wouldn't he? He'd always had a tender spot for his baby sister.

Mindful that Gracie still slept, Anna slid out of the car, leaving the door open for air, and straightened, groaning a little. Her muscles protested after all those hours in the car, to say nothing of the tension that had ridden with her.

She glanced down at the faded blue jeans, sneakers, and wrinkled shirt she wore. It might be less harrowing for Joseph and Myra if she'd arrived in conventional Amish clothes, but she'd certainly have drawn attention to herself driving a car that way.

Not giving herself time to think about their reaction, she walked quickly to the back door.

She knocked on the screen door, paused, and then knocked again, louder. Nothing. The inner door was closed—odd on a pleasant September day. She opened the screen door, tried the knob, and the realization seeped into her. The luck that had gotten her all the way here from Chicago had run out. No one was home.

She stood on the back step, biting her lip, frowning at the car. The dark blue compact, liberally streaked with rust, had been her friend Jannie's, and now it was hers, the only car she'd ever owned. Pete knew it well, too well. If he'd followed her—

That was ridiculous. Pete couldn't possibly have known where she was going. She had to stop jumping at shadows.

But her common sense seemed to have fled. All she could think was to get the car out of sight and submerge herself and Gracie in the protective camouflage of the Amish community as quickly as possible.

Joseph and Myra were away, but one of their horses might still be in the barn. If she could hitch it to the car, she could tow the vehicle out of sight. Hurrying, she checked the sleeping baby. Gracie still slept soundly, her head turned to one side in the car seat, a small hand unfurling like a leaf next to her face.

Gracie was all right. She just had to keep her that way. Anna turned and jogged toward the barn, urged on by the fear that had pursued her all the way from Chicago.

She slid the heavy door open and blinked at the dimness, inhaling the familiar scents of fresh straw, hay, and animals. From one of the stalls came a soft snort and the thud of hooves as the animal moved. *Thank heaven*. If the horse had been turned out in the field for the day, she might never have caught it.

The bay mare came willingly to her, nosing over the stall boards. It was Myra's buggy horse, most likely. Wherever they were today, they'd taken the one Joseph drove. Did he still have that big roan?

Lifting a lead line from the hook, Anna started to open the stall door.

A board creaked behind her, and she whirled toward the sound, her breath catching.

"What are you doing with that horse?"

A man stood in the open doorway, silhouetted against the light behind him. Not Joseph, for sure, but Amish, to judge by the outline of him and the cadence of the words he'd spoken in English.

Well, of course he'd spoken English. That was what he thought she was, standing there in her jeans and T-shirt—an English woman. A horse thief, maybe.

He moved toward her before she could find the words for an explanation, and she could see him better. Could recognize him.

"It's . . . Samuel Fisher, ain't so?" The Amish phrase she hadn't used in three years came readily to her lips. Samuel was her sister-in-law Myra's brother. Maybe Joseph and Myra had asked him to look after things while they were gone today.

He stopped a few feet from her, assessing her with a slow, steady gaze. Slow, she thought. Yes, that was Samuel. Maybe *deliberate* would be a kinder word. Samuel had never been one to rush into anything.

"So. Anna Beiler. You've come home, then."

He'd switched to Pennsylvania Dutch, and it took her a moment to make the mental change. After so much time away, she even thought in English.

"As you can see."

"It's been a long time."

"Three years." She shifted her weight impatiently from one foot to the other. She didn't have time to stand here chatting with Samuel. The baby could wake—someone could spot the car. "Do you know where Joseph and Myra are?"

He took his time about the answer, seeming to register every detail of her appearance as he did. "They've gone over to Fostertown for the day. Joseph didn't say anything to me about you coming."

"Why should he?" The words snapped out before she could moderate them.

Samuel's strong, stolid face didn't register much change—but then, it never had. His already-square jaw might have gotten a little squarer, his hazel eyes might have turned a bit cold, but that was all.

As for the rest—black suspenders crossed strong shoulders over a light blue work shirt, and a summer straw hat sat squarely on sun-streaked brown hair. He seemed taller and broader than he had when she'd last seen him. Well, they were both older. He'd be twenty-six, now, the same as Joseph.

"Joseph and I are partners in the business, besides him being my brother-in-law," Samuel said, voice mild. "Usually he tells me if he expects somebody, 'specially if he's going to be away."

"Sorry," she muttered. "I didn't mean to be rude. Joseph didn't know I was coming."

"Ja, I see. And you thought you'd take Betsy to go and look for them?"

"No, of course not." Her fingers tightened on the lead rope. "Look, Samuel, I need . . ."

How to explain? There wasn't any way. "I need to put my car in the barn or the shop, but the engine died. I thought I could pull it with Betsy. Will you help me?"

He kept her waiting again, studying her with that unhurried stare. Her nerves twitched.

"Well?" she demanded.

Samuel's firm mouth softened in a slow grin. "I see you're as impatient as ever, Anna Beiler. Ja, I will help you." He took the rope from her, his callused fingers brushing hers. "But I wish I knew what you are up to, I do."

She stepped out of his way as he opened the stall door, talking softly to the animal. He didn't seem to expect any answer to his comment, and she couldn't give one.

What could she say? She could hardly tell him that she'd come home because she had no place else to go—and that she was only staying as long as she had to. Little though she wanted to deceive anyone, she had no choice. Gracie's future depended on it.

.   .   .

Samuel looped the lead rope through the ring in the upright and went to get the harness. The deliberate movements gave him a few moments to consider. Was he doing as Joseph would want?

Well, Joseph might not be happy to have a car stowed in his barn, but he would be wonderful glad to see his little sister home again. Samuel knew him well enough to be sure of that.

He lifted the harness from its rack and carried it to where the mare stood patiently waiting. Anna was not quite so patient, moving back and forth like a nervous animal pacing in its stall.

"I'll harness her up and use a chain to attach her to the car. That should be plenty gut enough to move it, long as we're not going uphill."

She caught the harness strap on the other side of the mare as Samuel tossed it over, pulling it into place. "Where should we take the car, do you think? The barn or the shop?"

He considered. "Joseph might not want it in the shop, where people are in and out every day. Let's put it in the back of the barn for now."

If she was home to stay, she'd be getting rid of the car first thing, he supposed, so what difference did it make? When he'd first spotted the car, and then seen the woman going into the barn, he'd thought it was someone looking for the English couple who lived down the road. Anna Beiler had never entered his mind.

Anna ran her hand down the mare's shoulder, crooning to her, and then reached underneath to fasten a strap.

"Seems like you remember how to do this," he said. "I thought you might have forgotten, after living as an Englischer so long."

"It's coming back to me." Her voice was dry and clipped, all her softness saved for the animal.

Anna had changed, no doubt about that. Those jeans and shirt didn't leave a lot to the imagination. She'd always been slim, but now she was almost skinny.

The blond hair he'd always seen braided neatly back under her prayer covering was now pulled into an untidy knot at the back of her neck. Her slim shoulders were stiff, as if she couldn't let herself relax.

The strain showed in her face, too, in

small lines around her blue eyes and in the tight way she held her mouth. He remembered a rosy face always alive with feeling—either passionately happy or sad or angry. Anna had never done anything by halves. She'd always felt everything more intensely, it had seemed, than anyone else.

Now—well, she looked as if the outside world had knocked all that youthful spirit out of her. The English world could do that. His own experience had taught him well.

He veered away from that thought. What had happened to him outside had nothing to do with Anna.

"What took Joseph and Myra to Fostertown?" She asked the question as if tired of the silence rather than from any need to know. Or maybe she was trying to ease her own tension with talk.

"Myra's expecting again. I suppose you know that." He raised an eyebrow in her direction, not sure how closely in touch she'd stayed with the family.

"No." A faint flush stained her cheeks. "I didn't know."

"The doctor wanted her to have some special blood tests done at the clinic over in Fostertown, so naturally Joseph wanted to go with her. Your sister Leah is watching little Sarah."

"There's nothing wrong with Myra or the baby, is there?"

"Nothing I know about."

He'd seen the worry on Joseph's face lately when he looked at his wife, but if there was a problem, it would be Joseph's decision whether to tell his sister or not.

"How is Leah? And her family?" Anna put the question carefully, not meeting his eyes.

"They're well, as far as I know." He hesitated. How much had Anna been in contact during these past three years? "Your mamm . . ."

She stiffened. "I know about my mother's death."

"I wasn't sure." He picked up the chain and slung it over his shoulder.

"Because I didn't come back for the funeral?" She shot the question at him, hands on her hips.

Defensive, that's what she was.

"It's not my business," he said quietly, and began to lead the mare out of the barn, leaving her to follow.

Anna caught up with him in a few steps. "I'm sorry." She bit off the words.

He shrugged, a little uncomfortable. "It makes no matter. I'm sorry for your loss."

They headed for the car parked in the lane by the kitchen door. "I'm sure Joseph wouldn't mind if you left the car where it is for a bit," he ventured.

"I can't. I don't want to."

Which is it, Anna? Can't or don't want to?

He wouldn't ask the question, because it wasn't his business and she wouldn't tell him, but he did wonder. Something was going on here besides the obvious fact of Anna's return.

"What about you?" Anna glanced at him, maybe wanting to change the subject. "You fence-jumped before I left. When did you come back?"

"I wasn't gone long. Less than a year."

He had a feeling she wouldn't press him on it, not that he couldn't have evaded questions if he'd had to. He'd had plenty of practice.

But Anna wasn't really interested in him—not in what had taken him away or in what had driven him back. She was preoccupied with her own worries, only talking to fill the silence.

"You work with Joseph, you said?" She made it a question.

"Ja, he took me on as partner two years ago. That's my place over there." He jerked his head toward the neighboring house, surrounded by fenced pastures for his horses.

She followed the direction of his nod, staring at the two-story frame house. "That place was owned by an English couple, I thought."

"They sold up and moved south, to get away from the winters, they said. I'm still taking out the electric and such."

It was a big job, but he could take his time about doing it. He had only himself to please. He could do it as he wanted.

Anna shot another glance at him, maybe wondering why he was clean-shaven like a boy. "You're not married?"

"No." It was his turn to be short. He'd had practice evading that question, too, and it surely wasn't Anna's business.

They'd reached the car, and he spoke soothingly to the mare as he backed her up. Betsy was inclined to be a little skittish about anything strange, but he could talk her into doing this.

"Wait a second."

He stopped the horse where she was. Anna darted to the back door of the car and ducked inside. He heard the soft murmur of her voice.

And then she was out again, holding a baby in her arms.

He took his time absorbing that. Anna wouldn't be surprised that he didn't immediately respond. After all, she'd always thought him tediously slow, maybe even stupid, as he recalled.

So, Anna had come back with a child. The little girl looked to be about a year old, with rosy cheeks that hinted she'd just woken up.

Anna had no husband, it seemed. Her ring finger was bare.

Ach, this would set folks talking, for sure, the news flying around the valley faster than fast. As to how her family would take it—well, that he couldn't guess.

"This is my daughter. Her name is Grace. Gracie." Her chin lifted as she spoke, and he saw in her blue eyes a spark of the defiance that the old Anna had had in such abundance.

The child had blue eyes, too, round and wondering as he approached and held out his hand to her. Her hair was silky and as white-blond as corn silk. She considered him for a long moment, her face solemn, and then grabbed at his fingers and giggled.

He broke into a smile. "You're a fine little girl, you are, Gracie." He glanced at Anna and found her looking at the child, her face alight with a fierce, possessive love. "You look a bit like your mammi."

Anna's eyes met his then, wide and un-guarded just for a moment. That look, with all her defenses down, went straight to his heart and stuck there like an axe biting into wood.

"Denke," she said softly. "Thank you. Just let me find a safe place to put her, and I'll help you move the car. Gracie crawls like greased lightning."

"Ach, you don't need to be helping me. I'll take care of it." He jerked a nod toward the back door of the house. "The key is on top of the door frame. Go on inside with the boppli."

She looked as if she'd like to argue the point. Probably didn't want to be beholden to him if she could help it. But instead she nodded, took a bag from the car, and headed for the house.

He watched as she disappeared inside. Then he turned to the horse, patting her absently, his mind struggling to absorb everything that had just happened. Little Anna was back, and she had a boppli.

Small wonder she wore that look of strain. Her situation was difficult for sure. As for her future—that was beyond his imagination.

Relief swept over Anna when she closed the door behind her. At least now she was safe from the chance of being seen, to say nothing of getting away from Samuel's cool gaze.

Had he been judging her? She couldn't be sure, but the idea made her seethe. She'd thought she'd wiped out her quick temper during the difficult years away. Maybe she'd been wrong.

Or maybe it was being back that had her reverting to the old, rebellious Anna. That wasn't a pleasant thought. She'd need all the maturity she'd gained to negotiate the coming weeks, maybe months.

How long? How long until she felt it was safe to stop hiding?

Grace wiggled, fussing a little and reaching toward the floor.

"Down?" She took a quick glance around the kitchen, but of course Myra's kitchen, including the floor, was spotless.

She put Gracie down, smiling as she crawled quickly to the table and, using its leg for support, pulled to her feet, wobbling there. Gracie seemed ready to take a step, but she wasn't quite brave enough yet.

The smile faded quickly. In her bright pink romper and tiny sneakers, Gracie could not be mistaken for an Amish child, any more than anyone would think Anna Amish in her jeans. If she were to succeed in blending in here, that was the first thing that had to change.

"We'll make it," she promised, scooping Gracie up again and kissing the downy hair that curled around her ears. "We will. I promise. I love you, little girl."

Gracie giggled at the kiss and squirmed to be set down again.

"In a minute you can crawl. Right now, let's find something suitable to wear, for both of us."

She walked through the hallway, memory coming back as she did so. Joseph and Myra had been fortunate to be able to buy this house when they first married, thanks to the success of Joseph's machine shop. Her brother was clever with machines, adapting English technology to work in ways the Amish could accept. She felt a familiar impatience with the endless adjustments Amish people made to live in a modern world.

Upstairs, she found Joseph and Myra's bedroom without difficulty but hesitated, not liking to touch Myra's things without permission.

Still, if she knew her sweet, shy sister-in-law as well as she thought she did, Myra would be delighted to lend anything she owned. She'd also probably be vastly relieved to see Anna in traditional garb rather than English clothes.

Anna put Gracie down on the rag rug beside the bed and rummaged in the diaper bag for her favorite ball. "There you are. Be good while Mammi gets dressed."

Quickly, before her qualms overcame her, she looked through Myra's things. Luckily they were about the same size, so that shouldn't be much of a problem.

She found a dress and apron combination in a deep forest green hanging from a hook.

"This will work," she said to Gracie, who was picking at a dark red color in the rug with one tiny finger. "You'll be surprised when you see how I look."

She peeled off her jeans and T-shirt and pulled on a plain white slip. Next she slid the dress over her head. Funny, to feel it flutter around her legs. She frowned for a moment, trying to remember the knack of fastening the bodice with the seven straight pins, but it came back to her almost at once.

Now the apron, and the black stockings. Her sneakers would be acceptable, so she wouldn't have to raid Myra's shoes.

She stood for a moment when she'd finished, rubbing her palms on the skirt of the dress, until she realized that her hair was still pulled back in an elastic.

Again, her fingers seemed to remember what to do as she twisted her hair into a bun. She had cut her hair first thing when she'd decided to leave, as a gesture of independence, but she'd soon found it hard to deal with and let it grow again. It wasn't as long as most Amish women's, but the bun and kapp would hide that. She settled one of Myra's white prayer kapps into place.

Prayer. She'd done a great deal of that in the past year, struggling to find her way, struggling to hear God's comfort and guidance.

But often her frantic pleadings seemed to fall on deaf ears. Maybe she'd neglected God for so long that He had forgotten her.

She looked at Gracie. No, she hadn't been forgotten, or she wouldn't have this beautiful, precious child.

Denke, she whispered silently. *Thank You.*

It took her a few more minutes to find something of her little niece's that Gracie could wear, but finally she was satisfied. They would pass for any Amish mother and daughter. She could probably walk right past someone who'd known her in Chicago. Most of them would only turn to stare at the clothing, not noticing the woman who wore it.

That was the idea, she reminded herself, carrying Gracie back down to the kitchen. Dress humbly, modestly, so that you don't stand out or draw attention to yourself. It was the community of believers that was important, not any single individual.

She'd rejected that when she left, but now she needed it, would rely on it.

Once in the kitchen she put Gracie in the wooden high chair next to the table. "Let's find you something to eat. You must be hungry, ain't so?"

She blinked, a little surprised at herself. Would it be that easy for her to go back to talking Amish, thinking Amish?

And being Amish? The voice of her conscience questioned. *Are you ready for that? Or are you playing a part?*

She pushed the thought away. Get something for Gracie to eat—

The back door opened. Samuel stood there, filling the doorway, his mouth agape. This must be the first time she'd actually disturbed that stolid countenance of his.

"Do I look Amish again?" Sure of herself on this, at least, she watched him.

He lifted those level eyebrows that gave

him such a serious expression. "You forgot something."

"What?"

He pulled a paper towel from the rack
and handed it to her. "Amish women don't
wear stuff on their lips."

The lack of mirrors had done her in.
She'd forgotten the lipstick. Quickly she
scrubbed her lips with the towel until it no
longer came away with the slightest tinge
of color.

"Better?"

"Ja. You don't need that stuff anyway."

"That might almost be a compliment,
Samuel. If it weren't for your disapproving
frown." She let her irritation show in her
voice. "I should think you'd be a little more
understanding than most people."

Her tart words didn't make a dent in his
composure.

"Ja, I was a fence-jumper, too." The words
seemed heavy, as if laden with something.
Guilt, maybe? "That's how I know it's not
easy to come back. Do you think you can
be again the girl you were?"

"I don't want to be." The words came
out quickly, before she had a chance to
think that she didn't want to have this con-

versation with him. She shrugged. "I'm three years older. Maybe a little wiser, I hope."

"And you're certain-sure you're ready to be Amish again?"

The question pricked at her, sending her tension soaring. Did he see through her so easily? No, he couldn't possibly know why she'd returned. No one could.

She squared her shoulders, facing him. "My readiness will be a question for my family to answer." *Not you.*

"True enough." He glanced out the door at the sound of buggy wheels. "I suppose you'll know that soon. Here they are."

CHAPTER TWO

Myra passed another plate for Anna to dry. She gave her a shy smile, as if still getting used to having this unexpected guest in her house.

"You didn't have to help. I'm used to doing the supper dishes by myself, I am."

"I'm glad to do it." Besides, it might keep her from thinking too much.

Myra glanced across the kitchen to where almost-three-year-old Sarah played on the floor with her new little cousin, as if checking to be sure they were all right. So far, at least, the girls seemed happy to share the blocks, but who knew how long that would last?

Myra turned back to the sink, plunging her hands into the sudsy water. "It's wonderful gut to have someone to talk to over the dishes. To tell the truth, I missed this time with my sister once I was married." She flushed a little. "Not that I'd want Joseph to think I had any regrets. But we used to have the best talks while we were doing the dishes. I'll bet you and Leah did, too."

"Ja, that we did."

At the thought of her older sister, Anna's throat muscles contracted. Even with the ten years' difference in their ages, she and Leah had always been close. When she left, Leah had been the only one who seemed to understand.

She'd promised Leah that she'd stay in touch. She hadn't kept that promise. She hadn't been here for Leah's wedding or the birth of her little girl or when Mamm had died. Could Leah forgive that?

She cleared her throat, trying to evade those thoughts. Things she'd been able to banish to the back of her mind when she was far away were loud and insistent here, demanding answers.

"I want to thank you again for the use of the clothes." She brushed at a tiny soap bubble that had landed on her sleeve. "It's kind of you."

"Ach, it's nothing at all." Myra might not know just how to react to her sister-in-law's return, but she followed her generous heart. "I'm happy to share them. I'm not sure I have the black covering for church for a single woman . . ." She stopped, a flush mounting her cheeks. "I mean . . ."

"I'm not married." Anna pushed the words out, steeling herself for the response. This was how it would be, trying to explain herself to the family and the community. She'd better get used to saying those words. "But the white one is fine."

After all, how silly would that feel, to be wearing the single woman's black kapp with a baby sitting on her lap? She hadn't even thought of what it would be like to go to worship here again, to feel all those people watching her.

Myra, at least, had no condemnation in her eyes. "I'll get out another dress or two for you," she said, avoiding the subject of whether Anna would wear the black kapp expected of a single woman at worship.

"Denke," she said softly. Unexpected tears stung her eyes, and she blinked them away. She must be tired. She never cried.

It had been a very long day. She could only be thankful that Gracie had slept so much in the car. Of course that meant that now she was full of energy. The baby banged a block on the floor, getting a quick smile from Myra.

"Ach, your Gracie is such a bright little one. So active, too. She must keep you busy."

"She does that." Of course, back in Chicago, other people had cared for Gracie while she worked double shifts, trying to bring in enough money to support the two of them. That would seem strange to someone like Myra.

It wouldn't be necessary here, she realized. At least, not if the family welcomed her back.

She concentrated on the plate she was drying. If she looked at Myra, Myra might see the fear in her eyes.

Her heart filled with a longing she hadn't anticipated. If only the others reacted as

Joseph had . . . with concern, yes, but also with immediate love and support.

It all depended on Daadi; all three of them realized that. Even as they'd talked over the supper table, she'd known that was what lurked in Joseph's mind, behind his words.

Samuel hadn't been there, though he apparently usually took his lunch and supper with Joseph and Myra. He'd made an excuse to leave so that they could talk, showing more consideration than she'd expected.

The moment the meal was over and the silent prayer after the meal had been said, Joseph had pushed back his chair.

"I'll go over and tell Daad you're here." His smile had tried to reassure her. "That's the first thing, ain't so?"

It was what she had intended, if only the car had cooperated. Instead she'd landed here, putting her problems onto Joseph and Myra.

She rubbed the plate with the towel, trying not to think beyond the action of the moment, but she couldn't stop her churning thoughts.

"Joseph should be back soon." Myra probably meant the words to be reassuring.

She nodded. What was happening with Daadi? How was he reacting?

He'd always been fair. That was the first thing people said about Elias Beiler; he was fair.

But he'd babied her, just a bit, she saw now. The last of the family, the girl who'd finally come along nearly ten years after Leah—yes, Daadi had been easier on her, and she'd tried his patience sorely.

And now she was doing it again. Returning after all these years without a word, an unmarried woman with a baby . . .

She hadn't even come when Mamm died. It was all very well to justify it in her mind—happening as it did just when Gracie was born, when Jannie was dying. But Daad might not . . .

Myra touched her hand gently. "Don't worry so."

She tried to smile, but the effort failed. "I can't help it. If only Daad will see me, I'll tell him how sorry I am. I'll tell him—"

But what could she say? Back in Chicago, coming here had seemed a simple solution to the nightmare that surrounded her. She would come home and disappear into the tightly knit Amish community where Gracie would be safe. She hadn't thought enough about what it would mean both to her and to the family.

"Joseph will do a gut job of telling him." Myra patted her hand. "You can count on him."

Myra had always thought the sun rose and set on her young husband. Anna loved him, too, but she had a more realistic picture of Joseph's ability to communicate such difficult news.

She heard the clop of the horse's hooves in the lane, the creak of the buggy. Drying her hands twice over, she tried to swallow the lump in her throat. Joseph would have done his best, but what if it wasn't enough? What if Daad wouldn't see her?

The door opened. Joseph came in, his face impassive, and she took an impulsive step toward him.

"What did he say?" Her heart was in her throat.

"Ask him yourself." He stepped aside, and she saw that Daadi was behind him.

"Daadi . . ." Her voice caught on the words, her mouth dry. "I'm sorry . . ."

Before she could get anything else out,

her father had crossed the kitchen in a few long strides and swept her into his arms.

She couldn't have spoken then, not for anything. Her tears spilled over, wetting the soft cotton of his shirt, and she let them fall.

Strong arms around her, comforting her, just as Daadi had held her the time she'd fallen from the apple tree when one of the boys had dared her to climb higher. She'd broken her arm, and her next older brother, Mahlon, had earned a whipping for such a foolish dare.

Daadi had held her then, letting her cry, while Mammi ran for something to immobilize the arm. His shirt had felt as it did now—soft and warm against her cheek, smelling of the clean fresh air that had dried it.

She wasn't six any longer. She shouldn't weep on her father's chest. But it was so comforting to feel the safety and security of that embrace that she didn't want to let go.

"Ach, it's all right." His voice was husky. "Don't cry anymore, little one. It's wonderful gut to have you here again at last."

The love and forgiveness in his voice threatened to bring on another bout of crying, but she stifled it. She drew back, wiping her eyes with her hands.

"I'm sorry—" she began again, but he silenced her with a shake of his head.

"Enough of that," he said. "I must meet my new little grandchild."

Fighting for control, she nodded to where Gracie sat on the floor. Daad's eyes misted, his mouth trembling just a little above the beard that was nearly all white now. He moved to the children, squatted down.

Sarah threw herself at him, of course, and he hugged and kissed her, greeting her gently.

"So," he said, once Sarah was satisfied with her share of attention. He extended a hand to Gracie. "This is little Gracie, ja? Wie bist du heit. It's gut to meet you."

Gracie stared at him for a moment, her blue eyes round. She reached a chubby baby hand and grasped his white beard.

He chuckled. "Ja, that is real, it is." He held out his hands to her. "Will you come to me, Gracie?"

She studied him for another moment, as if trying to make a decision. Then she smiled and reached for him. Murmuring something so soft only the baby could hear, Daadi lifted her in his arms, holding her as close as he'd held Anna.

Anna blinked back tears that threatened to overflow again. *Now was the moment.* She should tell Daadi the whole story now. She should trust that when he knew, he'd help her.

But he was bouncing Gracie in his arms, his face filled with love. Joseph and Myra were smiling, arms around each other's waist as if they had to touch at this moment, too. And emotion she hadn't anticipated had a stranglehold on her throat.

"We must have some cake and coffee, for soon it will be time to put these little ones to bed." Myra wiped away a tear and hustled to the stove, lifting the coffeepot. "Komm, Joseph, fetch the applesauce cake from the pantry for me."

Joseph, with a quick wink at Anna, did as he was told. The moment when she might have spoken was gone.

Maybe that was just as well. She took the plates and forks Myra handed her and began to put them on the table, as swift and smooth as if she were back working in the restaurant again. Sooner or later she must tell Daadi, at least, everything about Gracie.

But later would be better, wouldn't it, when he'd had a chance to get used to having her here again?

And could she—should she—really tell him everything? Gracie was the important thing. Anna had to be sure of keeping Gracie safe above all, even if it meant putting a barrier between herself and her family.

"Now," her father said a few minutes later, feeding Gracie a small crumb of applesauce cake, "we must decide where you and the little one are going to live. Joseph, what do you think?"

He was consulting her brother, not her, and making the decision for her as automatically as he'd always done. Once that would have provoked an angry outburst. But she'd learned control during her time away. She couldn't afford to indulge in emotion now.

Joseph folded his hands and looked at Myra, and she gave a tiny nod. "Anna can stay here."

"That's gut of you both." Daad nodded, as if it was no more than he'd expected. "But Anna and her baby should have the right to move back into her old room at the farm, if she wants."

Now it was her turn to exchange glances with Joseph. Levi, their oldest brother, and his wife, Barbara, ran the farm with their growing family, while Daadi had moved into the small daadi haus. Living with Levi and Barbara would be like stepping onto a whirling carousel. Dizzying at best, even if she could contrive to keep from getting annoyed with Barbara's well-meant meddling twenty-five times a day.

"Denke, Daadi, but I think that would make things too crowded for Levi and Barbara." She glanced at Myra. "If you're sure . . . With another baby on the way, you might rather have your privacy."

Something, some faint shadow, crossed Myra's face, but then she was smiling. "Ja, we're sure. We have plenty of room." She reached across the table to squeeze Anna's hand. "And besides, it will be gut to have a sister in the house again."

Anna couldn't speak for the emotion that welled in her. She could only look at the faces around the table, reflected in the mellow glow of the gas lamp above them. Plain faces, filled with love for her.

And she sat here accepting their love, their help, and all the while she was hiding the truth from them.

The sun had barely finished drying the grass, but Samuel wanted to get in a few minutes' worth of working the new bay gelding on the lunge line before he started at the machine shop. With the line in one hand and a buggy whip in the other, he started the animal trotting in a wide circle around him.

The field next to the lane gave him a near view of Joseph's house, making it impossible not to think about Anna's arrival. And to wonder what had happened when the family found out.

The young horse, distracted by a car going past out on the blacktop road, broke gait, and began to canter. Samuel stopped it and started it again. Patience and repetition—that was what it took to make a gut driving horse.

The screen door banged as Joseph came out on the back porch, saw him, and waved. With both hands occupied, all Samuel could do was nod.

Joseph had certainly been wonderful

happy to see his baby sister again. He wasn't
one to hold grudges or dwell on problems.
Quick to forgive, forget, and move on. He
was sometimes too quick to want unpleas-
antness over, maybe. Joseph would sure
never be the one to ask hard questions.

Forgiveness was part and parcel of
Amish life, and usually in a case like this,
families welcomed the penitent home with
joy. Anna's situation was more complicated
than most, though. She'd come home with
a baby.

He frowned, narrowing his eyes against
the sun. Something else bothered him
about Anna's attitude. He couldn't quite
put his finger on it, but he'd sensed something. If you'd been through a challenging
situation yourself, it seemed to give you
an extra measure of understanding and
maybe an obligation to help someone else
going through it.

He backed away from that unwelcome
thought. Anna had plenty of family to as-
sist her through this difficult time, to say
nothing of Bishop Mose and the rest of the
community.

Elias Beiler had come to the house last
night with Joseph, not that Samuel had

been spying on his neighbors. He'd been in the midst of scraping tractor-patterned wallpaper off the walls of the bedroom that faced Joseph's place, and the windows had given him a clear view.

He'd just been thinking it was a bit of a shame he'd had to get rid of those tractors, put up by the elderly couple who'd sold him the house. They'd wanted to make the room special when their grandsons came to stay. He'd glanced out the window and seen Joseph's buggy pull up the lane, and recognized Elias sitting next to him.

So that was all right. If the head of the family accepted Anna and her babe, the rest would as well.

For some reason, the thought of Anna was like a splinter under his skin. He couldn't forget how she'd looked yesterday—drained and exhausted, with all that sassy cheerfulness wiped off her face.

He knew from his own experience that people didn't find it easy to shed the outside world. Anna had been gone three years. She'd had a child. That was very different from the usual young Amish male taking off for a few months or a year, with the thought always in the back of his mind that he'd come home when he was ready to be baptized, join the church, and marry an Amish girl.

Anna's experience was not like that, and more different still from his own.

Turning as he gave the command to walk, he saw her. He hadn't heard her come out, but Anna stood by the fence, the little girl in her arms. She was obviously talking to the child about the horse—something maybe little Grace hadn't seen in her young life.

He let the gelding walk for another moment or so, gradually drawing in the line so that the circle grew smaller. Finally he stopped him, rubbing his neck and murmuring words of praise in his ear. The bay pricked his ear to listen.

He turned. Anna was still there. Leading the horse, he walked over to her.

"Anna." He nodded. "Do you think the boppli would like to see the horse up close?"

"What do you think, Gracie?" Her voice was soft with love when she spoke to the child. "Look at the horsey. Do you want to touch him?"

Gracie babbled something that might have been approval, and he moved the horse a bit closer to the fence so that her small hand could touch its mane. The bay gave a little shiver of the skin, as if he'd been brushed by a butterfly.

"You look better today. Not so tired," he added quickly, thinking Anna might take offense at the comment sounding so personal.

She did stare at him for a second, but then she smiled, a little quirk of the lips that wasn't very convincing. "I did sleep well last night. And Gracie slept soundly in her borrowed crib, didn't you, love?"

She tickled the baby, and when Gracie chortled, Anna's face lit with pleasure, too. For a moment he seemed to see the girl she had been—always alive with emotion, ready to plunge headlong into anything.

"I'd think you could take it easy for a few days, now that you've got through the hard part of telling the folks you're here."

Her gaze evaded his. "I made peace with Daad, if that's what you mean. I haven't seen any of the others yet, except Joseph and Myra."

"As long as you're settled with your daaad, they'll all fall in line. You'll see."

She lifted her brows, blue eyes sparking a bit. "Is that the voice of experience speaking?"

"I guess it is." Maybe it was as well to change the subject before she got riled. "Was Joseph all right with where I put the car?"

She nodded. "You know how he is about machinery. He'll probably be taking it apart before long, just to see if he can figure out what's wrong."

"Ja, that's for sure. Joseph never met a machine he didn't like."

"I see you're still as attached to horses as you used to be." She patted the gelding's neck. "I thought you said you were working with Joseph in the shop."

"I am. The horses are just a little sideline. Somehow folks got the idea that I have a gift with unruly beasts. So they bring all their troublesome ones to me."

"You always had that talent. You helped my daad with that mare that tried to kick the buggy to pieces, and you were probably only about fourteen at the time."

He grinned, surprised she remembered. That day was still clear in his own thoughts, because it was the day he'd recognized his gift.

He'd been over at the Beiler place for some reason, had seen Elias putting the new horse between the shafts, Anna watching him. No sooner had Elias turned his head than the silly beast went crazy, rearing and kicking so fierce no one could get near him.

He hadn't stopped to think, just grabbed the horse's head and held on, talking softly all the time. He'd gotten a few bruised ribs for his trouble, but he'd calmed the animal down. He could still see Anna's shocked, scared face.

"I think that was the day I figured out soft words worked on horses, especially when they're trouble."

"This one doesn't look like trouble. He's a beauty." She rubbed the gelding's face, and he blew gently at her hand, accepting the praise.

"He's okay. This one I picked up for myself, off the harness track. He's a bit flighty, but he'll settle down in time."

There might have been a touch of pridefulness in the words, he warned himself. If he was gut with horses, it was because the Lord had given the gift, and no praise to himself for it.

The baby, maybe feeling left out, waved her hand at the horse, who jerked his head back, startled.

"There, now, silly beast." He spoke in the animal's ear. "You don't need to be afraid of a beautiful little girl like Gracie."

Anna caught the baby's hand, holding it still in hers. "Denke, Samuel. Of course I think she's beautiful, but I still like to hear other people say it."

"You're a proud mamm, is all. You're fortunate to have her, even if . . ." He let that trail off, since there was no gut way that he could see for that sentence to end.

"Even if I don't have a husband?" She said the words quietly, but her lips had tensed. "Husband or not, I am fortunate to have her, and I wouldn't trade that for anything."

It didn't come easy to him to talk about it, but he couldn't leave it at that, or Anna would think he was passing judgment on her.

"I should have just said that you're fortunate to have her, Anna. I don't know that I'll ever . . ."

He stopped, wanting to bite his tongue. That slip proved that he was better off as he was—deliberate in thought, slow to speak—because anything else got him in trouble.

"Don't you want to have a family?" Anna, of course, was on it in a second.

"Ja, sure I do." He turned to the horse, using that as an excuse not to meet her gaze. "I didn't mean anything else."

Anna was curious—he could feel it flowing from her. A few years ago, if she had been curious, she'd have fired questions until she got the answers she wanted. Now, it seemed, she'd gained a little control over her tongue.

He had to be grateful for that, because he wasn't going to show his feelings, not to her or to anyone else. It was enough that he knew for himself what his limitations were. He'd never take on anything that he couldn't be sure of carrying through. And marriage—how could he chance that? How could he know he wouldn't turn out just like his father?

CHAPTER THREE

Anna's stomach churned so badly that it would be a wonder if she could swallow a thing at the family picnic they were headed toward the next day. It didn't help that Joseph had suggested she and the baby ride with Samuel, since the larger buggy Joseph envisioned for his growing family was yet to be built.

Samuel's buggy rolled down the road at a steady rate, and thank goodness he didn't seem inclined to chat. She alternated between feeling that the buggy was getting her there before she was ready and thinking how slow it was in comparison to a car.

At least the horse wouldn't break down. She gave a fleeting thought to her own car, still safely hidden in the back of Joseph's barn. He hadn't mentioned it, and she wouldn't.

As for Daadi, he hadn't questioned how his erring daughter had gotten back to the fold. He'd just been happy to welcome her home.

Would the rest of them act as generously? She had no idea.

She glanced at Samuel, his big hands steady on the lines, and looked away as quickly. It seemed that as Joseph's partner and Myra's brother, Samuel was automatically included in family events. She'd feel a bit less stressed about this meeting if he weren't there looking on.

Or maybe she wouldn't. Maybe there was nothing that would lower her tension except getting this over with.

She cradled Gracie in her arms. The baby had been lulled to sleep by the movement of the buggy within minutes of starting the trip.

Samuel tilted his head to smile at Gracie. "Sarah always used to fall asleep like that in the buggy. I guess little ones like the rocking."

"I just hope Gracie doesn't wake up cross. She has a lot of relatives to meet. I want her to make a good impression." She touched a small, relaxed hand with her fingertip.

"Cranky? Myra says she's the best behaved boppli she's seen, including her own."

So he and Myra had been talking about Gracie, and, by extension, about her probably. Her cheeks warmed. She'd better get used to that. Her return would be the source of plenty of gossip in the valley, just as her leaving had been.

Then she'd just gone away, slamming the door on Pleasant Valley and its opinions. Now she had to find a way to bear the results of her actions.

"You should have been around when she was teething." It took an effort to sound relaxed. "We were both up most of the night, and me struggling to stay awake at work the next day."

"You had a hard time of it." He said it matter-of-factly, but she thought she caught an undertone of pity in his deep voice.

She shrugged, the sense of his pity making her want to squirm. But she wouldn't let him know that. "Not worse than a lot of other people, I guess."

She'd made her choices. She would live with the consequences.

The buggy slowed as Samuel followed Joseph into the lane at the farm. Now memories crowded in upon her, whispering relentlessly in her ear. There was the apple tree and the little seat hanging from a low branch that Daadi had fixed for her. Levi and Barbara's children probably used it these days.

Her gaze went to the window of her bedroom on the second floor of the neat white farmhouse. Who slept there now?

She'd been lucky, her brothers had always said, getting a room of her own. But Mamm had declared that with ten years between her and Leah, they shouldn't have to share.

Her stomach tightened even more at the thought of her sister. What was Leah thinking about her return? Anna hadn't been kind to her that last summer, yet Leah had been the only one who'd seemed to understand. Even when Anna lay in the hospital, to blame for the accident that had put her there, Leah had been by her side.

Anna cleared her throat. "How are they— What is everyone saying about my coming back, do you know?"

Samuel's broad shoulders moved slightly, as if he started to shrug but thought better of it. "There hasn't been much time for me to hear anything, now has there?"

"That sounds pretty evasive. You may as well tell me, whatever it is."

"Your brother Mahlon's eager to see you," he offered, as if that might make up for something. "You know he and Esther Miller married, don't you?"

"Ja." Thanks to Myra, she did. That had happened after she'd lost touch with Leah.

Not lost touch. The voice of her conscience was stern. *You broke off contact, because you didn't want to tell her what was going on in your life. Be honest with yourself, at least.*

"What about Levi?"

Her oldest brother had taken over the farm when it got to be too much for Daadi after Mamm's first bout with cancer. Levi was close to Daad—would that make his attitude toward her better or worse?

Now Samuel did shrug. "I haven't talked to him. No point crossing bridges before you get to them, is there?"

"This bridge is only a few feet away," she said. "If you've heard he's angry with me, I'd rather know."

"I see you still want to have all the answers, Anna. Just like you did when you were little." His lips curved slightly.

"Actually, I thought I had all the answers, as I recall." She'd been so sure of herself once.

Samuel gave a small sound that might have been a chuckle. "Ja, I thought I knew a bit about life before I jumped the fence. It didn't take long out there to show me how dumb that was."

"I know the feeling." She made the admission before she stopped to think that she didn't want to confide in Samuel. Or anyone else, if she could help it. "But about Levi—"

"You're as persistent as a horsefly, Anna. I don't know, but surely Levi and Barbara wouldn't be having everyone here to greet you if they were mad at you, ain't so?" Samuel's reasonable tone began to sound a bit strained.

"They would if Daadi wanted it." They'd respect his judgment outwardly, even if they disagreed. "Let me guess. It's Barbara, isn't it? She never liked me."

Samuel glanced at her face. "You didn't give her a lot of reason to like you, now did you?"

"Maybe not."

She'd been a rebellious teenager then. Barbara had been only too ready to give advice, and she'd been just as ready to resent it. Just as she resented the fact that Samuel seemed able to see right through her.

"Leave it," Samuel said, his voice gentling. "We're here. Everyone will get used to having you back. Things will be just like they were before."

He pulled up to the hitching rail, and the buggy stopped.

Samuel was right. They were here, and it was time to stop worrying and face everyone.

But he was wrong, too. Because things would never go back to being the same. They couldn't.

Samuel dropped to the ground before she could move. He took her arm in support as she stepped down, Gracie in her arms.

"It will be all right," he said, his hand warm and strong against her sleeve. "You'll see. They're your family. You can trust them, if you can trust anyone in this world."

Before she could respond to his unexpected support, she was swamped by a crowd of young nieces and nephews, all clamoring to see their new cousin. Head spinning, Anna tried to sort them all out. The children, at least, were glad to see them.

"Ach, what a noisy bunch of kinder." Daadi waded through the flock of grandchildren. "The boppli is sleeping. Can you not see that?"

But even as he spoke, Gracie stirred, lashes fluttering, and opened her eyes. She looked around wonderingly. With her cheeks rosy from sleep and her blond hair curling damply against her neck, she looked like a baby doll.

"She's near as pretty as my baby sister."

It took a moment for Anna to count up ages and realize that this tall young girl was Elizabeth, Leah's stepdaughter.

"Elizabeth, you're nearly a grown-up woman now, aren't you?"

Elizabeth's naturally serious expression relaxed in a smile. "I was eleven my last birthday, Aunt Anna. Can I carry Gracie? I help my mammi with Rachel all the time."

At a slight nod from Daad, Anna passed Gracie over. "She might be a little cross," she warned. "She just woke up."

But Gracie seemed entranced with her big cousin. She caught hold of the string of Elizabeth's prayer cap, and the girl grinned. "That's just what Rachel used to do when I held her. She's two now, so she doesn't like to be held so much, you know."

"Come along," Daad said. "No need to stand here when there's folks waiting to greet you."

Anna took a breath and hoped she didn't look as nervous as she felt. "I guess not."

They started toward the house, Elizabeth bearing the baby proudly. Her younger brother had Myra's Sarah by the hand, chattering away to her, and Levi's two boys were already racing each other to the porch, their little sister trotting after them.

The porch, and the waiting cluster of people. For a moment no one else moved. Anna's eyes seemed to see them as an outsider would, as a group of solemn, archaically dressed strangers. Then one figure started toward them, running a few steps, and Leah threw her arms around her.

"Anna. You're home at last." Leah pressed her cheek against Anna's, and Anna wasn't sure whether the tears came from her or her sister.

"Ja, I am." But even as she said the words, guilt pricked at her. Home? It was home, but not in the sense that Leah meant. Leah thought she was here to stay.

She'd given this life up three years ago. She belonged to the outside world now. This place was only a refuge, until she felt it was safe to leave.

Leah drew back, studying her face, her green eyes intent and serious. In spite of all the times they'd quarreled, Leah had been the one to understand her the most. She'd even understood why, after the accident, Anna had had to leave.

For an instant, panic edged through her. It was as if Leah looked right into her and saw all that she was trying to hide.

Anna turned away, hoping she'd done it quickly enough to mask her feelings, and returned her brother Mahlon's warm hug. She stood back, gazing up at him. "You can't still be growing, can you? You seem bigger to me."

"That's my Esther's fine cooking," he said, his ruddy face flushing with pleasure. He reached out and drew his bride to him. "You remember Esther, ja?"

"That I do." She hesitated a moment, not sure how to greet the girl who'd married her brother a year ago last November in a wedding she'd missed.

But Esther seemed to have no qualms about following her husband's lead. She pressed her cheek against Anna's. "Wilkom, Anna. Wilkom home."

Over her shoulder, Anna saw Leah picking Gracie up, holding her in a close embrace. Something that had been tense inside her seemed to ease. It was going to be all right, wasn't it?

Barbara marched off the porch, managing not to look at Anna. She clapped her hands. "The food is ready. Komm, we must eat while it is hot."

A moment of silence followed, and then came Daadi's voice. "We will all greet Anna first. Then it will be time enough to eat." He fixed Barbara with a firm stare.

A flush mottled Barbara's round cheeks. "Ja, ja," she said quickly. "I didn't mean anything else."

But she had. And maybe, despite the hugs and the welcomes, there were others who weren't best pleased to see Anna again.

By the time supper was over, Samuel realized he'd started to relax. Funny, that he hadn't recognized how tense he felt. Not for himself. For Anna.

They sat around the picnic table, all the adults. The children had gone off to play, the older ones watching the younger, except for Gracie, who sat on Anna's lap, chewing contentedly on a wooden rattle Leah had given her.

So things were all right between Anna and her older sister? He wasn't sure. On the surface, Leah had welcomed her warmly, but an outside observer like he was could see the awkwardness that still lay between them.

"More pie, Samuel?" Barbara held a slice of apple crumb pie out temptingly, but he shook his head.

"It's wonderful gut, but I couldn't find a

place to put it. Give it to your husband, won't you?"

"Ach, Levi will be having it for a bedtime snack, like as not." She moved around the table, but getting no takers for the pie, she slid back into her seat next to Levi. And fixed her gaze on Anna.

As if aware of that stare, Anna moved slightly. She was feeling uncomfortable, that was certain-sure. He remembered that feeling from his own return, even though the circumstances had been different. It was a sense of being caught between two worlds and belonging to neither.

She'd get over it. Even now she was joining in the easy talk from time to time. With the baby to consider, she had every reason to sink back into the life she'd left with no second thoughts.

Unlike him. She'd come back, he supposed, because she wanted to raise her child here. He'd come back because he had to.

That was the difference between them. He'd never know, not for certain-sure, whether his commitment was solid. Or whether, like his father, he had it in him to let everyone down.

"So, Anna." Barbara broke into a conversation about the right time for harvesting the pumpkins. "Why didn't you marry the boppli's father?"

Silence fell around the table, broken only by an indrawn breath or two. Barbara had the reputation of saying things other people didn't dare, but this time she'd outdone herself.

Anna had paled. A ridiculous longing to protect her swept through Samuel. She wouldn't want to answer a question like that here, in front of everyone. But wouldn't it be better to get it out, once and for all?

Please, Lord . . .

"Barbara, I thought better of you than to ask that. Anna's reasons are between her and God. The bishop will speak to her about it, not you."

Elias's voice was as severe as he'd ever heard it. Even Levi, who usually went along with his brash wife, seemed to shrink away from her.

It was true enough, what Elias said. But . . .

Trust them, Anna. Trust. I didn't, and I've grieved ever since.

"I . . . I didn't mean . . ." Barbara had turned brick red at the rebuke.

"It's all right." Anna seemed to straighten where she sat, as if preparing herself for a trial. Her hand caressed the boppli's head. She shot Samuel a glance. "Samuel reminded me that I should trust you. And I do."

She sucked in a breath. "There was never a question of marrying the baby's father. Gracie is mine—has been since her birth mother put her into my arms, but I didn't bear her. Gracie's mother was my dearest friend. I made a promise to her when she was dying that Gracie would be my daughter. She is, and she always will be."

CHAPTER FOUR

Anna held her breath, looking at the faces around the table. She shouldn't have blurted it out that way. What had happened to her resolve to let them believe Gracie had been born to her?

She couldn't do it. When it came right down to it, she couldn't lie to them. Ironic, after all the lying she'd managed to do during her rebellious rumspringa. That girl seemed pretty far away now.

Still no one spoke. They were waiting for Daadi, she knew. She couldn't read anything from his expression, and her heart grew cold. The others—well, there she saw doubt and questions.

Her gaze collided with Samuel's, and she looked away quickly. He shouldn't be here for this. It was private, between her and her family.

Except that maybe they weren't her family any longer. If they couldn't accept that Gracie was her child, she'd have to leave.

The thought was there, in her mind, when her father finally spoke. "You must tell us more, Anna. Help us to understand."

Convince you I'm telling the truth, you mean? The quick, defensive words were there in her mind. A few years ago they'd have spilled out of her mouth, but she wasn't that headstrong teenager any longer. She needed their help, and she'd have to submit to whatever they asked.

Submission. The word left a bitter taste in her mouth. That was the core of Amish life she'd always found impossible to accept.

Times change, so the saying went. More likely, time had changed her. She could accept anything for Gracie's sake. She wrapped her arms around her daughter, feeling Gracie's head pressing against her heart.

"I was going to school in Chicago and working as a waitress to pay my way." She chose her words carefully, needing to make them understand a world they'd never known. "Another of the girls working there needed a roommate, so I moved in with her."

They wouldn't be able to picture the rundown, dirty building or the cluttered apartment. Or imagine the triple locks on the door.

She took a breath. "Jannie, my roommate, had a boyfriend. Pete, his name is. He was in and out of trouble all the time, mostly for selling drugs."

Daad shook his head slowly, not in disbelief but in sorrow, it seemed. "That is a bad thing, it is."

"Jannie got pregnant, and I could see something wasn't right." That was one benefit of growing up Amish. She'd been around enough pregnant females, animal and human, to know what was normal. "I got her to go to the clinic. They found she had leukemia."

Someone around the table sucked in a breath. Leah. "Poor thing."

"Ja," Myra said softly.

"When she told Pete, he couldn't handle it. He just wanted out." She was consolidating into a few sentences the weeks of anguish, of comforting Jannie and trying to see the path ahead.

"Jannie . . ." How could she make them understand a waif like Jannie, rootless in an uncaring world? "She didn't have anyone. No family, no one who could help. When she lost Pete, she was desperate."

"So you helped her."

If there was a trace of surprise in Daadi's voice, she decided to ignore it.

"I was all she had." She took a shaky breath. "When she realized she wasn't going to live, all she wanted was to know that her baby would be safe." Jannie, who'd never seemed to have a mind of her own about anything, had proved unexpectedly strong when it came to her baby. "She asked me to raise her child, and I promised that I would. The nurse put Gracie into my arms minutes after she was born." She dropped a kiss on Gracie's hair, inhaling the sweet baby scent. "I knew she was mine in that moment."

A faint murmur of understanding came

from the other women. Barbara nodded. They knew that moment.

Daadi was frowning, though. "What about the father? He has the right to his own child."

She bit back angry words. They wouldn't help. Daadi could never really understand a man who would put his next fix ahead of his child. Daadi would always try to be fair, even to someone like Pete.

"He didn't want her." She cradled Gracie in her arms. That was true. Pete hadn't wanted the baby. "He signed the papers giving her away. She's my child, both in law and in my heart."

Her words seemed to linger in the silence that greeted them. She pressed one hand against the rough wood of the picnic table, willing someone to speak. No one did.

Rebellion rose in her. "You'd be happier if I came back an unwed mother," she snapped. "Would that be easier to forgive?"

"Don't, Anna." Leah might have been chiding a fifteen-year-old Anna for hiding English clothes in the barn. "You know that's not so. We're just trying to understand, ain't so?" Leah glanced around the table, seeking agreement.

Several heads nodded. Mahlon, her next-older brother, usually so happy-go-lucky, still looked faintly shocked, but he nodded, too.

To her surprise, it was Barbara who reached over to pat her hand. "You love her, whether she came from your body or not."

"Ja," she said softly. "Denke, Barbara." Too often her annoyance with Barbara's nosiness made her overlook the woman's warm heart.

"The Stoltzfus family, over by Big Creek, they adopted three English kinder," Samuel said, dropping the words in quietly.

"Ja, but they are a married couple." Mahlon glanced at his young wife, as if trying to gauge her opinion.

"You've all accepted my three young ones as family," Daniel, Leah's husband, said, wrapping his hand around hers. A blind person could see how much those two loved each other. To think she'd once been furious with Leah for considering marriage to Daniel.

"If the law agrees the baby is Anna's," Joseph said, "then we'll have no quarrel with the English over it."

Anna should have been grateful for their support. She was, for Gracie's sake. But still her rebellious spirit rose. They all thought they had a share and a say in her life. That was what she'd jumped the fence to escape.

"I will talk to Bishop Mose," Daadi said at last. "No one else needs to know anything but that our Anna is back with her child." He looked at her, and his face softened. "You are here, where you belong. You'll talk to Bishop Mose, kneel before the church, and be accepted back. It is what we've all prayed for, and we are thankful."

She nodded, lowering her face so that she didn't have to meet his gaze. How could she kneel before the church and ask them to accept her back when she didn't intend to stay? How could she hide among her own family without telling them the whole story about Pete?

A shiver ran through her. She seemed to see again the twisted anger on Pete's face, the maudlin tears he'd shed when he'd shown up at her door, demanding to see his baby, dismissing the papers he'd signed. Saying little Gracie belonged to him.

The baby's safety came first, no matter the cost.

"Ja, Daadi," she said softly. "Denke."

She looked up then. The others appeared happy, or at least relieved.

But Samuel—Samuel looked as if he saw right into her heart and knew what she was hiding.

"Hand me that wrench, will you?"

Samuel passed the tool to Joseph, smiling a little. There was nothing Joseph enjoyed more than a challenge like the one posed by the balky baler. "You won't be content until you've fixed it, will you?"

"Course not." Joseph looked up at him, grinning. "Converting tractor-drawn machinery to horse-drawn might seem like a step backward to the outside world, but to me, it is fun. Any real mechanic would feel the same."

The Amish ban on connecting to the power grid meant plenty of work for someone like Joseph, who could use a portable electric generator, powered by a gasoline engine, to run a welder. And because the end purpose was to keep horse-drawn equipment in the field, the bishops agreed to it.

"I guess I'm not a real mechanic." Samuel didn't need to be embarrassed about admitting it to Joseph. Joseph knew it as well as anyone, but said they made a gut team anyway.

Samuel could only hope that was true. Joseph's offer to go into business with him had come at a time when he'd desperately needed it. It had made him feel like a useful part of the community again. He wouldn't soon forget what he owed Joseph.

Which maybe partly accounted for how troubled he felt over Anna. Joseph cared so much about his little sister. It would be a shame if he ended up getting hurt.

Joseph gave the baler a frustrated tap with the wrench. "So tell me something."

"Ja, what? If it's something about the machine, you know it better than I do."

Joseph shook his head, concern slipping into his eyes. "What are people saying about Anna coming back? And the boppli?"

"I haven't said a word to anyone." That wasn't really an answer to the question, but maybe Joseph would let it slide. "Your daad didn't want us to talk about it." He shrugged, rising from where he'd been squatting next to Joseph on the rough floor of the shop. "I wouldn't, anyway. I remember how it felt, coming back, figuring every blabbermaul in the valley was gossiping about me."

"I know you wouldn't say anything, but I bet you hear plenty. I saw how everyone shut up fast when I stopped at the feed mill. They had to be talking about Anna."

"Ja, well, you know how folks are." Samuel shifted his weight from one foot to the other. "They're bound to talk, but soon as they see that things are all right with the family, they'll settle down."

At least, he hoped so. Anna's situation was a bit different from his. He hadn't come home with a baby.

"Little Gracie makes a difference," Joseph said, echoing Samuel's thoughts. Hands on his hips, he stared out the open shop door toward the house. "It's not like the usual."

No, it wasn't. The usual was a young man like he'd been, who, at the end of his rumspringa, decided to taste the outside world instead of getting married and settling down as people expected. Most of them came back, convinced they belonged here.

He'd come back. But the conviction— that was what he was missing. That was why he hadn't found a bride, despite the broad hints of his friends.

How could he, when he didn't know his own mind? When he didn't know how much of his father was in him, ready to burst out and bring the world crashing in on people he was supposed to love?

Joseph sighed, and Samuel knew his thoughts were still on Anna. "I guess we just have to ride it out until somebody else does something to get folks talking. It'll be better once Anna has seen Bishop Mose."

"Ja." If anyone could help ease Anna and her babe back into the church, it would be Bishop Mose. Samuel just wished he felt sure that was what Anna really wanted.

"Somebody's coming." Joseph stepped out into the sunshine, and Samuel followed him. "A car."

"Maybe the English are starting to hear how gut you are with the machines," he said, nudging Joseph.

"Not likely. If a thing doesn't run on the electric, they're not interested."

It was a pickup truck, not a car, bright red and shiny as could be. Samuel made a quick comparison to the rundown vehicle Anna had arrived in. This glossy piece of metal wouldn't want to be in the same garage as Anna's heap.

The Englischer got out, tugging his ball cap into place. With his jeans and flannel shirt, he looked like most of the English farmers in the valley, but most of them wouldn't be driving such an expensive rig. Farmers put their money into stock or equipment, not something fancy to ride around in.

"Good day." The man nodded, looking from one to the other of them. "I'm looking for Samuel Fisher."

"I am Samuel Fisher." Making the switch to English was easy enough. Dealing with reminders of the outside world was not. "How can I help you?"

"I'm Jase Bartlett." The man thrust out his hand. "Have a place over on Shady Point Road."

Samuel shook hands. The name was familiar, even if the face wasn't. "You have the horse farm, ain't so?"

"That's me." Bartlett didn't seem surprised

that he was known. He'd come to the valley more than a year ago and snatched up a farm that several Amish had had an eye on. He'd torn down the old farmhouse and put up something new, torn down the barns and sheds as well, putting in new stables and what seemed like miles of rail fences around acres of pastures.

"I've been hearing about you, Fisher. People say you're pretty good at training difficult horses. That true?"

Samuel kept his face expressionless. "I like to train horses, ja."

Bartlett raised his eyebrows. "The way I heard it, you're some kind of horse whisperer, able to get through to any animal."

The man seemed intent on making Samuel brag about himself. "Are you wanting some work done with one of your horses, Mr. Bartlett?"

Bartlett's face seemed to darken. "I've got a new gelding that's proving troublesome. Good breeding, and I paid a fancy enough price for him, but he's a mean one. Not that I couldn't break him of his bad habits myself, but I just haven't got the time right now. So, what do you say? You interested?"

Somehow Samuel thought that if Bartlett were able to train this expensive animal himself, he wouldn't be here. His instincts were telling him that both the man and the horse might be more trouble than they were worth.

"I am sorry, Mr. Bartlett, but working with horses is a sideline for me. We have much to do in the shop right now, and I don't think I'll have time to take on a raw animal now."

Bartlett's flush deepened. It seemed he wasn't one to take no easily. But before he could speak, Joseph clapped Samuel on the back.

"Ach, it sounds like a job made for you. Don't worry about the shop. We're not so busy right now that we can't spare you." Joseph switched to Pennsylvania Dutch to add, "Besides, a man like this will pay well."

"Sounds like your friend can spare you," Bartlett said quickly. "What do you say? If you do a good job, there's more work I can throw your way."

Samuel glanced at Joseph, who nodded encouragement. "Well, I guess I could give it a try. When did you want to bring the gelding over?"

The slam of the back door punctuated the question, the screen probably caught by the breeze. Anna stood on the back porch, seemingly frozen in place by the sight of the Englischer.

Then, before Jase Bartlett could turn to look that way, she whisked back into the house, closing the door behind her.

Bartlett rattled on, talking about the arrangements, and Samuel nodded and responded. But inside, he was back to wondering and worrying about Anna's return. Did he think she was telling the truth? That had been what Joseph really wanted to know, even if he hadn't come right out and said it.

The answer wasn't a simple one. Samuel did believe that what Anna had said was true. He just didn't believe she had told them everything.

The Englischer was gone. Anna pressed her hand against the screen door, surprised that her thoughts had taken that form.

Her alarm really had nothing to do with the fact that the man was different from the Amish, but only with the reminder of the outside world, where Pete might be looking for her.

That was foolish. The fear that curdled her stomach was irrational. She had to believe that.

But could she? Probably not as long as her memory of the last time she'd seen him was so vivid. He'd been high—she'd realized that the moment she'd opened the door.

Her fingers tightened on the handle she held now, as if she could go back, relive that moment, and not open the door.

That's what she should have done, but she hadn't. How was she to know? She hadn't seen or heard from Pete since long before Gracie was born. She'd hardly expected him to decide, after all that time, that he wanted to see the baby.

Not just see. Take. Her skin crawled with the memory. He'd gone from tears to fury and back again, talking wildly about running off with Gracie. He'd go to Mexico, or Canada, where no one would look for them. He'd be a good father to his little girl.

She's not yours. That's what she'd screamed at him. *She's not yours.*

He'd come after her then, tossing her out of his way as if she were a rag doll. Her ribs still hurt from where she'd hit the floor.

That was what her neighbors had heard. Two college boys, who hadn't seemed interested in anything more serious than girls and games, had rushed to the rescue, hustled Pete out, and told her to call the police.

She hadn't. Maybe she'd still been more Amish than she thought. The Amish didn't turn to the law to settle their problems.

Instead she'd packed up everything she could carry, put Gracie in the car seat, and fled.

She shook her head, trying to make the memory go away. Pete had never known anything about her background, so even if he wanted to come after her, he couldn't. The Amish, living off the grid, possessing no computers or cell phones or credit cards, could not easily be traced. They were safe here.

That should make her feel better, but she knew she wasn't going to be content until she was sure that visitor had nothing to do with her.

She went out onto the porch, picking up the basket she'd dropped when she'd seen the truck, and glanced across the yard. Joseph had disappeared, probably into the shop. Samuel stood where he'd been, watching her, as if he knew she would come and speak to him.

Swinging the basket as if the garden were the only thing on her mind, she went across the yard, the grass whispering under her feet. The walnut tree was heavy with nuts, the green pods starting to fall and blacken.

Mamm had always said the black walnuts were the most delicious—that they had to be because they were so difficult to harvest. She could help Myra with that, if she was still here. Samuel watched her, his face unreadable. She gestured with the basket.

"I'm going to get some peppers to roast. Myra wants to put some up."

He nodded, looking at her as if knowing that wasn't all that was on her mind.

Annoyance pricked at her. "Who was the Englischer?"

"His name is Bartlett."

He was telling her as little as possible. Why?

"Did he say anything about me?"

Now something did flicker in Samuel's eyes—surprise, maybe. "Mr. Bartlett has a troublesome horse he wants me to work with. That's why he came here, to ask me about the animal."

"I see." She tried to smile. "I'm glad you're getting some more business." She hitched up the basket. "I'd better get on with the peppers."

She started to turn away. Samuel reached out, his hand clasping her wrist. She stopped, startled, feeling the warmth of his grip.

"Why would you think the Englischer had come about you, Anna?"

"I . . . I don't." She'd been an idiot, asking him that. "I just wondered. I mean, I suppose my coming back made a lot of talk."

"Among the Leit." The Amish. "Why would the English know? Or care?"

"They wouldn't." She tugged at his hand, feeling the strength of his grip. "What are the Amish saying, then? You're in a position to tell them plenty, aren't you?"

His face tightened, making him look far

older than she knew him to be. "I would not do that, and I think you know it."

She'd rather hang on to her anger, but he was right. That didn't make her feel any more kindly toward him. She took a breath. "Sorry." The apology was ungracious, but it was the best she could do. "I don't believe you'd gossip about me."

He let her hand go, a smile flickering across his face. "I'm the last person who'd do that. I remember too well what it was like when I came back."

"Plenty of talk, I suppose."

"Ach, it soon died down. They found something else to talk about."

"*Someone* else, more likely." Her shoulders moved, as if to shake off the sense of people watching. Commenting. "That was one of the reasons I left. I hated everyone thinking they had the right to talk about what I was doing."

"Even when it was kindly meant?"

"That was the worst." He wouldn't understand. How could he?

Samuel's hazel eyes were serious, intent on her face. "You don't like people taking an interest in you."

"Not when it means they think they have the right to judge." Her temper flared again in an instant. "I didn't like it then, and I don't like it now."

He continued to stare at her without a visible reaction, his face impassive. "That might make it a little hard to go before the congregation with a humble heart, don't you think?"

How did he know to press on exactly the point that bothered her most? She fought down the surge of temper that only he seemed able to unleash in her.

"That's between Bishop Mose and me, Samuel. Or are you wanting to be chosen for a minister the next time it comes around?"

"I could not do that." He pushed that idea away with a quick, instinctive movement of his hands. "But I do know what it's like to come back after living English. I can see that something is wrong, Anna. If there's anything you want to talk about, anything you think maybe the others wouldn't understand—"

"There's nothing!" She snapped the words, not sure whether anger or fear predominated in her heart. "There's nothing wrong, and I'd be pleased if you'd mind your own business."

Clutching the basket, she brushed past him and hurried to the garden.

CHAPTER FIVE

Anna slid the skin from one of the peaches Myra had scalded, the fruit smooth and heavy in her hand. She hadn't done this in a long while, but the technique came back to her, as if her fingers remembered what her mind had forgotten. The aroma of the peaches, rich and sweet, filled her head, carrying her back to her mother's kitchen and the easy chatter of women working together.

Helping Myra can peaches kept her hands busy, but it left her mind free to worry about what the evening held. Bishop Mose would be stopping by after supper to talk with her. Daadi had sent word over this morning, which must mean he'd already spoken to the bishop about her.

What would Bishop Mose ask her? And how would she explain herself to him? She needed his acceptance if she was to stay here. She forced herself to loosen her grip on the peach before she bruised it with her worry.

Myra sliced peaches quickly into a bowl of water treated with a pectin solution to keep them from darkening. "The Elbertas are the best ever this year, I think." She darted a glance at Anna. "But you are not thinking about peaches just now. You are fretting about the bishop's visit, ja?"

"How did you know?" In the week she'd been here, Anna had begun to discover that for all her outward shyness, Myra could go straight to the heart of the matter.

"Ach, it's only natural, ain't so?" Myra's hands stilled on the peaches for a second, and then she clasped Anna's hand in a brief, wet squeeze. "It will be all right. You'll see. Bishop Mose will understand."

"I hope so."

But did she hope that, really? As she recalled, their district's bishop, wise with years, had a way of knowing what was in your heart. She wasn't sure she wanted him looking that closely into hers.

"I'm certain-sure," Myra said, her voice warm with affection.

"Denke, Myra." Anna's heart filled with gratitude for her sister-in-law's caring. "I appreciate your saying so."

Myra took the next peach. "Ach, I just thought maybe you wanted to talk to someone about it, and I'm the only one here. Or you could run over to Leah's, if you want. I can handle the canning myself."

"That's all right. I don't need to see Leah."

A chill settled on her heart. That was just as well, since it seemed Leah didn't want to see her. For all her words of welcome and her warm hug, Leah had made no effort to seek her out for a private talk since her return. It looked as if Leah wasn't ready yet to go back to being sisters.

She should try to look on the bright side of it. At least this way when she left, she wouldn't be hurting Leah again.

Her heart twisted. She didn't want to hurt anyone. If she could have found another place where Gracie would be safe, she wouldn't have come here.

She had to protect Gracie, no matter what, so she'd do what was necessary. She would submerge herself and her daughter into the Amish world until it was safe to come out.

And then what? How many people would she hurt when she went away again? If she could stay here while keeping her distance from the others . . . Well, that wasn't worth thinking about. It was next to impossible in a community like this. Nobody kept any distance, it seemed.

Myra lifted clean jars from the hot water bath, and together they began to fill them. The amber slices slid into the glass jars easily, making the glass seem to glow from within.

"Looks nice," Myra said. "Satisfying."

Anna nodded. "It does. I don't know why I used to try so hard to get out of helping with the canning."

Myra chuckled, smoothing a strand of hair back from her damp forehead with the back of her hand. "Ach, I was the same. Always thinking that Samuel had it better, because he got to work outside with Daadi."

"I'm afraid I just wanted to get out of the

work, period." Her thoughts had always been drifting off far from the farm, as she recalled.

"It's different now that the work is for my own family," Myra said. "I like to see the jars all lined up on their shelves and know that we'll be eating well all winter. And you, too. Your Gracie loves fruit as much as my Sarah does."

Myra's calm assumption that they'd be here for the winter to eat the peaches shook Anna, and it took a moment to reply. "She does enjoy her food."

Gracie seemed to have blossomed in the time they'd been here, her cheeks rounding, her chubby little legs getting sturdier. Maybe she was just thriving on all the attention she was getting and from being encouraged to try new things by her two-years-older cousin.

Where would she and Gracie be, come winter? She didn't know. Not here. By then Pete would have lost interest, or else he'd be back in jail.

She couldn't go back to living Amish, not after having been in the world for so long. Not after being free to make decisions for herself.

"I'm glad you're here." Again, Myra seemed to respond to her thoughts. "It's gut to have another woman in the house."

"You're nice to say that, but I'm sure you'd rather be alone with Joseph and your little Sarah."

She glanced out the window over the sink. The shop was clearly visible, and even now she could see Samuel's tall figure move past the open door.

She'd talked to Samuel at meals, of course, in the two days since she'd accused him of nosiness, but she'd been careful not to venture near the shop while he was there working. She didn't want another private conversation with him, maybe because her conscience was telling her that she owed him an apology. He'd been trying to help, and she had slapped the offer away as if it were an insult.

"With my mamm gone and my sister living clear out in Indiana, I've missed having a woman around to talk to, and that's the truth," Myra said. "Especially now." She rested her palm on the small bump under her apron, smoothing it protectively.

Anna had seen Jannie do the same thing, time after time. Unease shivered along her nerves as she thought of that trip Myra had made to the clinic the day she'd arrived.

"Myra, is something wrong?" The question was out before she could tell herself it was intrusive—as intrusive as Samuel's offer of advice.

Myra set down the jar she'd been wiping and stared at it for a long moment. "The doctor is concerned about the baby."

The words cut straight to Anna's heart. "Myra, I'm so sorry." She fought to keep her voice level. "You must be worried. What does the doctor say?"

"Just that I must have more tests. That the tests will show if the baby has problems." She pressed her hands against the edge of the sink, as if she needed to hang on to something, and then she turned a fear-filled gaze on Anna. "I try to have faith that it will be as God wills, but I . . . Oh, Anna, what if something is wrong with the boppli? What if I am not strong enough to handle it?"

Anna's throat was too tight to answer, her mind a jumble of images in which Jannie and Myra seemed to mix. She wrapped her arms around Myra. Myra clung to her tightly, her tear-wet cheek pressed against Anna's shoulder.

"It will be all right," she said, her voice soothing once she could speak. "It will."

But what if it wasn't? Things didn't always turn out for the best. Anna knew that only too well. How could sweet, sensitive Myra handle it if her baby had a serious medical problem?

Myra pulled back, grabbing a dish towel to blot her eyes. "I'm sorry. I shouldn't act so weak. It's just that sometimes I feel I must let it out, and I can't cry in front of Joseph. He doesn't know what to do when I cry, and it upsets him so."

Anna patted her arm. "You can cry in front of me anytime you want."

For as long as I am here. The words clung in her mind like a bramble caught on her skin.

"I wondered . . . I wanted to ask you . . ." Whatever it was, Myra seemed to have trouble getting the words out. She stopped, took a deep breath. "Anna, would you go with me when I have the tests? I don't want to keep taking Joseph away from the shop, and besides, it just makes him worry more. I'd go by myself, but I guess I'm just not brave enough."

"Of course I will go with you." What else could Anna say?

She was digging herself deeper and deeper into life here with every word, every deed. Caring too much. Letting people count on her. But she didn't seem to have any other choice.

Samuel had put in a busy day in the machine shop until late afternoon, when Joseph had chased him out, saying he knew full well that what Samuel really wanted to be doing was taking a look at Mr. Bartlett's horse.

They both knew that was true. So here he was, leaning on the fence of the training ring next to the lane and enjoying the slant of late afternoon sunshine, watching the animal.

Just watching. According to Bartlett, who'd driven the truck and horse trailer over early in the morning, the gelding was Star's Midnight Dream, but his barn name was simply Star, for the small white patch on his forehead. Otherwise he was a sleek, glossy black, well-fed, and shining animal, but with a nervous toss of the head and a leery roll of the eye that would make any horseman immediately wary.

So for today, Samuel was just watching.

Watching the horse, ja, but very aware of Anna, who'd just come out of the house with the baby on her hip. She seemed to bring little Gracie out every afternoon at this time, probably when the child got up from her nap.

Also part of Anna's routine, at least for the past few days, was ignoring him. Since the day she felt he'd spoken out of turn, that was.

Well, maybe he'd been wrong to speak. But he'd been in her place himself, teetering precariously on the fence between Amish and English, and when he saw someone else there, he couldn't help but reach out a hand. Speaking so to Anna had taken him beyond what was comfortable for him, but he'd done it. She hadn't been grateful.

The animal's ears flicked back, as if he heard something, and he rolled his eyes toward the house. Samuel took a quick glance over his shoulder. Anna and Gracie were coming toward him.

"Anna. And little Gracie." He held out his hand to the baby as he would to a wary animal.

There was nothing wary about Gracie. She'd obviously gotten used to seeing him, maybe connecting him in her mind with the horses she loved to watch. She grabbed his fingers, clutching tightly and grinning, showing off her two bottom teeth. She babbled something that might have been a greeting.

"Ach, I'm such a dummy that I don't understand. Is she speaking English or Pennsylvania Dutch?"

"It's getting hard to tell. Maybe she's already bilingual." There was a little strain in Anna's manner, but her words were friendly enough. "She and Sarah chatter away to each other, and they seem to know what they're saying, if no one else does."

"Sure they do. Just like the horses make their thoughts known, even if we don't understand them much of the time."

"I see you have a new addition." She nodded to the gelding, who threw up his head as if he knew she was talking about him.

"Ja, this is the horse belonging to Mr. Bartlett. Star, his name is, but I'm thinking Trouble would be more accurate."

"That's why Bartlett picked you. He thinks you can do what he can't."

"I'm not sure Mr. Bartlett would say that he can't." He couldn't stop a smile. "It's only that he doesn't have time, you see."

"I see. Aren't you going to start working with him today?" Her eyebrows lifted a little, so maybe that was a criticism.

"Are you still on English time, Anna Beiler? Still rushing to do things by the clock?"

"No." She looked a bit nettled. "I just thought, from what Joseph was saying about it, that this was a chance to take a step that could mean success for you."

"Success?" It was his turn to raise an eyebrow. She'd moved in the world's direction, for sure.

"Well, you know what I mean. If you're as good a horse trainer as Joseph says, maybe that's what you ought to be doing."

"What I'm doing is working in the machine shop with Joseph," he said flatly. "That is what I do, and I'm content."

Even as he said the word, he wondered. Was he content? He'd made his decision, and he'd abide by it. But whether it had been made with the heart or the head, he still wasn't sure.

Star, taking exception to a barn swallow that swooped low over the fence, tossed his head and trotted to the far end of the field, where he pawed at the ground a few times before dropping his head to the grass.

Anna watched him. "You'll have your hands full with this one, I think."

"Ja, you're right about that." He tickled Gracie's chin. "Gracie won't be petting Star for a while, that's certain-sure." He glanced from the baby's face to her mother's. "Are things going all right for you, Anna?"

"Fine," she said, clipping off the word. "Don't I look all right?"

"You're looking more Amish every day." He leaned back against the fence to study her. "I could say you still look a little nervous, but if I did, you might bite my head off."

Her lips pressed together for an instant. "Again, you mean. I should apologize for what I said the other day. I was rude. I know you were just trying to help."

"It's not a problem."

"You're kind to say so." She disentangled Gracie's fingers from her kapp strings, patting the chubby hand. "Maybe I am a little nervous. Bishop Mose is coming by to talk to me tonight."

So. Anna would face the bishop, and it bothered her. "Well, that's not so bad, is it? You've known him since you were born."

She nodded, but her gaze slipped away from his. "I guess that's so." She was silent for a moment, but her forehead was knotted. "When you came back, what did he say to you?"

He didn't especially want to remember that time, but he would, if it helped Anna.

"We talked. About why I'd left, and what it had been like out there." He jerked his head, but Anna would know he wasn't meaning the distant line of trees, but what lay beyond. "He talked about what it meant to come back. Asked me to be sure I was ready before I made the commitment to be baptized."

Anna nodded. She didn't look as if she

relished that prospect. "You went before the congregation then."

"Ja. Bishop Mose said I could wait for a bit if I wanted, but my mamm was sick, so it was important to do it right away." His throat thickened. His mother had been dying; they'd all known that. But she'd seen her son restored to the fellowship before she passed.

"Myra told me about her death. I'm sorry."

He nodded, not able to say more. Anna was pushing him down some roads he'd just as soon not take.

"You've seen the rest of it with others. I knelt before the congregation, confessed, was forgiven. And everything was like it had been before."

"Like it had been before." She repeated the words, but they didn't seem to give her much comfort.

"Don't look that way, Anna." Impulsively he reached out to her, wanting to wipe away that expression. "I came back because I had to, you see. Because of my mamm. It will be easier for you. I'm sure of it. After all, you came back because you wanted to."

For a long moment she stared at him, her blue eyes wide with some emotion he couldn't name. And then her lashes swept down, hiding it from him.

"Ja," she said, her voice flat. "I'm sure you're right."

"After supper" could mean most anytime, Anna decided as she and Myra washed up the dishes. Bishop Mose could show up soon, and she had to be ready.

Unfortunately, her mind was a blank.

Samuel had reminded her that she'd known Bishop Mose from her earliest memories, which was certainly true. She'd loved going to his harness shop with Daadi, and he'd always had a gentle word and a twinkle in his eyes for her. But that had been long ago, and this was now.

Myra, maybe sensing her discomfort, kept up a gentle flow of chatter that allowed Anna to simply smile and nod from time to time. Behind them, Joseph sat on the floor, playing with the two little girls as naturally as if Gracie had always been a part of their lives.

Funny, how that thought gave her pause.

If she'd come back here with Gracie right after Jannie's death, how different would the situation have been?

She didn't want to think about the answer to that question. She hadn't wanted to come back then, didn't really want it now. Her life was out there, in the world, where she could make up her own mind about things.

You came back because you wanted to, Samuel had said. *That will make it easier.*

Her stomach cramped. She hadn't wanted to. Everyone here seemed to accept that without question, but it wasn't true. And if Bishop Mose asked her point-blank, how would she answer?

She looked across the room, her gaze seeking her child. Gracie stood, balanced uncertainly, holding a block in each hand, waving them and laughing at something Joseph said to her.

Anna's heart turned over. She would kneel in front of the congregation, beg forgiveness, all to keep Gracie safe. The girl she'd been three years ago wouldn't have been able to humble herself in that way, but then she hadn't known what it was to have a child. For Gracie, she would do anything.

The clop of a horse's hooves came almost as punctuation to her thought. Bishop Mose must be arriving already.

He entered smiling, little Sarah running to meet him as if he were another grossdaadi. He scooped her up in his arms and spoke to her in a low voice. Gracie, following her cousin's lead, looked for a moment as if she'd let go and toddle toward him. Then she plopped down on her bottom and crawled across the floor. She grabbed his pant leg, and he stooped down and picked her up, too.

"There, little Gracie. What a fine girl you are, and almost about to walk already."

Gracie babbled something incomprehensible and patted his snowy beard. Anna's heart lurched. If only . . .

She let the thought trail away, not sure what it was she hoped. Just to get through this, maybe.

"Bishop Mose, you'll have coffee and peach cobbler, ja?" Myra was already pouring the coffee into a thick white mug.

"Ach, Myra, you know my weakness." He sat down at the table, a child in each arm. "Now, what shall I do with these two sweet girls?"

"Best let me take them, or they'll be spilling your coffee for you." Joseph lifted the kinder off Bishop Mose's lap, plopping them down with their toys. "Komm now," he said. "A few more minutes to play before bedtime."

"Joseph, you'll have cobbler now, won't you? And Anna?"

"I don't know—" she began, not sure how to respond. She'd expected the bishop to want to talk with her privately, and the living room was tidy as ever, with two chairs pulled together for a quiet talk.

"Komm, fress." Bishop Mose waved her to the table, seeming to read her thoughts. "Sit, eat. We can talk together while we have some of Myra's wonderful-gut cobbler, can't we?"

Nodding, she went to take her seat at the table. She probably wouldn't be able to choke down a bite, but if this was what he wanted . . .

Apparently it was. He dug into the cobbler with obvious pleasure, all the while sharing the latest news from town and comparing opinions with Joseph on how long the fine fall weather would hold. Myra perched on her chair, one wary eye on the kinder, and Anna knew that at the first sign of fussiness, she'd sweep them away to bed.

Anna toyed with her cobbler and waited for the moment when she'd have to answer the bishop's questions.

When he finally turned to her, his expression was as kindly as ever. "So, Anna, you've come back to us. You want to be accepted as part of the community again."

She nodded, discovering that her throat was tight. "Ja, I do." She tried not to think about how soon she might be going away again.

"And why did you decide to come back?"

That was the question she feared. She'd made up an elaborate answer she'd thought would convince him without telling any outright lies. And now she couldn't seem to say any of it.

She tried to imagine how her friends in the city would react to her fear of trying to deceive him. Classmates in her college seminar would no doubt mutter about outdated superstitions. The other servers at the restaurant would expect her to stand up for herself. If you don't take care of yourself, who will, they'd wonder.

Nothing either group thought had any-thing to do with life as it was lived in an Amish community.

"I . . . I needed to be home," she said, staring at the tabletop, her voice choking on the words.

"Ja," he said. "Then that is gut."

The silence grew between them, and after a moment she raised her eyes to his. "What do I have to do? Will I go before the church then?"

Her mind filled with the act of kneeling before the congregation to confess. Her wayward imagination presented her with an image of her sociology professor making notes on that, eyebrows raised in disbelief.

"Ach, we don't have to rush." The bishop held out his mug to Myra for a refill.

She lifted the pot from the stove, filling his mug and topping off Joseph's.

"Denke, Myra." Bishop Mose blew on his coffee and then took a sip before re-turning his gaze to Anna. "You ask what you should do, Anna, but you are already doing what I would advise, I think. You must sink yourself back into being Amish again. Help Myra and Joseph, come to worship, be a part of the community. Embrace with a whole heart what you rejected when you left. Can you do that?"

"Ja." She felt almost let down, as if she'd been prepared to make a grand sacrifice and then was told it wasn't necessary. "I can." Although as she thought of it, the "whole heart" part might be a little difficult. "Is that all?"

He smiled, maybe a little sadly. "Is there nothing you yourself think that you should do, Anna?"

She blinked, her mind scrambling. Had she forgotten something important?

"Any wrongs left over from your fence-jumping that need to be righted?" he probed, and she heard a trace of steel in his voice.

Wrongs she'd committed, in other words, in the passionate desire of her eighteen-year-old self to live her own life.

Her father, her sister, pained by her actions. Her mother dying while she was gone, and her not even here to say a last good-bye. The family whose buggy she'd hit while driving a car belonging to her English friends. More, probably, that she hadn't even thought of. She found she was pressing her hand against her heart.

"Ja," he said gently. "I see. You might want to do something about that, Anna."

She nodded, not able to speak. She'd been intent on hiding the truth from him, thinking herself a hero for being willing to humble herself outwardly before the congregation in order to keep her daughter safe.

Instead, Bishop Mose had turned her inside out. *What does the Lord require of you but a humble and contrite heart?* The scripture floated up from her subconscious. Bishop Mose had set her a task far harder than kneeling and confessing.

CHAPTER SIX

Samuel swept the floor of the shop, finding the routine chore relaxing. Anna's arrival had introduced a new element into the flow of their days—not unwelcome, but a bit disturbing, even so. He was one who liked knowing what was coming from one moment to the next, not that anyone but the gut Lord knew that for certain.

Finishing, he propped the broom in the corner, stepped outside, and pulled the door shut behind him, taking a moment to lock it. Once people in the valley, Amish and English alike, hadn't bothered to lock anything, but times had changed. He wasn't as much concerned about thieving as he was that some foolish kid would get into the shop and hurt himself.

Samuel stood in the afternoon sunshine for a moment, deliberately turning over in his mind his approach to the new horse. Star would be a challenge, no doubt about that. Someone had made the animal wary and defensive where humans were concerned, and it would take time and patience to overcome that.

And while he was thinking of wary creatures, Anna was in the yard, taking sheets down from the clothesline.

How had her meeting with Bishop Mose gone? He'd seen the bishop's buggy arrive last night, and he'd seen it leave again an hour or so later.

While he hesitated, wondering whether to approach her or not, she turned, caught sight of him, and nodded. He walked over to her, catching the end of a sheet that had drooped close to the grass.

"Denke." She took it, shaking the sheet out with a quick flip of her wrists, and started to fold it. "You're done for the day, are you? Or is my brother still tinkering with a job?"

"Tinkering, yes, but not on a job." He couldn't suppress a grin, knowing how predictable Joseph was on this subject. "Can't you guess where he is?"

She blinked, and then glanced toward the barn. "He's working on my car, isn't he? I guess it was only a matter of time."

"Joseph never met a machine he didn't want to take apart." He studied Anna's face. Was she content over Bishop Mose's counsel? He couldn't tell from her expression. "Still, when you sell the car, it would be as well to have it working."

"Sell the car." She stopped, turning her face away from him as she took a white pillowcase from the line. "Ja, I guess you are right."

Her reaction raised a few more questions in his mind, in addition to the ones that had been there since the day he'd found her in the barn.

"How did it go with Bishop Mose?" he asked abruptly. Maybe she'd tell him to mind his own business again.

Her hands stilled on the fabric for a moment. Then she folded the pillowcase and dropped it into the basket at her feet. "All right, I guess. Not exactly what I expected."

"The bishop can be a bit surprising at times." He waited.

For a moment it seemed she wouldn't speak. Then she gave her head a frustrated little shake. "I thought he'd say I must kneel and confess to the church. I'd do it, and then it would be over."

"He doesn't want you to do that?"

"He says there's time enough later for that. That I should get used to living Amish again, make things right . . ." She stopped, turning to a row of small sheets that must be from the kinders' beds.

Make what things right? "Bishop Mose cares more about what's in the heart than on outward forms, ain't so?"

"I guess so." She was frowning, her fingers toying with a clothespin. "Kneeling and confessing wouldn't be easy, but I'd do it."

Most folks came to that, sooner or later, when they'd transgressed. The difficult moments were soon past, and the relief at being restored to full fellowship was worth almost anything. But was that driving Anna? He wasn't sure.

"People think being Amish is about clothes and electricity. They see only the outside and judge by that. We know it's more about having a humble and obedient heart."

Her mouth tightened at that. "They wouldn't understand, even if you told them. The people I knew out in the English world didn't see much value in being humble. You must know that. You lived out there."

"Ja." He didn't want to talk about his time out among the English.

She seemed to sense that, looking at him with a question in her eyes. "I couldn't believe it when I heard you'd gone. You were the last one I'd expect to jump the fence. Why did you?"

"Not for the cars and the clothes, any more than you did." He tried to turn it back on her.

"I wanted freedom. I wanted to make decisions for myself, not just accept what other people told me." She tilted her head to the side, looking like the girl she'd been, full of questions and curiosity. "That wouldn't be what drove you."

"No." He'd walk away from Anna, but that wouldn't be fair. He'd been the one to start this conversation. "I went away be-cause of my father."

He saw her process that, remembering probably the talk it had caused when a middle-aged man with a growing family had jumped the fence, disappearing into the English world without a word of explanation.

"You wanted to find him?"

"Ja, but . . . not only that." His hands closed into fists, pressing against his legs. He wasn't ready to go further than that.

Her blue eyes filled with sudden sympathy. "You wanted to understand."

"Ja." *Coward,* he told himself. *You're not facing the truth.*

He didn't want to. And he certainly didn't want to talk to Anna about his reasons for leaving. Or his reasons for coming back.

It wasn't her fault that her return made him think too much about that time in his own life. Made him question too much.

He cleared his throat. "My daad—"

A bird cried harshly. He stopped, spinning to look toward the barn. That noise . . . Then he heard it again, and he started running. It wasn't a bird. It was Joseph, calling for help.

Anna raced toward the barn, a few steps

behind Samuel, fear running with her. Her heart stuttered in an effort to pray.

Please, God, please, God. The words kept time to her pounding feet. Joseph wouldn't cry out like that unless it was bad.

She plunged through the barn doorway behind Samuel and stopped, struggling to see in the gloom after the bright sunlight. Dust motes swam in a shaft of light disturbed by something.

By the car falling from a jack. She rushed forward, breath catching in her throat. Joseph lay trapped under her vehicle.

Samuel dropped to his knees next to her brother, not touching him.

"Hurry! Get him out! Why aren't you moving?" She shoved Samuel's shoulder and plunged past him, reaching for Joseph. She'd get him out herself if Samuel was too slow to do it.

Samuel grabbed her arm, yanking her back. "Don't touch him."

"We have to help him!" she blazed at him. She couldn't see Joseph's face, just his legs. He could be dead—

His legs moved, just a little. She could breathe again. "Joseph, can you hear me?"

The only answer was a low groan.

"Anna, listen to me. We can't pull at him. That would only make it worse." Samuel caught her by the arms, shaking her a little. "Are you listening?"

She stifled a sob and nodded.

"We need jacks to get it off him. Run. Ring the bell first—if the neighbors hear, they'll come. Then go to the shop. There's a jack on the bottom shelf to the right of the door. Bring it. Got that?"

She jerked a nod. Samuel was right. They needed help. She ran from the barn.

Sunlight stabbed at her eyes as she raced across the yard. She stumbled onto the porch, breathing hard, trying to form the words to pray.

Help Joseph, Lord. Please help Joseph. She reached, groping for the bell rope, caught it, and pulled hard and fast. The bell pealed out, its clamor alerting anyone within hearing distance to come.

Myra pushed through the door, eyes wide in a pale face. "Who?"

No time to break it gently. "It's Joseph. He's in the barn, trapped under the car. Samuel is with him. I've got to get a jack."

She grasped Myra's arm. "He's going to be all right."

No time for more. She turned and ran toward the shop. Behind her she heard the bell ringing again, sending its call across the quiet fields as Myra pulled and pulled on the rope.

The jack was right where Samuel had said it would be. Anna grabbed it and ran again, pain stabbing into her side. Even as she hurried toward the barn she could see men coming, running from the field beyond Samuel's where they'd been harvesting.

A cloud of dust on the lane from an approaching vehicle meant one of the English neighbors had heard, too. They'd bring a phone, maybe had already called 911.

For an instant she was one of them, furious at being without a phone in an emergency. Who lived this way? What if someday something happened to her baby and she couldn't get help?

She stumbled into the barn, clutching the jack. Samuel had already replaced the jack Joseph must have been using, and he had rigged up a lever with a heavy anvil and a barn post.

He grabbed the jack she carried.

"Has he said anything?" she asked.

"No." He tried to maneuver the jack into place. "It's better this way, Anna. Best if he's unconscious while we're getting the car off him."

How could he sound so calm? She clutched her hands together. But panic wouldn't help.

Myra ran into the barn, white-faced but tearless. "They are here—"

Others brushed by her then, men all alike to her dazed vision with their black pants and beards, hurrying to Samuel's side. Myra made an instinctive move, and Anna caught her before she could go closer.

"Wait, stay here. Give them room to work."

"Ja." Catching back a sob, Myra nodded.

A woman bolted into the barn—English, with a cell phone in her hand. "I've called nine-one-one. They'll be here soon." She put her arm around Myra, exchanging glances with Anna. "How bad . . . ?"

"Joseph is trapped under the car." The car. Her car, which shouldn't even be here.

"I'm Rosemary Welch." The woman was slim, in her early thirties, probably, wearing jeans and a flannel shirt over a white tee. She ran a hand through curly dark hair. "I'm sorry my husband wasn't home to help. What can I do? I've got my car. Do you want me to go for anyone?"

Myra didn't seem able to answer. She could only stare at the car, her whole being straining toward her husband's motionless body.

"I don't think so, thank you," Anna answered for her. "Thank you so much for coming and for calling the paramedics. We are grateful."

"No problem." The woman glanced toward the car, as if wondering what it was doing in an Amish barn, but she didn't ask. "I'll wait. I can drive Myra to the hospital if need be."

"Thank you," Anna said again. "Maybe the children . . ."

Myra seemed to rouse herself. "They were still sleeping when I heard the bell. Someone should go to them . . ." Her voice trailed away, as if she couldn't complete the thought.

Again Rosemary and Anna exchanged glances. "I'll look after them, Myra," Rosemary said quickly. "You stay with your . . ." She stopped, apparently not knowing who Anna was.

"I'm Anna Beiler, Joseph's sister. Some of the other women will come soon, I'm sure. If you could stay with the little ones until they get here?"

The woman nodded, already moving to the door. "Call me if you need me."

When she'd gone, Anna put her arm around Myra's waist. "You have gut neighbors."

"Ja." Myra seemed to rouse herself. "Do you think— Can't we go a little closer?"

Nodding, Anna led her around the side of the car, safely out of the men's way.

"They'll have him out in a moment. It will be all right," she murmured.

She didn't know that it would, and the fact that Joseph was still unconscious seemed bad to her, but Myra needed hope to cling to. They both did.

Samuel was directing the operation, the other men moving without question to follow his lead. He was calm and steady despite his anxiety for his friend.

The anger Anna had felt at him for not moving more quickly drained away, leaving her cold inside.

"Now," Samuel said.

She saw what they intended. The men were levering the car up, shoving jacks into place as it lifted. She held her breath. If it slipped . . .

It didn't. Samuel dropped to the floor, peering beneath the car. "Once more," he said.

Again they levered the car up, muscles straining, shirts darkening with sweat. The instant the jacks were in place, Samuel snaked his body under the car next to Joseph. She held her breath, praying, knowing Myra was praying, too.

She saw Samuel's hand gesture, and the men bent as one to slide Joseph gently out.

"He's alive," someone said, and Myra seemed to sag against her.

Thank you, Lord. Thank you.

Figures darkened the rectangle of sunlight in the open doorway. The paramedics had arrived and were moving quickly to Joseph, kneeling next to him in the center of a circle of Amish figures.

"You'll go with me to the hospital," Myra said, clutching Anna's hand.

"Ja, of course I will," she soothed.

But all the time her thoughts spun in a wheel of blame. This was her fault. She had brought the car to this place where cars were forbidden. If not for her, Joseph wouldn't be lying there, bloody and motionless. She should never have come home.

How much longer would they have to wait for word? Anna moved to the window of the waiting room, trying not to fidget, and stared out over the flat roof of the adjoining hospital wing. It had been hours, surely, since Joseph had been taken to surgery.

Please, Lord. *Be with my brother.* She fought to compose her mind to prayer, but her thoughts skittered helplessly in every direction. Now they fled to Gracie, and she yearned to be sitting with her at the kitchen table right now, spooning cereal into her mouth.

"You're not worrying about Gracie, are you?" Mahlon moved to her side, a cup of coffee looking too small in his big hand.

She tried to manage a smile for the

gawky teenage brother who'd turned into a responsible married man while she was gone. "How did you guess that?"

"Wasn't hard. You'd either be thinking about her or about Joseph."

"I'm doing plenty of thinking about him. And praying, too. If only . . ."

"Ja," Mahlon said. "He shouldn't have tried to do that by himself, for sure. But he's strong. He'll come through this fine, ain't so?"

He was asking for reassurance, she realized. Beyond his height and beard and outward maturity, she glimpsed the boy he'd been—a year older than she, but always seeming younger, the happy-go-lucky boy who'd tumbled into mischief without thinking.

"That's right," she said, trying to sound confident. "Nothing can keep Joseph down for long."

He nodded, pressing his lips together as if to keep them from trembling. "You don't need to worry about your boppli, either. My Esther will take gut care of her and little Sarah, too, for sure."

"I know she will." Mahlon's young bride had come straight to the house to take over the babies, while Levi's wife, Barbara, organized the folks who kept showing up to help.

Those who weren't taking over duties at home were here, it seemed. The waiting room had slowly filled up as word had spread through the Amish community.

She turned back to the room. Daad was talking to Bishop Mose in one corner, a few older men forming a supporting circle around them. With their dark clothes and white beards they looked like a cluster of Old Testament patriarchs.

Leah sat on one side of Myra, clasping her hand. Samuel was on the other, supporting his sister. Other Amish, their faces as somber as their clothes, waited with them, murmuring softly now and then.

Suddenly Anna saw them as her sociology professor would have . . . a strange, anachronistic group with their old-fashioned clothes and their identical hairstyles, talking in their own version of Low German interspersed with English words.

Different. Odd. He wouldn't have used those value-laden words, but that's what he'd have meant. She stared at them, feeling as if she were looking at an illustration in a textbook.

She blinked, trying to shake off the sense that she saw them from both inside and outside the group. Coffee, that was what she needed.

She skirted a small group of men and headed for the coffee urn. As she passed, a word from their conversation reached her. *Car.* They were talking about the car, of course, the cause of this tragedy. Her car, which never should have been in Joseph's barn to lure him to disaster.

Her hands weren't quite steady as she lifted the lever on the coffee urn, filling the cup. Naturally they'd be talking about it, even as they prayed for Joseph. She glanced again at Myra, her face tense with strain, and at the supporting figures on either side of her, hiding their own pain to comfort her.

Was this what it had been like the night she'd landed in this same hospital after the borrowed car she'd been driving had hit an Amish buggy? Had Daadi and Mammi grieved and been comforted by the community?

She didn't know. She hadn't even thought of it as she'd come out of the daze of medication, aware only of her own misery. Mammi, Daad, Leah—one of them, patient and loving, had always been next to her when she woke.

She'd repaid them with impatient words and stony silences, so obsessed with her own concerns that she hadn't even thought about what they were going through.

She spotted Bishop Mose coming toward her. She took a hurried gulp of the coffee, trying to wash away the shame that had hit so unexpectedly.

"Some coffee for you?" She reached for a cup, trusting that the movement hid her face for a moment.

At his nod, she filled the cup, adding the sugar she knew he used.

"Denke, Anna." He took the cup in a work-worn hand that was stained by the oils he used in his harness shop.

"People out there," she said, jerking her head toward the window, "they couldn't imagine a bishop who has to do his own job as well as his ministry."

Bishop Mose didn't seem surprised by a comment that had to sound odd under the circumstances. But then, it would take a lot to startle him.

"I guess that's true. But Paul still made tents when he was an apostle, ain't so?" He didn't seem to expect an answer. "How are you, Anna?"

She clenched her teeth, determined not to say what she was thinking. But the words slipped past her guard and came out anyway.

"It's my fault. If I hadn't brought the car here, none of this would have happened."

For a moment those wise old eyes surveyed her. "Joseph had nothing to say about what he did, then?"

"I didn't mean that." She fumbled for a way to express what she felt. "Everyone knows how fascinated Joseph is with machinery. I should have realized that if the car was there he'd start tinkering with it. I should have gotten rid of it."

"And Joseph should have known better than to crawl under a car supported by one old jack, ja? And all alone, besides, with no one there to help him. Ain't so?"

Somehow she'd rather cling to her guilt. Was that just another way of being self-centered?

Bishop Mose patted her hand. "We've all got plenty of real things to feel guilty about in this life, without taking on burdens that don't belong to us." He squeezed her hand briefly. Without waiting for a response, he moved off toward Myra.

Things to feel guilty about—she had those, all right. They'd been slapping her in the face ever since she'd returned. Her friends in Chicago would reassure her that she hadn't done anything wrong, that she'd just been trying to find herself, that she deserved to be free.

She didn't. The conviction landed on her. She didn't deserve that freedom she longed for so much. Not until she'd made things right with the people she'd hurt.

CHAPTER SEVEN

Samuel held Myra's hand in his, heart aching for his little sister.

Dear Father, give her strength. She will need it.

Strong wasn't a word he'd ever used to describe Myra. Their sister, Elizabeth, on the other hand—no one ever doubted Elizabeth's powers. Even though she came between Samuel and Myra in age, she'd bossed them all around from the cradle, and no doubt was doing the same for her husband and kinder out in Indiana.

Myra was the gentle, easily wounded one, and maybe closer to his heart for that

reason. He'd always thought he had to protect Myra. Until she married, of course.
Then she'd found her strength in Joseph. It
was a knife in his heart to think she might
lose that, all from a moment's thoughtless-
ness.

He should have insisted on going with
Joseph. He might have known Joseph
wouldn't be content to tinker around with
the car's insides. No, he'd have to test out
every bit of it, because that was the kind
of mind he had, endlessly curious about
every piece of machinery he saw.

"Samuel."

He jerked his mind back to the present,
realizing his name had been spoken more
than once, and stood to greet Daniel Glick,
Leah's husband.

"I just came from your place," Daniel
said, turning his straw hat in his hands.
"Everything is fine there. The kinder are
happy and the animals fed. I locked up
your house and saw to the horses myself."

"Denke, Daniel." He'd known, of course,
that everything would be taken care of.
That was their way in times of trouble.

"Is there any news?" Daniel lowered his
voice, glancing at Myra.

"Not yet." Samuel realized he was clench-
ing his hands and deliberately relaxed
them. "All we can do is wait. And pray."

"Ja. I am doing that, for sure." Daniel hesitated. He glanced at Leah, and it seemed
a silent communication passed between
them. "I was thinking that my oldest boy,
Matthew, might be some help to you in the
machine shop if Joseph is laid up for a while.
He seems to have a gift for machinery."

"He does that." Samuel had seen
enough of young Matthew to be aware of
the boy's interest. It was a sacrifice for
Daniel to be offering him, both because
Daniel could use the boy's help on his
own farm and because it was well known
that Daniel would rather see the boy a
farmer. "Let's talk to Joseph about it, soon
as he's able," he said.

Please, Lord . . .

"Things will change with Joseph laid
up." Myra looked up at them suddenly, her
face pinched. "I don't know how we'll manage."

"You mustn't worry about that now."
Samuel bent to pat her clasped hands. "It
will be all right. Joseph will be fine." She
needed to believe that.

Daniel moved off to a group of men. Leah stood, stretching a little, and Anna came to take her place on the plastic chair next to Myra. Someone offered coffee. Samuel waited. Prayed.

Finally the door opened. This time it was a doctor, a surgical mask hanging loose around his neck. He looked a bit startled by all the people there, gazing from one to the other.

Myra rose, Samuel and Anna standing with her. "My husband . . ." she began, and her voice wavered.

"Mrs. Beiler." The doctor looked relieved to have her identified. "Perhaps you should come out into the hall to talk."

"Komm, Myra." Samuel reached for her, but Anna already had her arm around Myra's waist. Together they walked through the door with her, Elias Beiler following them.

The door swung shut, cutting them off from their people, but not from their support. He could still feel them there, hoping and praying. Myra clutched Anna's hand. They'd grown close in the short time since Anna had returned.

"He's come through the surgery very well," the doctor said quickly, as if not wanting them to imagine anything else. "His vital signs are good, and he should be regaining consciousness soon."

"Can we see him now?" Elias asked, as if he couldn't believe his son was all right until he saw for himself.

"He's still in recovery now, but I'll have a nurse come for you as soon as you can see him."

Myra nodded, tears welling in her eyes. Samuel could tell that she hadn't caught much more than that Joseph was alive.

The doctor started to turn away. Surely there was more they should know . . .

"How extensive was the surgery?" Anna's crisp voice had the doctor turning back to them. "What exactly are his injuries?"

Again surprise marked the doctor's face. Had he not expected intelligent questions from them?

"The head injuries aren't severe. He has a concussion. There's some damage to his left eye, but we believe it will heal in time. He's very bruised, so don't be alarmed by that when you see him."

Anna nodded. "What else?" She clearly didn't intend to let him get away until they'd heard everything. Her years in the English world had taught her something of persistence, it seemed.

"The injuries to his chest were more serious. Several broken ribs, a punctured lung."

Myra sagged a bit at that, leaning against Anna's shoulder.

"He will be all right in time?" Samuel put the question he knew was in Myra's mind.

"He has a long recuperation in front of him, but he's young and strong. I don't see any reason why he shouldn't get back to normal, given time."

Elias put his hand against the wall, relief coming over his face.

"Denke." Myra's voice was little more than a faint murmur.

The doctor nodded. Then he walked briskly away.

Myra wiped at her tears with the palm of her hand, the way she had as a tiny child, and the gesture tugged at Samuel's heart.

"He's going to be fine," Anna said. "You see, Myra. Everything will be all right."

All right, in time. Samuel's mind spun with the changes it would mean for all of them until Joseph was well again. The shop, the horses, Myra's pregnancy . . .

Myra murmured something to Anna, their heads close together. She'd grown to depend on Anna so quickly, he thought again. It was gut, surely, to have Anna there at the house with all that the future held.

Except that Anna might not be the best person to depend upon. She might do exactly what she'd done before—she might run away.

Anna slipped out of Joseph's hospital room. With all the rejoicing going on, she wouldn't be missed. After nearly a week's stay in the hospital, Joseph would be coming home tomorrow.

Myra had seemed a different person when she heard the news. She couldn't be happy until she had him home with her, to spoil and care for.

Thank you, Lord. Anna murmured the silent prayer as she hurried into the elevator and pushed the button for the lobby.

For days she'd been looking for an opportunity to call her friend Liz in Chicago, but that normally simple task had proved unexpectedly difficult. Phone booths seemed to be a thing of the past now that everyone had cell phones. Everyone but the Amish, of course.

However, she'd spotted a lone pay phone in a hall off the hospital lobby. She could call her friend, find out what she needed to know, and be done in time to meet Rosemary, Myra's English neighbor, in the lobby for the ride home.

Rosemary had been a huge help with rides over the past week. The church members had taken over everything else that needed to be done, but that they couldn't do.

The woman intrigued Anna. Childless, with a husband who traveled for work much of the time, Rosemary nevertheless didn't have a job. That fact had certainly worked out to the family's benefit this week.

Anna started down the hall at a quick pace, saw the woman at the reception desk glance up at her in surprise, and slowed down. That was something else to get used to. There was seldom a reason to hurry in

Amish life, unlike the frantic pace of her routine in Chicago.

Her luck was in—the pay phone wasn't in use. She dug out a huge handful of coins and stacked them on the ledge. Now, if only Liz wasn't working the lunch shift . . .

The phone rang four times, and then the machine picked up. Anna bit her lip in frustration. When would she have another opportunity to call?

"Liz, this is Anna. Annie. I'm sorry to miss you—"

"Annie!" Liz picked up, cutting off her message. "Is it really you? Girl, I've been worried. Why haven't you called? Is Gracie all right? Where are you?"

It took a second to get back into the rhythm of Liz's rapid-fire questions. The last one Anna certainly didn't intend to answer.

"I'm fine. Gracie's fine. I'm sorry I didn't call sooner, but there hasn't been a chance."

"Nonsense."

Liz's sharp-tongued retort was typical. When Anna had first gone to work at the restaurant, she'd been more than a little scared of the woman. Liz had been a server at Antonio's for as long as the restaurant had been in business, and she didn't put up with slackers or sass.

Since Anna had worked hard and kept her mouth shut, Liz had had no complaint. She'd proved herself to be a true friend during the rough times.

"I've thought about you often, but things have been complicated."

Liz couldn't know how complicated. How good it would be to sit in Liz's cozy living room right now, feet up, eating popcorn and watching an old movie on television. That had been their favorite evening in, since Anna couldn't afford a babysitter and a trip to the movie theater.

"You can always find time to pick up the phone," Liz said, but there was affection under the tart words. "You sure that baby's okay?"

"She's doing great. Trying to walk, babbling all the time. She likes it here."

"So where is here? You haven't told me yet where you are."

Liz always came to the point. Anna didn't want to lie—probably couldn't lie.

Liz knew her about as well as Leah did. Maybe better, in some ways.

"It's best if you don't know. Then you won't have to lie if Pete asks you."

"I don't mind lying to Pete," Liz said easily. "But maybe you're right, at that. If I don't know, I can't make a slip. And Pete's been making a pest of himself."

Anna's stomach tightened. She'd been telling herself that Pete would have given up by now, but she knew that underneath, she'd been afraid of this. "What did he do? He didn't hurt you, did he?"

"He did not. He knows I'd see his sorry self in jail before he could count to three if he laid a finger on me. Honest, sweetie, that's what you should have done instead of running away."

"Maybe so." But she wasn't like Liz. For all the bravado she'd shown when she left home, she had an innate reluctance to make a fuss, to draw attention to herself, and above all, to go to the law.

Amish didn't go to the law to solve their problems. If they were harassed too much to ignore, they'd move on rather than fight.

"Well, it was your choice. If you need money—"

"No, nothing like that." Anna knew perfectly well that Liz had little to spare. "I just want to know what Pete's been up to."

"Hanging out around the restaurant, 'til Antonio got fed up and threatened to call the cops. That made him back off, but he's talked to everyone you know, trying to find out where you've gone."

Her heart sank. "I hoped he'd forgotten about us. Maybe he really does care about Gracie."

"Well, he had a funny way of showing it if he did." Liz had a core of solid common sense, and it showed. "Knocking Jannie around the way he did, and then cutting out on her when she needed him the most. You take my word for it—this is just a whim. He thinks he wants the baby because he can't have her. That's Pete all over, always wanting what he can't have."

"I hope you're right." Prayed she was right.

Pete's sudden interest in Gracie was the one twist Anna had never expected. He'd signed the relinquishment papers giving up his parental rights before Gracie was born, doing it with a sneer and a cutting comment. Why did he have to come back?

Anna rubbed her forehead tiredly. She'd better wind this up before she ran out of coins.

"I wouldn't worry too much," Liz said. "He's either going to lose interest because it's too much work to go on looking, or he's going to end up in jail again for dealing. Either way, you don't need to be afraid of him."

"I'll try not to. Thanks, Liz. I hate to cut this short, but my ride's probably waiting for me."

"You kiss that baby for me, okay? And call me again when you can. And Annie? Don't worry. It's bad for you. Gives you wrinkles."

"Okay, okay," she said, laughing a little in spite of herself. "I'll call you again when I can."

She hung up but sat for a moment, pressing her fingers against her forehead, trying to swallow the lump in her throat. It had been so good to hear Liz's no-nonsense tones and even better to feel the sturdy affection that lay behind the words.

But the news Liz had delivered hadn't been what Anna had hoped. She'd longed to hear that Pete had disappeared back into the underworld he usually inhabited, and had lost interest as soon as she was gone, but apparently that wasn't the case.

She straightened, scolding herself. She couldn't give in to discouragement. She and Gracie were safe here. Besides, Myra and Joseph needed her. She couldn't desert them now.

The only trouble was that the longer she stayed, the harder it would be on everyone when she left.

Well, she'd deal with that when she had to. She rose, turned, and saw Samuel leaning against the wall opposite her.

Her temper flared. "Were you listening in on my phone call?"

He pushed himself away from the wall, no shadow of returning anger in his face. "It's not my business who you call, Anna. I was looking for you because Rosemary is waiting."

She'd almost rather he snapped back at her, instead of being so reasonable. "Sorry." She bit off the word and started back down the hall.

He fell into step beside her. "I tried to stay in touch with my English friends when I came back. But it just didn't work."

"Why not?"

He shrugged. "I guess we didn't understand each other's lives anymore. We didn't have anything to say to each other."

"That won't happen with Liz. We're too close for that."

He pushed the door open, holding it for her. "I hope you're right, if that's what you want. But maybe in the long run you'll drift apart. That doesn't mean the friendship wasn't strong, just that it was time for it to end."

In the long run she wouldn't be here. She might not be lying outright about that, but with every word, every thought, she was deceiving people. She'd thought it wouldn't matter, as long as Gracie was safe, but it did.

"I just want to go over the records for the shop." Joseph tried to push himself up from the rocking chair in which he'd been settled. He grimaced in pain, and Anna helped Myra ease him gently back down.

"I'll get the books, all right?" That was

the last thing Anna thought Joseph should be doing after the exhausting day he'd had coming home from the hospital, but he'd reached the point of irrationality.

She exchanged glances with Myra and saw that her sister-in-law was thinking exactly what she was. If Joseph were a cranky toddler, they'd put him to bed no matter how he objected.

Daadi, sitting in the rocker across the room, cleared his throat. When Anna looked at him, he nodded slightly.

All right, she'd get the books. She headed out the back door, pausing on the porch step to listen to the stillness.

Dusk had settled over the farm, easing away the day's work, telling them it was time for rest. It reminded her of the story-book she'd read to Sarah and Gracie when she'd settled them in bed, all about the mother creatures of the farm putting their babies to sleep.

Thank goodness the rest of the family, except for Daadi, had finally gone home. They'd meant well, she supposed, gathering around to share the happiness that Joseph had left the hospital at last. But she'd seen the pain and exhaustion on his face.

She walked across the lawn, frowning when she realized that the shop door stood open, framing a rectangle of light from a lamp.

Samuel must still be there.

She stopped in the doorway. "Samuel, you are working late."

"Ach, not working exactly." His hand was arrested on the point of extinguishing the battery-powered lamp that stood on the workbench. "Just clearing up a little. What brings you out here?"

"Joseph. He won't settle down and go to bed. He wants to look at the records."

"He thinks I won't keep up with the paperwork, that's all." Samuel grinned, shaking his head. "And he'd be right about that. But should Joseph be taxing his eyes with figures?"

"Probably not, but he's past being sensible. Maybe if he sees for himself, he'll be content to go to bed where he belongs."

"Stubborn, that's what he is." Samuel pulled a dark green ledger from a shelf. "I will go in with you, if that is all right, and tell him everything is under control. He might believe it."

"I hope so." She waited in the doorway while he turned off the lantern and joined her. "*Is* everything under control?"

Samuel didn't speak for a moment, his face somber in the dimming light. "I'm not so gut as Joseph is at the work. Nor so fast. I'm thinking I should maybe send the gelding back to Mr. Bartlett. I'm not going to have time for him and the shop as well."

"You can't do that." The words were out before Anna thought about them. "The horses mean so much to you. You can't give that up. I mean, I'm sure Joseph wouldn't want you to do that," she added hastily.

"Denke, Anna." He stared across the fields toward his barn, as if longing to be there now. "But I can't let Joseph down when he needs me."

"I guess not." She couldn't argue with that. "Why not wait a few days before you do anything? Let things settle down a little before you make a decision."

"You give gut advice," Samuel said, smiling. "I'll think on that. Wait and see how Joseph is after he's had some rest."

"Rest is exactly what he needs. Even the trip home tired him. He should have been in bed hours ago, but he wouldn't go while people were here."

"Maybe he enjoyed the company after a week in the hospital."

"If it were me, I'd rather be alone."

He tilted his head, eyes crinkling. "Myra had a cat when she was little. Foolish creature tangled with a groundhog and came out the worse. The cat crawled under the barn to nurse its wounds, and Myra cried herself sick until I went in after it. I was bleeding worse than the cat by the time I got it out."

Anna found she was laughing as they reached the porch. "That's me, all right. Don't come near if you don't want to be scratched."

"I'll keep it in mind." He took a step toward the porch.

Anna caught his arm to stop him, and he instantly turned to her.

"Just one thing before we go in . . ." She should mind her own business, but she couldn't stop herself. "Remember what I said. Don't give up on the horse unless there's no other way."

He stood still, his gaze fixed on her face. "Denke, Anna." His voice was soft, his head tilting so that they were very close in the quiet evening. She felt the corded muscles of his arm, strong under her hand, his skin warm against her palm.

Her breath caught. His eyes seemed to darken, but maybe that was a trick of the light. The moment stretched between them, as fragile as glass.

Then he was turning to the house. "Maybe we'd best go in."

She nodded, moving quickly up the three steps to the porch and across it to the door. They'd better, before she let herself be so silly as to imagine she felt something for Samuel.

He followed her into the living room. Myra stood next to Joseph, her hand on his arm. "Komm now, to bed. The books will wait until tomorrow, ain't so?"

"Ja," Samuel said quickly. "There's nothing here for you to do tonight. Get some rest, and we'll talk in the morning."

Joseph shook off his wife's hand, frowning either from headache or frustration. "Everyone should just stop telling me what to do. I'm fine."

Myra looked at Anna—the wordless exchange of mothers who know the signs of overtiredness in young children. The sensation of understanding and being understood jolted her, coming so close on that moment outside with Samuel. A flicker of panic went through her. She didn't want to be fitting in here. She didn't belong here any longer.

Without a word, Samuel handed Joseph the ledger. Joseph opened it, stared at the page for a moment, and then slammed it shut, pressing a hand to his forehead.

"Useless," he muttered. "I'm useless. I can't even see the page to keep the books for you. What gut am I like this?"

Samuel's face tightened, a muscle twitching next to his lips. Anna knew what he was going to say, and she was helpless to stop him.

"I can handle the business until you are well. You must not fret over it. I'll send the gelding back to the Englischer so I can concentrate on the shop."

A protest rose to her lips, but she stifled it. This wasn't her business, remember?

"Oh, Samuel, you mustn't do that." Myra's face puckered. Poor Myra was on the verge of tears, worn out by her worries for Joseph and her fears about her pregnancy.

"Myra . . ." Anna wasn't sure what she intended to say, but she didn't get a chance.

"That is enough." Daad's voice was quiet, but it carried a firmness that wouldn't be denied, reminding them that he was the authority in the family. He rose from the rocking chair where he'd been sitting, watching them all. "Joseph, you are too tired to be thinking about the business. Your job now is to rest and get well so that you can care for your wife and family."

For an instant Joseph looked mulish, but then his gaze fell, and he nodded. "Ja, Daadi."

"There is no need for Samuel to give up his work with the horses. I have spoken to Daniel and Leah. Their boy Matthew will come every day, starting tomorrow, to work in the shop. I also will help. If more is needed, Mahlon can come in the evenings. Anna can take over the book work. She is gut with that."

He was telling them what to do without

the least doubt that they would obey. For an instant the old rebellion flared in her.

She slammed the door on it. She was a woman grown, not a heedless teenager. If she expected the family to take her and Gracie in, she had to do her part.

"Ja, Daadi," she said.

"Komm now." Daadi took Joseph's arm, and Samuel moved quickly to his other side. "It is past time you were in bed."

CHAPTER EIGHT

Samuel led Bartlett's gelding toward the ring he used for training. He hadn't expected to have time to work with the animal today, sure that despite what Elias Beiler said, he'd have to give up training the animal until Joseph was well again.

That would mean giving up entirely, he was sure. The little he'd seen of Bartlett had suggested the man wasn't endowed with much patience. If Samuel couldn't do the work on his timetable, he'd find someone else.

But to Samuel's surprise, by three in the afternoon he and young Matthew had gotten through the day's work, and with a bit of assistance from Elias, they'd begun to catch up on tasks that he'd let slide while Joseph had been in the hospital.

Matthew was keen on anything mechanical—that was certain-sure. Daniel was going to end up being disappointed in his wish to see the boy a farmer. There wasn't much point in arguing with a God-given gift. Probably the younger son would be the farmer in the family.

So the burden of the shop had eased, but another had come to take its place. Samuel couldn't stop thinking about those moments with Anna last night.

They'd been talking, that was all, just being friendly. He'd even been thinking what a relief it was that Anna was talking to him as she might to a brother, instead of an enemy.

Then she had put her hand on his arm, and he'd looked into her eyes, and he'd felt as if the world were not steady under his feet. He'd gone on one of those carnival rides once, when he was a teenager, where the floor suddenly went out from under you. It had been like that—confusing and exciting all at the same time.

His life wasn't a carnival ride, and he wasn't looking to make a commitment to anyone. Maybe he never would be. The thought of his father sent coldness through him. So he had to show Anna that he wanted to be her friend. Nothing less, but nothing more, either.

It was about time to show Star that he wanted to be friends, too. He led the animal to the center of the ring and stopped, unclipping the lead line and holding him by the halter. Star was getting to know him now, and he consented to having his forehead rubbed.

Talking softly all the while, he let go of the halter and walked around the animal. Star's ears moved toward him, his eyes watching Samuel warily.

When he'd gotten behind him, he flicked the line lightly toward Star's rump. The gelding's head jerked up, the whites of his eyes showing, and he trotted toward the fence. Another flick of the rope sent him cantering around the ring.

Samuel kept his gaze on the horse, turning to face him as Star circled, flicking the rope occasionally to keep him moving. The animal had beautiful conformation and a smooth, fluid gait. Mr. Bartlett had chosen well when he bought him.

But something or someone had made the horse cautious, even afraid of humans. Samuel had asked around, knowing the interest horsemen had in other people's animals. Word was that Bartlett had been ready to give up on the animal before he'd shown up here. A pity that would have been to let one person's mistake ruin such a fine animal.

Samuel was barely aware of time passing as he worked the horse, first in one direction, then in the other. When Star finally began showing signs that he wanted to stop, Samuel coiled up the line, turning away from the horse as if losing interest.

His senses alert, he waited to see what the animal would do. Was he ready to extend some trust? Star took a few steps toward him, head down. Then a few more. Finally he nudged Samuel's shoulder with his nose.

Pleasure welled up in Samuel as he turned toward the horse, giving him a strong rub on the forehead. "You are a fine boy, you are."

He walked away a few steps. Sure

enough, the gelding followed him. He circled to the right, letting Star follow, until he was facing Joseph and Myra's place. And stopped. Anna stood there, watching him.

The surge of pleasure he felt at seeing her was even stronger than his pleasure with the horse—strong enough to remind him of his decision. He must show Anna that he wanted to be her friend, nothing else. He couldn't let her feel awkward with him because of a moment's unguarded attraction. He also couldn't let her think there was anything more between them.

He walked toward her, the gelding following him. "I'm sorry," he said as he reached the fence. "I did not realize you were here."

"I didn't want to interrupt you when you were working." She was staring at Star, who had stopped a few feet away from the fence, eyeing Anna much as she did him. "Is this the same animal that was so skittish the last time I saw him?"

"He's settled down."

"You mean *you've* settled him down. I watched you working with him. That's amazing."

He shrugged. "Nothing so special about it—it just takes patience and gentleness."

"If that was all, anyone could do it. I've never seen a horse bond with a person so fast."

"Horses are herd animals, and he's missing his herd. I just helped get him wanting to be a part of my herd."

She looked unconvinced. "How can you possibly know what he wants? Honestly, Samuel, it's as if you can read his mind."

"Not his mind." He smiled at the idea. "But since the horse can't say what he's thinking or feeling, you have to learn to read his movements and reactions to understand him."

She thought that over, nodding slowly. "That's exactly what a mother does with a baby. Those first weeks are so scary, because you haven't a clue to what they want. And then, when you're ready to tear your hair out, you realize you've figured out what every cry and every movement is saying."

"It's much the same, I'd say." Her comments had set him wondering. "You had little Gracie from the time she was born?"

"Ja. Jannie never came out of the hospital after her birth." Anna's eyes clouded with the words. "She was able to hold the baby once, but that was all. Then she just slipped away from us."

He'd never met Jannie, but he could picture the scene just the same. "I'm sorry for your loss. It must have been ser hard for you."

"I loved her like she was my own sister. I guess I felt responsible for her, too, because she didn't have anyone."

Neither did you, Anna, he thought but didn't say. "Couldn't the doctors do anything for her?"

She shook her head. "They said Jannie might have lived a little longer if not for the stress of the pregnancy, but I know she never regretted having the baby."

"And you've never regretted taking her, that's clear."

"Not for a minute." Anna's lips curved in the way they did whenever she mentioned Gracie. "Even when she kept me up all night when I had to go to work early. Even when she scared me half to death running a fever."

What must it have been like for Anna, raised in a family and community that supported each member, to have dealt with such a life-changing experience all alone? He couldn't imagine.

"Gracie is lucky to have you."

Her eyes shone with unshed tears. "I'm the lucky one. She's exactly what I wanted most in the world, but I never knew that until I held her in my arms."

He hesitated. "Gracie's birth father—he doesn't want her at all?"

Tension tightened Anna's mouth. "He signed the legal papers giving up all his rights to her months before she was born. He just walked away."

The words set up an echo in Samuel's heart. His father had walked away, too. He'd thought that once he found his father, maybe he could understand his leaving, but he hadn't understood. He never would.

When he was growing up, folks had always said how much he was like his daadi. He'd thought then that nothing could be any better than that.

Anna was looking at him, maybe wondering why he was quiet for so long. Pain gripped his heart, and he tried to shove it away. Anna seemed to have the power to bring out all the thoughts and feelings he tried to forget, and for an instant that an-gered him.

"Did you want to see me about some-thing?" The question was too sharp, honed by the unsettling memories of his father.

Anna blinked a little, her face tightening at his abrupt tone. She took a step back from the fence, as if she shouldn't be there.

"It's not urgent. I've put together a simple way for us to keep track of the income and expenses, that's all. I'm sure you want to work with the horse now, so I'll show it to you later."

She turned, walking away with her head erect.

He'd upset her. They'd been talking like friends about something that was painful to her, and he'd cut her off as if he didn't care. He didn't like himself much at that moment.

But maybe her anger with him was all for the best. He couldn't let Anna start to depend on him, because he didn't trust himself enough for that.

This was right, he reminded himself firmly. So why did it make him feel so bad?

People were staring at them. Anna sat next to Myra in the waiting room at the medical clinic. She clasped her hands together in her lap, staring down at them, and willed herself not to mind.

She'd forgotten what it was like to be the object of that rude gawking. In the city, she'd been one of thousands of people, all busy with their own concerns, not so much as making eye contact with those they passed in the street.

Here, in these clothes, she was an object of curiosity. She'd always hated that. She hated it now.

She glanced at Myra and gave herself a mental kick. She should be comforting Myra at this moment, not absorbed in her own feelings.

She touched Myra's sleeve. "Maybe it won't be much longer."

At least she didn't have to be concerned that anyone else in the waiting room would understand the dialect. That was one advantage of their differences.

"Ja." Myra grabbed her hand and clung. "This test—do you know anything about it?"

"Didn't the doctor tell you what to expect?"

Myra shook her head. "He told us all the

risks of the test, and that I should have it anyway." Her fingers clutched and strained. "Anna, what if it hurts the baby?"

Anna wrapped the straining fingers in hers. "Listen, it's going to be all right. I remember when my friend Jannie had to have so many different tests, and she came through them fine."

"Did she have this amniocentesis?" Myra said the word carefully in English, there being no equivalent in Pennsylvania Dutch.

"Ja, she did." Anna had gone straight to the computer on campus then and looked it up, so that she and Jannie would be ready. "Why did the doctor say you had to have this test? Was it because of something that showed up on a blood test?"

Myra nodded. "The doctor said so. He has many Amish patients, so he knows about the inherited diseases."

That was one of the perils of being Amish. With most of the community descended from the same small group of ancestors, the chance of genetic abnormalities showing up was greater. Anna's heart twisted as she thought of her own healthy child.

"What will they do to me?" Myra's eyes clouded with worry.

"I'm sure the nurse will describe it to you." It might have saved Myra some apprehension if the doctor had explained when he'd ordered the test. "They'll do an ultrasound to see exactly where the baby is. Then the doctor will put in a long needle and take out a tiny amount of the fluid around the baby to test."

Myra closed her eyes for a moment. Anna seemed to see Jannie, face pale, closing her eyes at the prospect of yet another test, trying to shut out the bad things.

"Denke," Myra murmured, opening her eyes. "I feel better when I know what to expect." She patted Anna's hand and released it. "Let's talk of something else."

"All right. What?" She was willing to cooperate, although she suspected Myra wouldn't be diverted so easily.

"Are you sure you are willing to take care of the books for the business?"

"It's no trouble at all. I'm happy to help with the shop."

Except for the fact that Samuel seemed to be avoiding her these days. He still hadn't managed to find time to talk with her about the simple system she was trying to set up to keep track of expenses.

"You mustn't take notice if Joseph fusses at you about it. He thinks no one can do it but him."

"I won't let Joseph worry me."

As for Samuel—well, obviously he had been embarrassed by the foolish little surge of attraction between them. Maybe he'd thought she was growing too attached to him. Warmth came up in her cheeks at the thought.

"Something is wrong between you and Samuel," Myra said, again seeming to read Anna's thoughts.

Was she so transparent? Her first instinct was to deny it. "What makes you say that?"

Myra shook her head. "I know my brother too well. I can see what's happening. He likes you, and that makes him nervous."

"It's nothing—I mean, he doesn't like me that way. We're old friends, that's all."

Myra seemed to catch back a sigh. "He likes you," she repeated. "I saw it, and I

hoped . . . Well, I know I shouldn't matchmake."

"No, you shouldn't." Anna's stomach
twisted at the thought that people might
have been talking about her and Samuel.

"He's never been exactly outgoing with
girls. Slow and steady, that's our Samuel."
Myra's smile had a tinge of sadness. "But
after our daad left, it seemed like he turned
inward. Mammi tried to get us to talk about
it, but Samuel never would."

"He was about sixteen, wasn't he, when
your daad jumped the fence?"

"Ja. We were all sad and hurt, but Samuel took it the hardest. He and Daadi were
always so close, you see. Samuel just
couldn't understand it. He couldn't talk
about it, either."

Anna remembered when Ezra Fisher
left. The valley had buzzed with little else
for a couple of weeks. It wasn't unusual for
a teenage boy to take off, but for a man in
his forties with a wife and family—that was
practically unheard of.

And then a few years later, Samuel had
gone, too.

She hesitated, but the pressure to ask

was too strong to ignore. "Was that why Samuel jumped the fence?"

Myra's face clouded. "I don't know, not for certain-sure. He never talks about it. But I think he wanted to find Daadi. To find out why he left."

"Did he?"

Myra shrugged. "He doesn't say. He came back when Mammi got so sick. He tries to act as if everything is the same as before, but it's not. I just wish he could be happy again."

Anna's throat was tight, and she couldn't seem to come up with anything reassuring to say. Whatever was going on with Samuel, it was all tied up with his father's desertion. She couldn't begin to understand him, but she knew enough to be sure that giving in to their mutual attraction would be a big mistake for both of them.

"Mrs. Beiler?" A nurse, clipboard in hand, looked inquiringly at them. "We're ready for you now."

Myra stood, her face white and set, and walked toward the woman.

Apprehension shivered through Anna, and she murmured a silent prayer as she followed them. If this was bad news, how would sweet, gentle Myra find the strength to cope with it?

Anna took a deep breath and slid down from Daad's buggy, reaching up to take Gracie as Daad handed her down. Already, a boy in his early teens was running up to take the horse and buggy and lead them off—that would be his duty at the worship service this morning. The buggies would be parked in neat rows, while the horses were tethered in the shade, content to stand there for as long as it took.

If she could have found any excuse to avoid attending church this morning, she'd have grabbed it. She'd suggested that she stay home to take care of Joseph, allowing Myra to go to worship, but Myra wouldn't hear of it.

Probably Myra was happy for some time alone with her family. She'd been unusually quiet in the two days since her amniocentesis, taking a nap Friday afternoon at Anna's urging and spending most of yesterday making a new dress at the treadle sewing machine.

Worrying, most likely. Anna dropped a

light kiss on Gracie's forehead. Gracie smiled and patted her face in return.

The loving exchange heartened Anna. She glanced at her father. "I'll join Leah, Daadi. We'll be fine."

At least, she hoped they would. Sitting with a baby through a three-hour worship service could be a challenge, to say nothing of the fact that this was her first appearance at church since she'd returned.

"I'll walk over to her with you." Daadi held out his hands to Gracie, and the baby lunged toward him, smiling, already delighted with her grossdaadi after such a short acquaintance.

Daad must know Anna was apprehensive. Carrying Gracie, walking with her to where the women assembled before the worship service . . . that was a gesture of his support. Some of the tension eased out of her.

The service today was being held at the Stoltzfus barn. During the week, the family would have spent hours sweeping and scrubbing until it was as clean as any church building.

Anna still had vivid memories of how much work that preparation had entailed when they hosted church at the farm. Mammi had enjoyed it, though, almost as if all the preparation was a part of worship.

The benches would have come by wagon from the last host family. They'd be arranged in rows in the barn, along with copies of the Ausbund, the hymnal, even though most people knew the hymns by heart.

The white barn gleamed in the September sunshine. Beyond it, in the hedgerow, spires of sumac had already turned color, looking like so many flames.

Men stood in quiet groups or shook hands soberly, their white shirts, black pants and vests, and straw hats setting them apart from the world. When the weather grew colder, they'd add black jackets, and the straw hats would give way to black felt.

Daadi marched across the stubble of grass toward where the women were gathering, grouping themselves by age. Fortunately, Anna would be seated with other young mothers who'd probably be sympathetic if Gracie started to fuss.

She hoped so, anyway.

Heads turned to watch them as they

passed. Probably her cheeks were pink. She kept her gaze down, trying to ignore their interest. It would be a poor repayment for Daadi's thoughtfulness if she gave in to the desire to glare at people.

Her story would have spread throughout the church district by now. Did they believe it? Or were they thinking, whispering, that Gracie was probably her out-of-wedlock child?

"Here is Leah." Daadi greeted Leah and her little daughter, Rachel, before handing Gracie back to her, kissing the baby's soft cheek as he did. "I will see you after worship."

"Denke, Daadi," Anna said, but he was already moving off toward the group of older men.

"Wilkom to worship." Leah touched her sleeve lightly. "It's gut that you are here."

"Brave, don't you think?" Anna lifted her eyebrows in a question.

"Ach, don't say that," Leah said. "Folks are just happy to see you back, that's all."

"I hope they'll still be happy after they see how Gracie is during the service."

Anna bounced the baby in her arms. She wiggled, reaching toward the ground, reminding Anna of how Samuel read the body language of the horse. Gracie was certainly making her wants known.

"You can let her down now, if you want," Leah said, glancing down at her two-year-old, Rachel, who was busy pulling up blades of grass.

"If I do, I'm afraid she'll scream when I pick her up again."

Leah smiled. "We've all heard that before. If you need to bring her out during the service, Mary Stoltzfus has a bedroom ready on the ground floor for changing and feeding."

"We'll probably have to use it."

The commonplace exchanges made Anna feel better. Leah was talking to her easily now, more like her old self again. Maybe all it would take to relax the constraint between them was time.

Leah had understood, at least a little, when she had left. Would Leah understand why Anna had come back?

Her mind backed away from that thought. She couldn't tell Leah all of it, any more than she could tell anyone else. If the community knew that Gracie's father was after her, what would they do?

She glanced at the sober faces around her, at the quaint, old-fashioned clothes, at the barn where they would worship. They wouldn't understand. How could they? They didn't have experience with anyone like Pete, and couldn't envision the ugly underbelly of society where he lived. They might think that as Gracie's father, he had a right to take her, no matter what papers he had signed. Even Daadi, with his innate fairness, might think that.

Anna's arms tightened around Gracie, and she recognized the truth. She'd been thinking that Leah was putting barriers between them, but she was just as guilty of that herself.

Anna was the one who didn't dare cross the boundaries. She couldn't trust Leah or anyone else with the truth about Pete, because she didn't know what they might do.

However she might wish it otherwise, the chasm between her and Leah could not be mended. Not now, at least, and maybe not ever.

CHAPTER NINE

Gracie slept on Anna's lap, lulled into an early nap by the long, slow unison hymns that had opened the service. The first time Anna had attended an English service, a praise band had led the congregation in music so loud and fast that it had made her head spin.

She'd come to appreciate the lively songs in time, and now the long, slow, quavering notes of an Amish hymn sounded almost like bagpipe music. She patted the sleeping baby gently. Gracie appreciated Amish hymns, it seemed, just as she did buggy rides.

Next to Anna, Leah sat with her head bowed. On her lap, Rachel folded and re-folded a handkerchief, totally absorbed in the task. For just an instant Anna could feel herself at that age, sitting on Mammi's lap, doing the same thing.

On the other side of Leah her dearest friend, Rachel, for whom Leah's daughter was named, sat with her little ones close to her side. Anna had been cautious, see-ing Rachel again, knowing that if Leah had talked to anyone about her rebellious sis-ter, it would be Rachel. But Rachel had greeted her with a smile and a kiss.

Anna had never been quite so content as the teenagers here seemed to be. She glanced toward the section of benches where teenage girls sat, their dark dresses neat, white aprons pinned over them, heads bowed. Behind all that conformity, someone must feel as restless and rebel-lious as she had at that age.

And now here she was again, not rest-less or rebellious, just out of place. She was as separated from everyone else here as she was from Leah.

She bit her lip, staring down at her shoes. Maybe she was wrong about Leah. Maybe she could trust Leah with her fears about Pete. And even if she didn't, why did that have to keep them from being close? Everyone had secrets they didn't want to share.

And if you do, what then? her conscience asked. *Someday, when it's safe, you'll leave, going back to raise Gracie in the English world.*

When she did, she would break her sister's heart again. It would be even worse than the first time, worse than not being here when Mammi died. Grief took hold of her throat, so sharp and hard she could barely breathe.

Bishop Mose stood to deliver the long sermon. She tried to focus on his words, blocking out every disturbing thought.

The bishop began to speak about forgiveness, that cornerstone of Amish faith. Forgive as you would be forgiven. His voice was firm, but gentle and compassionate as always.

She hadn't expected to be bothered by the service today, beyond a little awkwardness. She'd assumed she could sit through it, saying her own prayers, thinking her own thoughts.

She couldn't. The detachment with which she'd been able to view the singing had vanished. Bishop Mose seemed to be speaking directly to her, and when he mentioned the Prodigal Son, she felt as if she'd been dipped in boiling water.

She tried to shut out his message. She couldn't. Her emotions battled, tearing at her, and she had to fight to keep back tears.

Gracie jerked awake on her lap, probably sensing her emotions, and started to cry. Anna cradled her, patting her, but it was no use. Gracie wailed, and Anna wanted to wail with her.

Murmuring an excuse to Leah, she slid out of the row, carrying Gracie quickly toward the door and out into the sunshine.

The moment they were outside, Gracie stopped crying as abruptly as if Anna had thrown a switch. She inhaled deeply, feeling her own anguish subside—still raw, but eased.

She jumped when Leah slipped an arm around her waist.

"Are you all right?"

"Ja. We're fine." She bounced Gracie in her arms as she started walking toward the farmhouse, pretending that Leah's concern was for the baby, not for her. "She stopped crying as soon as we came out."

"Gut." Leah walked beside her, holding little Rachel's hand. "But it was not Gracie I was worrying about. It was you."

Apparently Leah wouldn't let her get away with evading the question. Anna took another deep breath, trying to compose herself. She mustn't say anything, not when her emotions were so raw. It would be too easy to say more than she should.

She shouldn't, but the words burst out of her anyway. "I'm sorry." Her voice choked. "I wasn't here for Mammi. I'm so sorry."

"Oh, Anna." Leah's arms went around her, warm and strong and comforting, as they'd always been. "I know you must grieve over Mammi, but she loved you. She didn't blame you."

"I should have been here. I don't even know how—" She stopped, not sure she wanted to hear details.

Leah drew back so that she could see Anna's face. "Mamm was very peaceful at the end. I think maybe she always knew the cancer would come back, and she'd accepted it. She died at home, with Daadi holding her hand. She just seemed to slip away between one breath and the next, like stepping through a doorway."

Anna felt as if her heart were breaking. "I should have been here. How could she forgive me for not being here?"

Leah wiped the tears from Anna's cheeks. "You know the answer to that question, now that you have a child of your own. You never stop loving. Never stop forgiving."

"Ja, I guess so." She glanced at Gracie, who was staring at them with wondering eyes. "I just wish I had been here to say good-bye."

Leah patted her arm. "You're here now," she said simply. "That's enough."

She should say now that she'd be leaving. Say it quickly, before she hurt Leah again. But she couldn't. Gracie's safety was at stake.

You could stay. The voice spoke quietly in her heart, startling her with a possibility she hadn't even considered. *You could stay.*

No, she couldn't. She fell into step with Leah, moving toward the house.

She couldn't go back to living this way. Her independence was too important to her. She couldn't give that up.

But they love you here. They love Gracie. You could be safe.

They mounted the steps toward the porch. The scent of coffee floated out of the open door, announcing that someone was anticipating the end of the worship service. Voices came with the aroma, clearer as they moved into the house.

". . . should be on her knees before the congregation, she should, not sitting there as if she's done nothing wrong—"

The speaker, realizing she had company, cut off her words.

Too late. Anna stopped, vaguely aware of Leah's arm going around her.

She couldn't deal with this. Clutching Gracie, Anna pulled free, turning to flee across the yard, stopping only when she realized that there was nowhere to go.

Leah reached her a second later, taking her hand. "Anna, it's all right. Don't listen to them. They don't know—"

Anna shook her head violently. "Don't. They only said what everyone else is thinking. I don't belong here anymore."

"Wait, here is another handful of receipts." Samuel passed the papers over to Anna, who sat next to him at Joseph's desk in the shop, trying to make sense of their bookkeeping.

She took the receipts, raising her eyebrows a little. "Are you sure that's all?" She obviously wasn't impressed with their system.

"I hope so." He hitched his chair a little closer to the desk, frowning at the stacks of papers. "I did tell you that I'm no gut at the paperwork, ain't so?"

"You did." She sorted through receipts, her face intent on organizing. "But you're not the only one. Some of these date from before Joseph was hurt."

"We get so involved in the work, you see." That wasn't much of an excuse, but Anna nodded.

"I didn't realize how busy the shop was. You have almost more work than you can handle," she said.

"Ja. Between the needs of dairy farmers to use machinery to meet government regulations and all the small businesses our people now run, it's commonplace to use hydraulic and air pumps powered by diesel engines. So that means more machines to be repaired or converted all the time."

"So Joseph's love of tinkering has paid off, I guess." But her face was shadowed when she said the words, and he suspected she was thinking of the accident. She didn't speak of it, though, just focused more intently on the receipts.

The activity did give him a chance to study her face and wonder how much she was hiding behind her concentration on the work. Myra had told him about Anna overhearing Mary Stoltzfus's unkind words, having heard about it in her turn from Leah. If Anna had thought to keep it quiet, she'd be disappointed.

Myra had been near tears when she told him. With all her tender heart, she wanted to see Anna settle down and be happy here.

Anna will not talk about it, she'd said. *She should. You try to get her to speak, Samuel. You've been through it, so you know.*

Ja, he knew. And he cared, but it was dangerous, talking to Anna about his time away. Talking would reveal his own still-raw places. And whether Anna would be helped if he did—that he didn't know.

Anna tapped a stack of receipts into

neatness and fastened them with a paper clip. "You've got to do better," she said, frowning sternly at him. "You and Joseph both. These tax records have to be in order for the quarterly payment."

"Ja, I know." He ran his fingers around his collar. He had a healthy respect for the IRS, and he didn't want to make any mistakes, especially with Joseph laid up. "You tell me what to do, and I'll try to do it."

"I think the simplest thing would be for you to put every scrap of paper for the business into the boxes at the end of every day." She gestured to the small cardboard boxes she'd placed on the desk, one marked for income and one for expenses. "Don't try to enter them into the ledger. I'll take care of that."

"Gut, gut. Nothing would make me happier."

"I hope Joseph feels that way." A faint line appeared between her brows. "I wouldn't want him to think I'm interfering."

"He'll not think that. And even if he does . . ." Samuel hesitated. "You'd know it was just the pain and frustration speaking, ain't so?"

She nodded. "It's hard for him to be laid up this way, I know."

"He should be happy you understand so much about keeping the books. I'd be lost in a blizzard of paper if I tried."

A smile chased the worried look from her eyes. "My boss used to say that. The owner of the restaurant where I worked. He was a wonderful chef, but he couldn't keep track of finances at all, so I helped him with that. He liked to say that was why he gave me time off for my college classes."

"It sounds as if he was a gut friend," Samuel said, wondering how he could possibly lead the conversation into what had happened at worship. Myra was counting on him to do it.

"Antonio always said the people who worked at his restaurant were like family, and that's how he treated us. Jannie worked there, too. That's how we became close."

"I'm glad you had friends there," he said. "It can be lonely out there among the English."

She nodded, her eyes darkening, and he thought she'd experienced that loneliness, too.

"But you decided to come back," he ventured. "I guess, with the boppli, you wanted to raise her with your real family."

For a moment something a little startled showed in her eyes and was quickly hidden. Then she nodded. "Gracie has loved it here."

She almost sounded as if she were saying good-bye. Maybe he'd just have to be blunt about it.

"I heard what happened with Mary Stoltzfus yesterday. You are upset."

She pressed her lips together. "It was nothing. Do you have a copy of the last quarterly tax form?"

He passed the form over. "Ironic, that was. Seems to me Mary Stoltzfus would have been better off in the barn hearing Bishop Mose talk about forgiveness. Maybe she'd have learned something."

Anna's hands stopped moving on the ledger. She pressed them flat against the pages, staring down. He heard the soft inhalation of her breath.

"It's not easy to forgive," she murmured. "Or to be forgiven."

"No. It's not." He thought about his own return. Forgiveness was never easy, especially when it was yourself you had to forgive.

"When you came back . . ." she began, but then stopped, shaking her head. "Never mind. It doesn't matter."

"It does matter." He startled himself, as much as her, when he put his hand over hers on the ledger. He could feel her tension in the taut muscles. "I don't know that it helps you, but when I came back, I had doubts about belonging again. Fears about how other people would accept me, but mostly doubts about why I came back."

She looked up then, eyes surprised and intent. "You doubted yourself?"

He wanted to back away from it, deny that he doubted, then or now. It seemed a weakness, admitting it. But how could he help Anna's struggles if he didn't?

"I came back because my mamm was sick. I had to, and I wanted to. My family needed me." He paused, not wanting to put it into words. "I came back for gut reasons, but not because of faith. When I knelt before the congregation, I knew they forgave me, but I felt like a fraud." His voice thickened. "Sometimes I still do."

It was very quiet in the shop, so quiet

that all he could hear was the sound of his own breathing.

Then Anna gave a little sigh. "Denke, Samuel. Thank you for telling me. For being my friend."

Friend. The word echoed in his mind. He had thought he wanted to be Anna's friend, but all at once he knew he wanted to be more than that. And the idea scared him half to death.

"No, no, Sarah." Anna gently removed the toddler, who was trying to reach the squeezer they'd set up on the picnic table in the yard, ready to do a big batch of tomatoes. "That's not for little ones. You and Gracie play with your ball."

She tossed the ball across the lawn and watched Sarah run after it, her sturdy little legs pumping. Gracie stood, waving both hands in the air as if she'd fly. Apparently deciding she could go faster crawling, she plopped onto her bottom and sped after her cousin.

"These tomatoes probably look like a bucketful of red balls to them," Myra said, pouring a pail of tomatoes into the hopper.

Anna shoved the wooden plunger down

and began turning the crank. "Wouldn't they have a grand time with them? We once went to a tomato battle . . ." She let that sentence die out.

"You and your friend?" Myra didn't seem bothered by the mention of Anna's life in the English world.

Anna nodded, watching the tomato juice pour out of the squeezer into a bowl. "Jannie and some other friends. It was a tomato festival at the county fairgrounds."

Liz had gone. And Carl, the boy Anna had dated for a month or two before realizing they had nothing in common other than sitting beside each other in class. Pete had been there for a while, grumbling and complaining.

Then he'd disappeared for an hour and come back, bright and talkative. She should have realized what that meant, but she'd been too naive, and was just glad that Pete wasn't making Jannie miserable any longer.

"And they threw tomatoes at each other?" Myra cleaned the next batch, hands moving quickly as she cut out any bad spots.

"Ja." Anna smiled, forcing thoughts of Pete and his drug use out of her mind.

"Picture a game of eck ball, only with tomatoes."

Myra giggled. "That sounds like fun. Nobody seems to play eck ball much anymore."

Eck ball, or corner ball, was a uniquely Amish sport. "Maybe boys don't like getting clobbered with that hard ball."

"You'd never get me doing it, that's for certain-sure," Myra said. She glanced at the tomato juice, seeming to measure the amount. "I was thinking I could cook down some sauce and make spaghetti when the family comes on Friday."

"I seem to recall everyone telling you that you weren't supposed to fix a thing," Anna said. "This is to be a chance for everyone to visit with Joseph, not to give you extra work."

"Ach, spaghetti is easy enough, and I know the children like it. Besides, it is Gracie's first birthday we're celebrating, so we have to make cake, too, ja?"

Gracie's birthday. Anna's heart clutched at the thought. "I can't believe she'll be a year old already."

"I know what you mean. When Sarah turned one—" She stopped, swinging around as the back door opened. Daad appeared, supporting Joseph as he made his way slowly out onto the porch.

"We thought we'd come out and watch you work," Daadi said.

Joseph nodded, pressing one hand against his ribs. "Got to make sure you're doing it right."

"You'd best be careful, or I might come after you with these tomatoes." Anna held up red-splashed hands.

Joseph chuckled and then groaned, clutching his ribs tighter. "Ach, don't make me laugh. It hurts too much."

"Then you'd best stay away from these two little girls." She nodded to Sarah and Gracie, who were rolling across the grass like a pair of puppies. "They're being a circus."

He smiled, his face looking less drawn every day, it seemed. "They make me feel gut." He settled in the chair Myra held for him, looking up into her face and saying something soft that made her smile and touch his cheek despite the tomato stains on her hand.

Anna's heart squeezed. The love between Myra and Joseph seemed to grow stronger with this adversity over Joseph's accident and with the waiting to hear the results of Myra's amniocentesis.

She had been waiting these past few days, too, and she wasn't sure what she was waiting for. A sign, maybe. Stay? Or go?

Her emotions had been all over the place. She hadn't even realized until she sat in worship on Sunday morning that she'd been considering staying. Thinking about being Amish again, forever. Committing herself to bringing Gracie up Amish.

Then had come that overheard nastiness, and she'd found it impossible to hang on to her emotions. Luckily no one had been there to see but Leah.

Of course they'd all found out anyway. If you wanted to keep anything to yourself, you'd better not belong to an Amish family, where one person's trouble or joy belonged to everyone.

She should have been annoyed that Samuel, of all people, had been the one to speak to her about it. Should have been, but wasn't. Samuel had been through this situation, so he knew. And he cared— cared enough to talk about his own deepest feelings to her.

Since then, they hadn't had a private conversation. They'd both been busy, constantly surrounded by other people. Still, if he'd wanted to, he could have found some excuse to be alone with her.

She glanced across the lawn. With the workday over, Samuel had gone on to his second job, working the big gelding. They were in the ring now. By this time, the horse was following him around like a puppy dog.

Daad gave her the next pail of tomatoes. "I thought I'd help you and let Myra have a break."

She nodded, watching as Joseph held out his arms to his small daughter. Myra bent over them, her hand moving, probably unconsciously, to stroke her belly.

"Are they going to be all right?" Anna asked the question softly, turning to her father as if she were a small child again.

"It will be as God wills." Daad's fingers closed over hers on the handle. "They will deal with whatever comes, with His help."

She nodded, tears stinging her eyes. Her emotions were just too close to the surface for comfort.

Daadi busied himself with cleaning the

next batch. "Little Gracie likes to watch Samuel with the horses, doesn't she?"

Anna nodded, a little surprised by the change of subject. "Samuel certainly has a gift for training horses. I never thought he'd have that skittish animal practically eating out of his hand."

"Samuel knows how to be slow and patient. The creatures sense that. After all the troubles with his daad running away and his mamm dying, he's turned into a gut man." Daadi glanced at her, his eyes bright with curiosity.

She saw instantly what he was thinking, and she took a mental step back. Daadi would be only too ready to jump into pairing them up, just like everyone else in the community. Matchmaking was their favorite sport, far more popular than eck ball had ever been.

"Daadi, there's something I've been wanting to talk to you about." Something she should have done before this, probably. "About the family . . ." She paused, surprised that her throat had tightened up. . . . "The family that I hit with the car."

That had been the determining factor that finally sent her over the fence. Driving an English friend's car, coming upon the Amish buggy on the dark road . . . For months she hadn't been able to remember any of it, and even now she remembered very little. But it had been the final straw in her rebellion, the thing that sent her careening into a world she had been ill-prepared for, for all her eighteen-year-old bravado.

"Aaron Esch and his wife and kinder," Daad said, seeming unsurprised. "Ja, what about them? They were shaken up, bruised a bit, but no one was seriously hurt. You knew that then."

She had known it, but only because Leah had told her. That should have been her first thought upon awakening in the hospital. Instead, she'd been wrapped up in her own concerns.

Glancing at Gracie leaning against Joseph's knee, Anna realized that even though the past years had been difficult, maybe they'd knocked the selfishness out of her.

"I never talked to them. I never told them how sorry I was. There must have been a lot of damage to their buggy, too." She had just walked away, taking refuge with her

English friends, and leaving her family to deal with the consequences.

"I took care of having their buggy repaired. That was only right." Daadi's face was grave, not minimizing what had happened, but not accusing her either. "Those Englischers, the ones that owned the car, I heard they wanted to give Aaron money so he wouldn't go to court, but naturally he wouldn't take it."

Naturally. That wasn't the Amish way, and they wouldn't take money for following the Ordnung, the unwritten rules by which all the Amish agreed to live.

"I wish I could repay you for that. It must have been a lot—"

Daadi stopped her with a hand on her arm. "There's to be no talk of repaying between family, Anna. You are my child. Would you want little Gracie to repay you?"

"Gracie hasn't broken the law. Or broken her mother's heart." Her throat choked on the words.

"Perhaps a mother's heart is made to be broken, over and over," he said gently. "That seems to make it stronger. As for the Esch family, if you want to ask their forgiveness, you can. Why don't you mention it to Esther? They're her second or third cousins, so she'd know how to talk to them."

"I will." She'd forgotten that Mahlon's wife was kin to the family. Asking their forgiveness wasn't much, but it would go a little way toward clearing up the mess she'd made before she left.

"And while we're talking about cars . . ." Daad paused, studying her face. "I'm thinking it might be time for you to get rid of the car of yours that's sitting in Joseph's barn."

She could only stare at him, astonished at the strength of the negative feelings that rose in her at the words.

She'd been thinking about staying, true. But to get rid of the car . . . maybe her reaction was telling her that she wasn't ready for that at all.

CHAPTER TEN

Anna walked along the road toward Rosemary's house, two loaves of pumpkin bread in the basket on her arm, with a sense almost of having escaped. She ought to feel guilty for thinking that, but it had been so long since she'd been alone that she couldn't seem to help it. She loved her family. She was grateful to them for taking her and Gracie in. Still, she couldn't help the feeling of being slowly smothered.

That was what she missed most about life in the English world. Not the presence of electricity at the flick of a switch or the ability to flip on the television and see what was happening in the world.

No, what she missed was more basic than that. Independence. The ability to live her own life and think her own thoughts. Most of all, sometimes just to be alone.

She turned in at Rosemary's mailbox, walking down the gravel driveway toward the house. The loaves of pumpkin bread she carried were a thank-you from Myra, who'd been fretting that she hadn't done anything to repay Rosemary for all the rides she'd given while Joseph was in the hospital.

The drive rounded a stand of hemlocks and the house came into view. A long, stone one-story, it sat in an L-shape around a fieldstone courtyard furnished with a loveseat, chairs, and an umbrella-topped table. A gas grill snuggled against one of the walls, looking far more elaborate than most people's stoves.

When Anna reached the door, Rosemary pulled it open before she could ring the bell.

"Anna, how nice! It's good to see you. How's Joseph doing? And Myra? Is the business going okay without him?" She took Anna's arm, practically hauling her into the house.

Smiling at the enthusiasm, Anna handed Rosemary the basket. "Some pumpkin bread from Myra, with all her gratitude for your kindness. And they're well." It took a moment to adjust to speaking English again, but then it seemed the most natural thing in the world. "Joseph is pretty antsy at not being able to do things, of course."

"Of course. Men are always terrible patients." Rosemary headed for the back of the house, beckoning her. "Come into the family room and have some coffee. I'm dying to talk to you."

Anna followed her past a formal dining room and equally formal living room. "You have a lovely home."

Lovely, but the rooms were so perfect they didn't look as if anyone used them.

"It's all right." Rosemary seemed to dismiss the space. "We really live back here."

The hallway opened into a large family room where sunshine streamed through a skylight. The kitchen was in one corner, separated from the rest of the room by a counter. White leather couches formed a semicircle in front of a stone fireplace. The glass panels of French doors gave a view of a landscaped garden with a decorative pond in the center.

Rosemary was in the kitchen, already pouring coffee into two mugs. "You will have coffee, won't you? You just have to stay and visit."

"Yes, thank you." Whether you were English or Amish, a cup of coffee was always a good excuse to sit and talk.

"Over here." Rosemary, carrying the mugs, led the way to a round table next to the doors.

Anna joined her, inhaling the scent of the flavored coffee. "What a lovely garden."

"Not bad," Rosemary said. "But it doesn't really fit here." She shrugged. "We thought we wanted to live in the country, but then we built a house and put in a garden you could find in the suburbs of any big city. Weird, isn't it?"

"Maybe so." Anna hadn't been thinking that, but now that Rosemary had pointed it out, she realized that what she said was true. The house and garden were a contradiction in the middle of farmland.

"So tell me." Rosemary leaned toward her across the table. "I've been hearing about you coming back after, what was it . . . three years away?"

"About that." Apparently it was too much to hope that the English, at least, wouldn't be interested.

"Why come back after that long? Because of the baby, I suppose." She answered her own question.

"Yes, because of Gracie." That was true, though not for the reason most people seemed to think.

"So this story that the baby is actually the child of a friend—is that true?"

Anna felt reasonably sure her mouth was agape.

Rosemary laughed. "That's me, tactless to the end. Sorry about that, but I figure if you want to know something, you ought to come right out and ask."

Anna found she was returning the smile. The words had been said in such a friendly tone that it was impossible to take offense. Rosemary reminded her of Liz . . . forthright and honest.

"I don't mind telling you. Yes, Gracie really is the daughter of a close friend who died shortly after she was born. There wasn't any other family."

"Sad. But the baby has ended up with plenty of relatives now, right?"

"Right."

"We built this big house thinking we'd have babies to fill it." Rosemary's eyes were shadowed. "It hasn't happened. Not yet, anyway."

"I'm sorry." She wanted to ask what the doctors said about Rosemary's chances of getting pregnant, since she wanted it so much, but she barely knew Rosemary, despite the woman's quick friendliness.

"No sense in brooding about it. That's what my husband says." She waved her hand, as if trying to dismiss the subject. "You must have found it tough, getting used to the real world after growing up Amish. How on earth did you manage all alone?"

"I had some English friends who helped at first." They'd soon fallen away, though. They weren't family. "Even so, I wasn't nearly as prepared as I thought I was. Getting a job, finding a place to live, getting my GED— all of it was new."

Funny, that no one else had asked that. Her family seemed to consider her life out there a blank page. Samuel, who knew what it was like more than anyone, had only talked about the adjustment of returning.

"Rough." Rosemary took a gulp of her coffee. "Was any of it what you expected? Was it worth it?"

She considered. "The independence was great. Just being able to decide things for myself was so different from anything I was used to."

"Yeah, but there are downsides to that—like not having anyone care if something happens to you." Rosemary sounded as if she understood that personally.

Anna nodded. That had been the worst of it. "I made friends, eventually. People who became like family to me." She shook her head. "I'm sorry. I'm talking too much about myself. Tell me about you. Where are you from?"

That was always a safe question in the outside world. People always seemed to be from someplace other than where they were. If you asked an Amishman that question, he'd look at you blankly.

"Originally Los Angeles." She shrugged. "My husband changed jobs a lot at first. Always onward and upward. You know how that is. We saw this area when we were driving to Pittsburgh for a job interview. He had this vision that we'd settle down in the country, live close to nature, and he'd quit working so hard, but he never will." She lifted her hands in a giving-up gesture. "He's gone most of the time. Truth is, I'm bored."

That was how Anna had always felt as a teenager, bored out of her mind by the sameness of life here. Now—well, now she didn't have time to be bored. Amish or English, she didn't have time for that, not with a child to raise.

"So tell me." Rosemary's curiosity apparently wasn't slaked yet. "Are you really going to stay?"

The blunt question gave her pause. She thought about her reaction to Daad's comment about getting rid of the car.

"I don't know," she said honestly. She glanced at the clock. "I should be getting back."

"Do you have to?" Rosemary shook her head. "Well, sure, you've got stuff to do, I know. That's the Amish. Always busy. Maybe if I didn't have electricity, I wouldn't be bored." She smiled, standing when Anna did. "Listen, come back any time. Whenever you want to feel like an Englischer again."

"Okay, I will." Funny, how easy it was to fall back into an English way of speaking.

"Great." Rosemary gave her a quick hug. "See you later."

Maybe Rosemary just wanted someone to talk to, but that didn't really matter. Anna had found a friend, and she hadn't even realized that she needed one.

Anna stood on the back porch, Gracie in her arms, watching the family gathered in the backyard for the picnic. With the meal over, adults settled in their seats to talk, while the children, too restless to wait for the cake and ice cream, chased each other around the yard or lined up for turns at cranking the handle of the ice cream maker.

Once again Anna had that dizzying sensation of seeing them as an outsider did. Who were they, these people who dressed so strangely and spoke a different language? That was what an outsider would see.

An outsider would see her as one of them. Same clothes, same language, same mannerisms—quiet, unassuming, humble.

No outsider could look at her heart and know what was happening there. Sometimes even she couldn't.

Gracie tugged at Anna's kapp string, one of her favorite occupations. Anna caught the chubby little hand and kissed it, making Gracie laugh. Certainty settled in her.

What she felt or didn't feel at this moment didn't matter. The only important consideration was keeping Gracie safe.

"Anna, you're keeping that beautiful boppli to yourself, ain't so?" Mahlon's Esther hurried up the porch steps, Mahlon close behind her. "Let me put these dishes in the kitchen, and then I want to take her." She paused to coo at Gracie. "She remembers Aunt Esther, don't you, little schnickelfritz?"

Gracie babbled something incomprehensible, clasping her hands and then stretching them up, as if ready to fly out of Anna's arms.

Anna was swept with the need to hold her close. *Don't be so eager to fly away, little bird. You need your mammi still.*

Would she ever feel ready to let Gracie go? Somehow she doubted it.

Mahlon held out his hands to Gracie. "Come and see me, little one."

Gracie hesitated for a moment, giving him a coy smile. Then she lunged into his arms. Laughing, he lifted her over his head, making her shriek with glee.

"Careful," Anna warned. "She just had her supper. You don't want applesauce and mashed potatoes all over you. Maybe I should take her."

Mahlon settled Gracie high in his arms. "You're just jealous because she wants Uncle Mahlon now. I'll look after her." Before Anna could answer, he marched off the porch with the baby.

Gracie would be fine with him. Maybe Mahlon didn't know a lot about babies yet, but he wasn't the careless boy he'd been. He was a grown man, perfectly capable of watching Gracie. Probably he and Esther would be starting a family of their own before long.

Anna should be helping Myra bring out the birthday cake instead of standing here worrying. She headed for the kitchen, her thoughts flickering to the girl she'd been. That girl had never taken responsibility for a thing, if she could help it. She couldn't have imagined how she'd feel as a parent.

"Anna, look at the cake Leah brought."

Myra was cutting thick slabs of chocolate cake. "Barbara brought snitz pies. Maybe get that cream out to go with. And the birthday cake is all ready except for lighting the candle."

Nodding, Anna went to the propane refrigerator for the whipped cream. She had made the cake herself that morning, yellow cake with white frosting, trimmed with pink icing. She wasn't good enough with icing to write Gracie's name, but Gracie wouldn't know.

There would be no photos to hold the memory. The ban on cameras irked her, but then, she wasn't likely to forget this day. "Shall I take coffee out then?"

"Ja, that would be fine." Myra looked up, her cheeks flushed. "Joseph looks gut tonight, ain't so?" Her eyes grew concerned. "I was afraid he'd be too tired for this. You don't think it's too much for him, do you?"

Anna glanced out the kitchen window. Joseph sat in the rocking chair they'd carried out for him, a pillow at his back to cushion the sore ribs and a footstool under his feet. He was deep in conversation with Samuel and Leah's Daniel, young

Matthew nearby listening in respectfully to his elders.

"Joseph looks fine right now," she said. "We can keep a close eye on him in case he starts getting tired."

"Ja, you're right." Myra shook her head. "I worry too much, but . . ." She hesitated, and Anna knew without more being said that she was thinking about the babe she was carrying and the test results she was still waiting for. "I'm glad you're here, Anna. I don't know what we'd do without you just now."

"I'm glad, too," she said, picking up the coffeepot.

To her surprise, that was true. The trouble with the car that had landed her at Joseph and Myra's door seemed to have brought her to the right place at the right time. Whatever the future, she was here with them now.

The future. She carried a tray with cups and coffeepot to the door, pushing the screen open with her hip. Let her mind go there, and it would start spinning again. With no money and no viable transportation, she couldn't leave now if she wanted to.

Samuel saw her coming. He jumped up

to take the heavy tray from her, his fingers brushing hers. "I'll carry that for you."

"Denke, Samuel." She withdrew her hands quickly, afraid someone might see. Might comment.

"He just wants you to hurry back for the cake and pies," Joseph said, smiling. "He's still hungry."

"I think you're talking about yourself, Joseph," Daniel put in. "A man needs plenty to eat when he's recovering, ain't so?"

Joseph patted his lean stomach. "Wouldn't hurt, I guess."

"There's a piece of cake and pie with your name on them," Anna assured him.

She glanced around for Gracie, and found her sitting in the grass with Sarah. They both had small wooden toys their grossdaadi had carved for them—a duck for Sarah and a dog for Gracie. The end of the picnic table held a stack of other gifts for the birthday girl.

Sarah held up the duck in front of Gracie's face. "Quack, quack, duck."

"Quack," Gracie parroted. Everyone laughed, and Daadi bent to pat her head.

Heart full, Anna turned back to the kitchen for the birthday cake.

When she came back out, the mood had changed. She sensed it the moment she approached the adults, reading it in the lowered voices and troubled faces.

"What is it?" She put the tray of cake down.

"Nothing," Mahlon said quickly. "It's nothing."

"Barbara was just telling us the gossip that's going around," Samuel said evenly, his gaze meeting hers.

A surge of gratitude went through her. Samuel understood better than anyone that she'd rather know than guess.

"What are they saying?" She stood stiffly at the end of the picnic table, feeling like the accused.

Barbara's normally ruddy cheeks were flushed even more. "Levi says I should have kept my mouth shut, and maybe he's right. But that Mary Stoltzfus is just plain mean-spirited."

"Barbara . . ." Levi said.

"Well, she is." Barbara glanced at her boys, chasing each other around the oak tree. "Maybe because she had no kinder of her own, she always thinks she knows more than anyone. Well, she was wrong about our Anna, and I told her so right to her face, right there in Mueller's store."

A mix of feelings roiled in Anna— surprise that Barbara had stood up for her mingled with annoyance that she'd done it in so public a place, along with anger at Mary Stoltzfus and her interfering.

"What is she saying?" She managed to say the words evenly.

Barbara's color deepened to a dull brick shade. "That little Gracie is really your child, and that the rest of the story is a pack of lies. And I said to her, 'Mary Stoltzfus, you should be ashamed and on your knees in front of the congregation yourself. Elias Beiler himself saw the papers making Gracie our Anna's adopted child, and the bishop is the one to know Anna's heart, not you.' That's what I said, and I'd say it again." She looked around, as if wanting someone to argue with her.

Anna couldn't say a thing. That Barbara, of all people, should be the one to spring to her defense—well, as Samuel had once pointed out to her, she'd never given Barbara much cause to like her. Her throat was almost too tight to speak, but she had to.

"Denke, Barbara. Denke."

She'd have tried to say more, but Gracie picked that moment to take two wavering steps. Even before Anna could exclaim about it, Gracie suddenly seemed to realize what she was doing, wobbled, and fell onto her hands and knees. More surprised than hurt, she burst into tears.

Daadi reached her before anyone else could. "There, there, little one." He scooped her up in his arms, cradling her against his chest. "You're all right, ain't so? You're just learning to walk. It takes a few tumbles to learn something new."

Gracie sniffled a time or two and smiled, with an effect like the sun coming from behind the clouds. She patted his beard. "Ga-da," she announced proudly.

"Ach, she's trying to say grossdaadi, the little dear," Esther said.

Murmurs of agreement, of love, sounded. Daadi's eyes were bright with tears as he smiled and kissed Gracie.

Anna tried to swallow the lump in her throat. She wanted Gracie to be safe, and so she was. The family would give Gracie more than Anna ever could alone.

And if, in the end, she decided they

should leave, at least Gracie would have known their love.

Longing welled up in her. Anna wanted to say something, do something, that would show what her heart couldn't express.

She thought of the car—two cars, really. A car had taken her away from them, and another had brought her back again. That was the car that was parked in the barn, mute cause of Joseph's pain.

She patted Gracie, secure in her grossdaadi's arms. "Daadi, I think it's time to get rid of the car. Do you know someone who would haul it away?"

He nodded, his eyes bright, his expression telling her that he knew exactly what she was saying.

"Ja, Anna. I will take care of it for you." He clapped his hands, getting everyone's attention. "Komm, it's time we lit the candle on that birthday cake."

Anna slipped out the back door into the dusk, much as she had when she'd been a teenager. Back then, she'd have been planning to hitch up Mamm's buggy and go off to meet her friends, sometimes Amish but more often English.

Now, she simply wanted a few minutes to herself—that, and to find the toy dog Daadi had carved for Gracie. Somehow in the midst of all the cleaning up, the toy hadn't made it back into the house.

She stepped down off the porch and switched on the flashlight she carried. She'd never find the small object in the grass without it. If the house had electric lights on the outside, as so many English farmhouses did, she could throw a switch and illuminate the whole area.

The Amish dictum had usually been that if it runs on batteries and doesn't depend on a connection to the power grid, it's acceptable. With the advent of so many other battery-operated gadgets, from boom boxes to cell phones and iPods, the lines had to be drawn over and over again.

She swept the flashlight beam across the yard in an arc. Could she get used to this way of life again?

She could give up electric lights, she supposed. But could she give up her independence after all she had gone through to get it?

The flashlight beam picked up a glimmer of white, and she stooped, but it was only a paper napkin, probably blown off the table.

She wanted to give Gracie the best life possible. Was an Amish life the best for her? What about college, a profession, all the things that the outside world considered important? The more she thought about it, the more she felt as if her head would explode.

"Have you lost something, Anna?" Samuel's voice came out of the dark beyond the range of her light. She swung around, the beam striking his blue shirt, his tanned face.

He put up a hand to shield his eyes from the glare, and she lowered the torch immediately.

"I'm sorry. You startled me. I didn't realize anyone was out here."

"Just making the rounds of the barn and henhouse," he said, moving closer.

"Don't you need a light for that?"

He gave a low chuckle. "It's not dark out yet, Anna. Switch that off and let your eyes get used to it. You'll see."

When she didn't move, he put his hand over hers on the flashlight and turned it off. She began to protest, and he held up his hand.

"Just wait."

They stood, not speaking. The rhythm of the evening settled over her—the rustle of the breeze among the tall sunflowers along the fence, the chirp of crickets, the lonely call of some night bird, answered by the whoo-whoo of an owl.

Her tumbling mind seemed to still along with her body. She inhaled. Exhaled. Saw the rhythmic flashes of the lightning bugs rising from the grass.

Gradually, as if the lights went up slowly in a theater, she realized she could see. Her eyes picked out the picnic table, the chairs, even a ball one of the children had forgotten. And there, in the grass almost at her feet, the small carved dog.

She bent and picked it up, closing her fingers around the smooth wood. "This is what I was looking for. Daadi made it for Gracie. I must have dropped it when I was taking her in."

"Ja?" He took the dog from her, turning it over in his hand. "I saw her playing with it, but I didn't realize Elias made it. He's a gut grandfather, he is."

"And father." Daadi understood so much, it seemed. All the things she didn't say.

"Ja." The word came out a little rough, and she remembered about his own father, who'd lost himself voluntarily in the English world, leaving his family to fend for themselves.

"I heard what you said to him about the car," Samuel said. "It's ser hatt for you, giving that up."

So hard. She nodded. "That car was the first one I ever owned. The only one, maybe. I guess it meant freedom to me."

"Ja, I know. I wanted a car first thing when I jumped the fence."

She should go in, but it sounded as if Samuel wanted to talk. Given Myra's worries about him keeping everything to himself, she couldn't discourage him. She sat on the picnic bench and patted the space next to her.

"Komm, sit for a minute. Tell me about it."

He folded his long frame onto the bench, propping one elbow on the table behind them. "Not much to tell. I found out that it's not so easy to get a car when you don't have a job or a credit card or even a telephone." He shook his head. "I was so green. Totally not ready for what it was like out there."

She studied his face in the dim light. "Why did you go, then? It seems so out of character for you. You were never a rebel."

"Like you," he said, his teeth flashing in a smile.

"Like me," she agreed, not even sure now what had been so important about that rebellion of hers.

Samuel looked down, his face growing serious. "It was my daad's leaving, first off. It unsettled all of us. I kept trying to fill his shoes, thinking I'd be able to go on without him."

"But you couldn't," she finished for him.

"I tried. I got baptized into the church, I courted Rebecca Miller, and we talked about marrying. But the closer it came, the more doubts I had. Mamm was still grieving about Daad, and I couldn't seem to feel right about anything, not knowing why he'd left. I got it into my head to go after him."

It made sense, and it also made her reasons for leaving seem frivolous in comparison. "You risked so much."

"I did. The church doesn't look lightly on baptized members leaving. I could have talked to Bishop Mose, explained what was in my mind. That's what I should have done. Instead I went running off, not telling anyone what I intended, hurting my family even worse."

His voice roughened, and the sound hurt her heart.

She touched his hand lightly, wanting to comfort him. "I'm sure your mamm understood."

"I hope so. But it pained her. It made it seem like I was siding with him." His fingers curled around hers, as if he needed something to hang on to.

"Did you find him?"

He was still for so long that she thought he wouldn't answer. Then he took a ragged breath.

"I found him. You know, I pictured him living in a shack someplace, maybe drinking himself to death, ashamed of what he'd done." His fingers clutched tighter and he stopped, as if he couldn't go on.

"It wasn't like that," she guessed, trying to help him along.

"No. Instead I found he had a whole different life, living with a woman who had a farm outside Columbus, Ohio. He looked prosperous and happy. He was so at ease that you'd think he'd never lived any other way, even though it was her money that put the clothes on his back and the car in his driveway, I'd guess." His words were heavy with bitterness.

"I'm sorry." Anna tried to imagine it and couldn't.

"I felt like I'd never known him. Like maybe he didn't even know himself."

Through the bitterness, she sensed what it was that Samuel feared. She longed to comfort him as she would Gracie.

"You're not like him. You're not."

"I hope I'm not. But how would I know for sure? When I came back, Rebecca wanted to pretend my leaving had never happened, but I couldn't. I couldn't marry her, not knowing if I wouldn't suddenly make up my mind to walk away."

"You wouldn't," Anna said again, searching for a way to convince him of what she saw so clearly. "You're not someone who gives up once you've set your hand to something."

Surely his endless patience with the horses, his steadfast determination to run the shop for Joseph, proved that.

He was shaking his head, and she put

her hand to his cheek, wanting to stop him. To comfort him. But his skin was warm against her hand, and the touch sent that warmth shimmering along her skin.

He looked at her, something startled and aware visible in his eyes even in the dim light. The breath caught in her throat.

Then his head came down, and their lips met. She ought to pull away, but she couldn't. She caressed his cheek, felt his arms go around her, drawing her close, and lost herself in his kiss.

After a long, dizzying moment he drew his lips away slowly. Reluctantly, it seemed. He brushed a trail of kisses across her cheek before he pulled back and looked at her.

"I didn't mean for that to happen," he said gravely.

"Neither did I." She could only be surprised that her voice sounded so calm.

"But I'm not sorry." A smile lit his face with tenderness. "I'm not sure what it means, but I'm not sorry."

He rose, clasped her hands for an instant and then let them go. "Good night, Anna. I'll see you tomorrow."

She put her fingers to her lips, watching him stride off toward his place until the gathering dusk hid him from view. She didn't know what it meant either, but for once, she wasn't running away.

CHAPTER ELEVEN

Are you still working on that old corn binder?"

Samuel looked up at the sound of Joseph's voice to see him leaning in the shop doorway. "As you can see. This time I'm going to get it working if I have to rebuild it from scratch. Should you be out here?"

Joseph moved a few more steps, listing a bit, and lowered himself to the wooden chair next to the desk. He was still hurting, clearly.

"Not according to your sister. She put me in a chair in the yard like she was putting a puppy in a pen and told me to stay there."

Samuel grinned. "Myra's getting a bit bossy, I'd say. Still, maybe you ought to go back out there and behave before she catches you. She might blame me."

Although truth to tell, he was glad to have some company about now. It might keep him from reliving over and over those moments with Anna last evening. He kept catching himself staring into space with a silly grin on his face.

"Ach, it's not going to hurt me to sit here a bit instead of out there in the yard. I'll take the blame if Myra catches me."

"That you will." Samuel tinkered with a stiff bolt, finding that his stubborn imagination still refused to be diverted from the image of Anna's face in the moonlight.

The why of it was simple, wasn't it? Anna had been a lovely girl, one anybody would want to kiss. When she'd come back, a grown woman, he'd thought at first that she looked hard, with her English clothes and her tight, wary expression.

Changing to Amish dress had made her fit in, but it had taken time for the wariness to fade. She probably hadn't even realized how her expression had countered her clothing.

Now it seemed that the bright, sassy manner and pert look of her teenage years had mellowed into a very appealing maturity.

Joseph's chair squeaked as he moved. "Do you think Anna is settling down all right?"

The question, coming out of the blue, made Samuel instantly guilty. Did Joseph know about last night? How could he? Anna wouldn't have gone in the house and said she'd been kissing him—that was certain-sure.

Samuel cleared his throat. "She seems contented enough."

At least he thought that was true. They had all been too busy since the accident to do much sitting around and thinking, except for Joseph, who probably had too much time for that.

"Ja, she does," Joseph agreed. "And she's keeping busy, what with helping Myra and taking care of the boppli."

"Then what has you so worried?" A thread of uneasiness went through Samuel.

"I guess I was just thinking about the girl she used to be, always running from one thing to the next, always so enthusiastic. She's changed."

Samuel sat back on his heels. Joseph's thoughts were following the same trail as his, though not for the same reason.

"She's grown up, is all. She probably took some hard knocks out there in the English world. That would change anyone." It had changed him.

"I guess." Joseph's gaze seemed to look into the past. "When I think about how she used to be, I remember that we all wished she'd settle down, especially when every boy in the district was looking at her." He smiled. "You, too, as I recall."

"Ach, no, not me." Samuel studied the bolt he'd just detached. "Well, maybe I looked at her from time to time. Such a pretty girl, who wouldn't look?"

"Well, then," Joseph began.

"I knew she'd never have time for someone like me," he added quickly. "I was too much a stick-in-the-mud for Anna."

He hadn't been last night, though. He wasn't the only one enjoying that kiss. They'd both grown and changed in the past three years.

"That Anna never wanted to take responsibility for anything." Joseph stretched a bit and then winced, putting his hand to his side. "Then the baby was dropped in her lap. Nothing takes more responsibility than being a parent does."

"True." Samuel gave Joseph a questioning look. "But I'm thinking you surely didn't come out here to talk about how your sister has changed. What is worrying you about her?"

"Not worrying, exactly." Joseph linked his hands together. "Just thinking about Myra and the new boppli. Myra's getting so she depends on Anna a lot."

Samuel mulled that over for a moment. "You're afraid Anna might go off and leave Myra flat, is that it?"

He had to admit that the thought had crossed his own mind a time or two. The longer someone spent in the English world, the less likely it was that he or she would ever come back to stay.

"It could happen. I don't want to think that, either for Anna's sake or ours." Joseph's forehead furrowed, the lines of his face deepening. "Myra needs all the support she can get right now. This worrying about the boppli . . ." He let that trail off.

"I know," Samuel said softly. "I am praying about it, too."

Joseph nodded, the corners of his mouth pinching in. "If only there was something I could do to make this waiting easier for Myra. Whenever she sees me looking at her, she puts on this smile like everything is fine. It near to breaks my heart."

If Joseph could do something, anything, he probably wouldn't fret so much. It was the inactivity that was eating at him, as much as anything, Samuel guessed. Joseph was used to working hard, dawn to dusk, not sitting in a chair, waiting to heal.

He gestured toward the corn binder's innards, knowing they made more sense to Joseph than to him. "Can you take a little look at this? Would it do any gut to tear this down already?"

Bending forward, Joseph peered at the machine, but he quickly sat back with a muttered exclamation. "Ach, I can't get my eyes to focus enough even to see. What if I never do? What will happen then?"

"Your eyes will heal," Samuel said quickly, regretting that he'd said anything about the binder.

"How do you know?" It was nearly a snarl.

"They will." He tried to sound sure. "You just have to give it time, like the doctor said."

Joseph nodded, but Samuel didn't think he was convinced.

Nor was he himself convinced. He'd been hoping that in a week or two, Joseph would be able to come back to the shop. If he couldn't . . .

Well, if he couldn't, then Samuel would carry on, even though he was beginning to think he might want to work at something other than the machine shop for the rest of his life.

Maybe he'd have begun to think that anyway, once he'd started working with that horse of Mr. Bartlett's. But Anna had something to do with the turn his thoughts had been taking lately. She'd stirred him up, making him think of possibilities. Maybe he'd been too mired in routine since he'd come back.

That was one characteristic that hadn't changed about Anna. She'd always come into any group and sparked it up. She might have grown up in many ways, but she still seemed to have that effect on people.

On him.

. . .

If any of her friends from Chicago could see her, they wouldn't believe their eyes. Anna knelt in the garden, picking the last of the peppers for the relish she'd told Myra she'd make.

She held a bell pepper in her hand, feeling the weight of it, then lifted it to her nose to inhale its freshness. Her city friends thought relish was something you bought at the grocery store.

She knew perfectly well what she was doing. She was keeping her mind occupied and her hands busy so she wouldn't think about those moments with Samuel. Those kisses.

It was funny, how she'd ignored him when she was a teenager. He was Joseph's friend, nothing else. She'd thought him slow and maybe not too bright.

But there'd been nothing slow about those kisses. And Samuel was bright enough when it came to the horses he trained, to say nothing of how he kept the shop going and supported Myra and Joseph.

Standing, Anna stretched her back and glanced over at the cucumber vines to see if any cukes remained, but the vines were brown and withering.

A movement caught her eye. Samuel came out of the shop and started for the house. Then he spotted her. He veered off the straight course and headed for the garden. A flutter of excitement in the pit of her stomach made her feel as if she were sixteen again.

"Anna." A smile teased the corners of his mouth. "Busy, I see."

"I told Myra I'd make some end-of-the-garden relish this afternoon. If I haven't forgotten how to do it, that is."

"It'll come back to you." He pushed his straw hat back on his head, glancing at the farmhouse, his brows drawing down. "Myra chased Joseph back into the house a bit ago. I hope he didn't overdo it, coming out to the shop."

"You didn't have him hauling any machinery, did you?" She tilted her head back to smile at him, her instinctive reaction startling her a little. Was she actually flirting with him?

It had been so long, she wasn't quite sure. For the past year she'd been so busy and burdened just struggling to survive that she hadn't even thought about men.

"No, I didn't." His smile flickered. "He's

not getting better as fast as he thinks he should. He wants to be back at work in the shop. I think he's secretly convinced that nobody can do it as well as he can."

"I don't believe that. He was just saying this morning what a great job you and Matthew and Daadi are doing. He feels bad that you can't spend more time with the horses, I know."

Samuel's broad shoulders moved in a shrug. "It makes no matter."

"But it's important to you. Working with Mr. Bartlett's animals could open new doors for you." She was probably saying too much, but wanted him to have his chance.

"Ach, I can be patient about that. It will work out as God wills."

Anna picked up the basket. "I've never been especially patient."

The fine sun lines around his eyes crinkled. "I remember that about you, Anna. You always had to push things along to make them happen faster."

"I guess so." Memories pricked at her. "Sometimes that didn't work out so well."

"Was it better, out among the English? Did things go fast enough for you there?"

He stood there as patient as if he had

all day to talk to her. Maybe it was that patience that had tricked her into thinking him slow.

"Things were always happening out there, I guess. The months went by so quickly. It was all I could do to get by, especially after Gracie was born. I didn't have time to think about whether I was bored or not."

He nodded. "I found it hard to keep up out there. Even knowing English, it was still like they were all talking a different language. And so fast. I'd be sorting out one thing and they were on to something else."

She remembered that feeling. "Once all I heard was English around me, I found I started to get better."

"Maybe you were more ready for it than I was," Samuel said.

She considered that. "When I left, I thought I was prepared because I had English friends. I wasn't."

Those first months had been indescribably difficult. A dozen times she'd been ready to come home, but something—pride, maybe, or stubbornness—had kept her going.

"We weren't intended to be prepared for English life," Samuel said. His eyes seemed to warm as they rested on her face. "Now that you're back, you're living a life you're prepared for. Even down to remembering how to make garden relish."

She laughed. "That's yet to be seen. But I'd best get going on it."

"One thing, first." He paused, as if not sure how to say it. "The county fair opens on Wednesday."

He stopped, and she waited. "Ja?" she said finally, when it seemed he was stuck.

He cleared his throat. "Joseph wants me to go and look over the equipment displays. I thought . . . well, maybe you would want to go with me."

For a moment she could only stare at him. Her instinctive reaction was to pull back. It had been too long. She wasn't ready.

"That . . . that would be nice, but I can't leave Gracie with Myra. She has enough to do."

"We can take Gracie along. She will like to see all the animals."

Anna had a sudden image of the three of them walking around the fair, looking like a family. "Samuel, I can't. People would say that we are courting."

He lifted an eyebrow. "Is that such a bad thing? Anyway, I thought Anna Beiler didn't care what folks thought about her. Ain't so?"

That had been the old Anna Beiler, the one who was careless with the people she loved. Now she knew better. If you lived in a community, you had to care what people thought.

But she also knew she wanted to go. She wanted to have a day with Samuel and the baby, to see how they were together.

It meant stepping into deep water, didn't it? Did she have the courage?

She took a breath. "Ja, Samuel. Gracie and I would like to go to the fair with you."

The house hadn't been this quiet since the day she and Gracie had arrived. Anna washed vegetables in the sink, trusting that neither of the two little girls would wake from her nap when she was in the midst of making the relish.

It was certain-sure that if one woke, the other would, too. Already Sarah and Gracie were more like sisters than cousins, looking for each other first thing every day.

She paused, staring down at the pepper in her hand. It was irrational, wasn't it, to feel almost . . . well, jealous that Gracie had so many other people in her life now. But for all these months, she'd been everything to Gracie. And Gracie to her.

If that changed . . . well, it should, shouldn't it? Amish or English, children grew, and their worlds grew, too, becoming larger than just mommy and baby. Maybe the question she was really skirting around was whether she ought to be moving into a relationship with Samuel.

What relationship? She called on the skeptical part of her mind. A few kisses, a single outing together . . . that didn't make a relationship. In modern society—but she wasn't in modern society, was she?

She got out the wooden chopping board, as comfortable now in Myra's kitchen as she'd been in her own tiny nook of a kitchenette back in Chicago. It had been a relief to come in from the garden and find that Joseph was taking a nap, apparently tired out from walking this morning, and Myra had gone to the store for groceries. That had put off the moment when Anna would have to tell them that she and Gracie were going to the fair with Samuel.

Not that Joseph and Myra would raise any objection. Quite the contrary. They'd have trouble hiding their elation, probably, and that would be enough to make Anna want to back out.

Maybe she should anyway. Maybe . . . The sound of a car in the driveway cut short that line of thought. She leaned over to look out the window over the sink, to see Rosemary sliding out of her late-model SUV.

Anna dried her hands on the dish towel and went to the door. She hadn't expected to see the English neighbor again so soon. She'd enjoyed their conversation and the taste Rosemary had given her of the world she still missed, but she suspected none of the family would smile upon her developing a friendship with an Englischer, thinking it too tempting. Which it probably was.

"Rosemary, how nice to see you." She reached the door before the woman could knock. "Myra is out now. She'll be so sorry she missed you."

"No problem." Rosemary took the open

door as an invitation and walked into the kitchen, her glance sweeping over the peppers, onions, and cauliflower on the counter. "Looks busy in here. I was hoping you'd have time for a cup of coffee."

"There's a pot on the stove," Anna assured her. "I'd love your company, as long as you don't mind if I keep on with this. I'm afraid the girls will be up from their naps before I've finished."

"Always busy," Rosemary commented, making herself at home and pouring her own mug of coffee. "I never saw anybody who liked work as much as the Amish."

"Oh, I don't know. I saw some pretty fierce workaholics when I lived in Chicago."

"Was that where you were?" Rosemary came to lean on the counter next to her, carrying the mug, obviously ready for a chat.

Anna nodded, sorry she'd let that slip. She'd be better off to keep that part of her life private. Still, what could it hurt for Rosemary to know she'd lived in Chicago?

"Maybe you're right." Rosemary shrugged her shoulders, staring a bit glumly into her coffee mug. "Here's my husband rushing off on another business trip just a day after he got home. Apparently the company can't get along without him for more than twenty-four hours."

"I'm sorry." Anna responded to the note of disappointment in Rosemary's voice. The woman was lonely, that was all, with her husband away again and apparently no prospects of the child she longed for.

"Oh, well, that's life, right? At least when he's not here I can eat a frozen dinner and snuggle up in front of the television with an old movie."

"*It Happened One Night*?" Anna suggested.

"*Casablanca*," Rosemary said. "If you want a good cry, you have to watch Humphrey Bogart giving up the woman he loves for the greater good. Hey, I thought Amish didn't watch movies."

"They don't." We don't, she corrected herself. "I had a friend in Chicago who loved all the old Clark Gable and Humphrey Bogart movies. We'd get together on a Sunday afternoon and watch them."

For a moment Anna longed to be in Liz's small apartment. The sensation was so strong that it was almost a pain. She was swept with that sense of being two different people—of English Annie looking contemptuously at Amish Anna.

"So what exactly are you making?" Rosemary left the subject of old movies abruptly.

"Relish. My mother used to call it end-of-the-garden relish because you put in whatever's left in the garden. It's delicious." She gestured with her paring knife at the array of vegetables on the counter.

"Hmm. I guess, if you say so." Rosemary sounded doubtful. "It seems like an awful lot of work just to use up leftover veggies. I'll bet I don't go through more than a jar of relish in a year."

"We do eat a lot of relishes. Haven't you heard of the Pennsylvania Dutch seven sweets and seven sours?"

"I guess I've seen it on restaurant signs, but I didn't know you had to make it from scratch. Don't Amish believe in buying food at the grocery store?"

Anna had to smile. Rosemary was obviously intrigued by her Amish neighbors.

"The Amish shop in stores. That's where Myra is now, at the grocery store."

"Well, then." Rosemary tapped a manicured fingertip on her mug. "Why bother to go to all this work just for a jar of relish? Or is it religious? Do you believe that God wants you to work this hard?"

Anna tried to sort out her thoughts, knowing she wasn't the person best suited to be explaining Amish beliefs to anyone.

"I don't know that any Amish person would put it that way, exactly. Most Amish want to work the land if they can. They take pleasure in raising the food their families will eat, and it does taste better than something that's been processed to death."

"Maybe so." Rosemary sounded doubtful. "I guess I don't get this whole living close to the land thing. Richard—that's my husband—he seemed to think he'd be happy puttering around the garden, but now that he has one, he doesn't have the time anyway."

"Everyone isn't suited to country life." That was the most noncommittal response she could think of. She certainly didn't want to discuss Rosemary's husband with her.

"That's me," Rosemary declared. "In fact, I'd think that was you, too."

Anna's knife slipped, barely missing her finger. "What do you mean?"

"Well, just that you were away for what—

three years? Is it really possible for some-body to come back and be Amish again after that?"

Anna's jaw clenched. It was a question she'd asked herself, but she decided she didn't care to hear it from someone else.

Rosemary's expression said she knew she'd gone too far. "Listen, I shouldn't have said that. My trouble is that I'm alone so much, when I do have somebody to talk to, stuff just falls out of my mouth."

"It's all right." It wasn't, but the woman had apologized.

Rosemary set her mug in the sink. "I re-ally did have a reason for coming today, besides being nosy. I wanted to ask if you'd like to work for me a few hours a week. That big house gets to be too much for me to keep clean. You could set your hours when-ever you want."

A refusal hovered on her lips. She had so many responsibilities here, with Joseph still not working. But a job would put some money in her pocket, money she wouldn't have to account to anyone for.

"Say twelve dollars an hour?" Rosemary asked, rushing the words. "That sound about right?"

If she had even a little coming in, she wouldn't have to feel so dependent on the family. And if she needed to leave . . .

She shut that thought off quickly. Hadn't she been telling herself that maybe this was the right life for her and Gracie? If she were really sure of that, she wouldn't be thinking that way.

So maybe she wasn't convinced. Maybe she didn't know her own mind at all. And Rosemary was still waiting for an answer.

"Thank you, Rosemary. I'd like to do some work for you."

CHAPTER TWELVE

As soon as they walked through the gates at the county fairgrounds, Anna knew she'd made a mistake in coming with Samuel. What had she been thinking?

The crowds flowed good-naturedly along the rows of stalls, aromas of a dozen different foods filled the air, and from the distance came the shriek of the rides. It was familiar, and at the same time it scared her.

It was one thing to be Amish again at home, among people who loved her. But when she'd ventured out, even in the church, her acceptance hadn't been complete. The memory left a bitter taste in her mouth.

And here she was back in the English world again, as an Amish woman.

"What is troubling you, Anna?" Samuel seemed to have an uncanny knack for reading her moods.

"Maybe it would have been better if I hadn't come." She glanced down at Gracie, asleep in the stroller Samuel was pushing. "If *we* hadn't come. It feels odd, being here like this."

"Because people are staring at us?"

"I hadn't even noticed that, but now you've given me something else to worry about."

He smiled at her tart tone. It was oddly freeing, knowing she could talk openly to Samuel in a crowd and no one would understand them.

"It hasn't been that long since I was one of them." She nodded toward the nearest clump of English who passed.

"Anna, you were never like them."

"Not those people in particular," she said. Maybe she shouldn't have picked a group of Goth teenagers, all in black, as an example. She shot a sideways glance at the piercings and dyed hair. "And they think we look odd."

"So we do, to them." Samuel was unaffected, no matter how people gawked. "You are Amish again now, Anna. That's how it is for us."

Her eyebrows lifted. "Is this a test?"

"Only if you see it that way. Only for your own sake, not anyone else's."

"I don't understand."

He gave a quick glance at the kids. "Those teenagers dress as they do because they want to be looked at. We dress as we do in obedience to God and the church, to remind us that we are to be separate."

A group of preteen kids in jeans and T-shirts, out of school for the first day of the fair, raced around them, jostling the stroller just enough to stir Gracie. She gave a startled cry.

"Ach, little girl." Samuel bent over the stroller before Anna could move. Unfastening the harness, he picked her up. "There, now. It's all right. There's nothing to be scared about. I have you."

He spoke in Pennsylvania Dutch, and Gracie quieted almost at once, as if she understood every word. Or maybe it was the slow, calm way he spoke that made the difference. Gracie, like the skittish horse, responded to his tone.

If they stayed, Gracie would grow up knowing the dialect, not even learning English until she went to school. If. Anna wanted to give her unruly mind a shake. It wasn't like her not to know what she wanted.

"Let's get a funnel cake and sit down for a few minutes until she feels like going back into the stroller," Samuel suggested. He nodded at a stand with long wooden picnic tables and benches under a blue-and-white canopy.

"Ser gut." Anna pulled the diaper bag from the stroller. "I'll give her something to drink while you get the funnel cakes."

By the time Anna had settled on a bench with Gracie chugging from a sippy cup, Samuel returned. He was balancing two paper plates filled with the powdered-sugar-coated treats.

"We could have shared one," she said as he sat down next to her.

"Speak for yourself." He grinned, holding a small piece out to Gracie. "Gracie and I will eat one ourselves, we will. Funnel cakes are wonderful gut, Gracie."

Gracie took the fried treat from his hand and lifted it tentatively toward her mouth. She stuck out the tip of her pink tongue and touched the sugar. Suddenly her dimples showed, and she crammed the whole thing into her mouth, then reached eagerly toward the plate.

Anna laughed at Gracie's delight, giving her a squeeze. "Just a little more. Too much funnel cake can upset a tiny tummy."

"It tastes like the fair, that's what it is," Samuel said. "They never taste quite the same when we make them at home."

"Better not let Myra hear that." Myra had decided to make funnel cakes yesterday as a treat for Joseph, since he wouldn't be going to the fair this year.

"I didn't say they were better," Samuel protested. "You know, that's my first memory of the fair. Sitting on my daad's knee eating funnel cake." For an instant, sorrow shadowed his eyes.

"For me it was caramel apples," she confessed, memory taking her back to that childhood taste. "Mahlon and Joseph always had to have their cotton candy, but I wanted a caramel apple. When we were little, we couldn't wait for September so we

could go to the fair. It was even more exciting than school starting."

Samuel nodded, understanding, and
gave Gracie another small piece of funnel
cake.

"It wore off when I was a teenager," Anna
said. "Then I just wanted to be like my
English friends."

"Plenty of us are that way during our
rumspringa. You weren't the only one who
hid jeans and T-shirts in the hay mow and
learned to drive in some English friend's
borrowed car."

"I didn't want them to see me as Amish.
I thought I could keep that part of my life
separate."

"Ja, kids are still trying that. Look at the
haircuts on some of the teenage boys in
service on Sunday morning. They didn't get
those cuts in the kitchen with their mother's
scissors."

If he was trying to make her laugh, he
succeeded. "I know. I noticed. If they want
to hide it, they need to be a bit more subtle."

"Annie!"

The exclamation had her turning toward
the sound. The next thing she knew, she
was being enveloped in a hug.

"You're back. I never thought I'd see you again. Where'd you disappear to? Don't you remember me? It's me, Shelley."

Anna disengaged herself. "Of course I remember you, Shelley." The hair that had once been brown and curling was now blond, done in a sleek, smooth style that just brushed Shelley's shoulders. Instead of the usual teen uniform of jeans and T-shirt she'd worn in the days before the accident, Shelley wore a pair of slacks and a bright, silky top.

"Never mind me," she exclaimed. Apparently she still talked in exclamation points. "I want to hear all about you. Look at you, with a husband and baby!"

"I don't . . ." Anna could feel herself blushing, but before she could think up an explanation, Shelley grabbed her arm.

"Let's sit down and have a cup of coffee together, okay? I want to catch up on everything."

"I don't know . . ." She glanced at Samuel. He waited, his face impassive.

"Oh, come on. It'll be fun."

"I would like to find out what happened to all of them." She said the words quickly in Pennsylvania Dutch to Samuel. "Do you mind?"

He stood, giving Gracie a little pat. "I will go and check out the farm machinery. I'll meet you back here in about half an hour. All right?"

She nodded. Of course it was. She had every right to catch up with her old friends. But as Samuel turned away, she caught the disappointment in his eyes. If this outing had been a test, it seemed that she'd failed.

"Not bad," Shelley said, sliding onto the bench opposite Anna and watching Samuel walk away. "If you like them solid and disapproving."

"Samuel didn't disapprove of you. He just didn't want me . . ." She let that trail off, since the thought didn't help.

"He doesn't want you hanging around with your old teenage friends," Shelley said. "I get that. How long have you two been together?"

"We're not. I mean, we're just friends."

This was more complicated than she'd expected. She wanted to make contact with Shelley again—to feel that their friendship had been real. She'd left so soon after the accident that she hadn't had a chance to talk with her.

"So, friends. Tell me more." Shelley's bright eyes flicked to the baby. "What about the baby's father? I thought you Amish didn't believe in divorce."

"We weren't married." She hesitated. If she didn't want to tell Shelley everything, it would be better not to say anything.

We're friends, aren't we? Her younger self seemed to be protesting. *We tell each other everything.*

"Wow," Shelley said. "And you went through with having the baby? But I guess you people wouldn't go for any other option."

Other option. Anna's arms tightened protectively around Gracie. "No," she said, her voice strangled.

"Well, looks like it all ended up okay," Shelley said cheerfully. "I sure wouldn't want to be settled down with a family right now, though. Just getting through school is hard enough."

It was probably safer to talk about Shelley's life than hers. "You're still in college?"

"Still." She sighed. "I'm just home now because my mom got all nostalgic about having everyone here for my dad's retirement party. I'm headed back to campus tomorrow."

"This must be your last year. Do you have any career plans?"

"No, I have another year. I changed majors too many times. It's accounting now, and I have to stick with it whether I like it or not. My dad says he's not going to pay good money for me to party and change my mind every five minutes."

That sounded exactly like the Shelley Anna used to know, and she smiled. "I'm sure there are plenty of good jobs for accountants."

"At least I'll be able to find a job in the city where something's happening." Shelley gave the fair a dismissive glance. "Did you hear about Casey? She got into UCLA, the lucky thing. Never comes home anymore."

"No, I didn't." Since she'd barely known Casey, it was tough to generate any interest.

"It's true. And Megan did get into Juilliard, but she dropped out her first semester. Couldn't stand the pressure."

"What about Jarrod?" Anna had been dating Jarrod that summer. She'd thought she was in love with him.

Their romance hadn't survived for more than a month or two after she'd left home. Still, she cared what happened to him.

"He's at Penn State. Runs track, got into a top fraternity."

Their lives seemed so different from hers that it was hard to find something in common. This was what Samuel had meant when he talked about drifting away from his English friends. Shelley seemed years younger than she was, even though Anna knew they were the same age.

"So you and Jarrod . . ." Shelley tipped her head to the side. "That didn't last long, did it?"

"No. After the accident we sort of went in different directions. But I'll always be grateful for the way his family helped me then."

"Well, they owed it to you," Shelley said. "Jarrod never should have let you drive their car. Naturally his folks wanted it settled quickly and quietly, before somebody got the bright idea of suing them for damages."

Anna took a moment to absorb that. It had never occurred to her that there was any reason other than kindness for their help.

"Nobody would have sued them," she said finally. "The other family was Amish. They wouldn't go to court any more than mine would."

"Other family?" Shelley looked blank.

"The family in the buggy we hit. Don't you remember?"

Shelley had been sitting next to her in the car that night. How could she have forgotten those terrifying moments—the lights striking the orange triangle on the back of the buggy, the realization that they were going too fast . . .

Gracie fidgeted in her lap, as if sensing her discomfort, and made a little sound of distress. Anna bent over her, soothing her, trying to get control of herself.

Anna didn't remember. She hadn't, in all these years, remembered anything about the accident. Those fragments that had flashed into her mind—she didn't want them there.

"Sure, I remember now." Shelley shook her head. "Sorry. It's been a long time since

I thought about that. Anyway, at least nobody got hurt."

Anna could only stare at her. "I did."

"Oh, yes, well, I guess I forgot that you were in the hospital afterwards. But you're okay, right?"

Shelley had forgotten. She hadn't come to see Anna in the hospital, hadn't gotten in touch.

Anna looked back at her teenage self with a sense of surprise. Had she really thought that Shelley was her friend?

Anna had known true friendship from both Amish and English people, but what she'd had with those kids wasn't it. She seemed to be seeing that whole time more clearly now.

They . . . Shelley, Jarrod, the rest of them . . . they'd been into the novelty of introducing an Amish girl to the wild side of life.

And she'd been no better. She'd welcomed their company because they were the perfect means of rebellion, not because she cared about them. It wasn't very pretty, but it was true.

Anna cleared her throat, trying to think

of something to say. There wasn't anything, it seemed.

"It has been so nice to see you, Shelley." Anna rose, putting the diaper bag in the stroller basket. "I must go now."

"Right, sure." Shelley glanced at her watch and gave a little shriek. "I've got to go, too. Listen, stay in touch, okay?"

Anna nodded. But she wouldn't. Neither of them would. She understood that now.

Samuel barely needed to touch the lines to convince Blackie to turn onto the county road. The old horse knew the way home as well as he did, maybe better. He'd chosen to drive old Blackie today, not wanting to trust one of the younger animals in fair traffic. Even Blackie had been a bit twitchy from time to time with all the excitement.

They could both relax now. There'd be little enough traffic on this back road.

He glanced at Anna. She'd been quiet while he'd negotiated the busy road around the fairground, but he'd caught a glimpse of her hand gripping the side rail. Now she patted the sleeping baby in her lap, her face tilted down.

"Did you enjoy the fair?" he asked, wanting to break the silence.

She nodded. "Gracie loved seeing all the animals up close. And that sausage sandwich we had was definitely overload."

He grinned, relieved to hear her sounding normal. "Too bad you didn't have room for one more caramel apple."

"Ach, don't remind me." She patted her stomach.

"Well, you have to eat the thing that means fair to you."

She sobered, glancing at him. "It bothered you when I wanted to talk with Shelley. I'm sorry."

That was a little more plain speaking than he'd expected from her, and it took him a moment to reply. "It wasn't exactly how I'd pictured our day at the fair together. For a second I wondered if you'd set that up."

She looked up at him, eyes wide. "I didn't."

"No, I know that. I could tell you were surprised to see an old friend there."

But her eagerness to talk to the English woman had made him stop and think about where he was going with this interest in Anna. Since his own return, he'd avoided showing attention to any woman, fearing his own character.

And if he did think about committing to someone, it needed to be an Amish woman who was strong in her own faith. He could hardly say that about Anna.

She pressed her lips together, making him wonder what she was thinking.

"Shelley and I are not friends anymore," she said finally.

He nodded. "That happens." He'd predicted that, in fact, but he didn't think she'd believed him.

She shook her head. "She and the others . . . it seems as if they're just kids playing at being grown-ups. Waiting to start their real lives. I can't believe I wanted to be like them."

He clucked to Blackie, who had taken advantage of his distraction to slow down. "It's not so odd. Most of us go through a time of wanting the freedom our English friends have." He suspected that her concern ran deeper than that, though.

Her eyes were shadowed. "I'm not sure that they ever were my friends." A car went by, sending out a spray of loose gravel, and she seemed to wince.

"Maybe, maybe not." He wouldn't say things just to make her feel better. "Sometimes English kids want to hang around with the Amish just for kicks. To make fun of them, like. But I'm thinking you had other English friends who were real, like Gracie's birth mammi."

Anna's smile flickered, chasing some of the shadows from her eyes. "That's true enough, but I didn't think to hear you say it."

"Ach, I don't discount the value of friends, even with folks who are very different. Take that horse of Mr. Bartlett's, for instance."

"The horse?" Her eyebrows lifted. "Now you're comparing me to a horse?"

He grinned, glad to see the liveliness coming back into her face. "Now, just hear me out. That animal was nervous as a cat at first, kicking at the stall bars, knocking over his water pail, making a nuisance of himself every time he was in the barn. So I got the loan of a goat from Aaron Zook."

"A goat." Her lips were twitching.

"Ja, a goat. Don't you make fun of me now, Anna Beiler. Those two animals got to be friends in no time at all, though they're as different as can be. Calmed that nervy horse down in no time flat, that goat did."

"So I get to be either a horse or a goat, do I?"

"Ach, you're definitely the horse, if you must be one or the other. Strong and high-spirited, but a mite uneasy in a new place."

"This isn't a new place—" She stopped, her head swiveling as a car roared up behind them.

He didn't bother to look around, concentrating on keeping his hands steady on the lines. The driver gave a loud blast on the horn, and the car swerved around them. Blackie, used to motor vehicles, flicked an ear at it, nothing more.

Samuel turned to Anna, but a casual comment died on his lips. Her face was dead white, her lips trembling, and she clutched the child fiercely against her breast.

"Stop—please stop. I have to get down. I have to!"

The hysteria in her voice sent a shock through him. "It's all right, Anna. They didn't hit us."

A farm lane led off to the right through a grove of trees. He turned Blackie into it and off onto the grass, then brought the buggy to a halt. He let the lines drop, knowing Blackie would be content to stand there indefinitely.

"Anna—" But before he could get out more than her name, she slid down from the buggy, carrying the baby. She rushed a few steps away and stopped, her shoulders shaking.

He jumped to the ground and went to her, approaching as slow and easy as if she were a wild creature. "Anna?" He reached out gently to touch her arm. "Was ist letz? What's wrong?"

She was trembling. A wave of caring had him putting his arm around her before he thought that she might not like it. But she didn't pull away.

"Was ist letz?" he said again. "That car passing so close—did that frighten you? Blackie is used to traffic."

She shook her head. "The accident." Her voice choked on the words.

Easy, he cautioned himself. Take it slow. "The accident," he repeated. "The one you were in with those English kids."

She nodded, head down, pressing her cheek against the head of the sleeping child. "I know what happened. They told me when I woke up in the hospital. But I never really remembered it."

"You had a head injury." He'd gone to the hospital once, like most of the community. And he'd helped out with Joseph's work, freeing him to see to his family. "Sometimes people don't remember."

"That's what the doctors said. That probably I'd never remember. But today, when I was talking to Shelley, a little of it flashed into my mind. And just now . . ." She stopped, as if she couldn't go on.

"When that car raced around us, it made you remember." He patted her shoulder, wishing he could take the pain away.

"I was driving. Jarrod said he'd teach me. They kept telling me to go faster, laughing, saying there was nothing on the road."

Her words seemed to gain momentum as she spoke, as if she couldn't get them out fast enough.

"It was exciting, racing through the dark, seeing the road curving ahead in the headlights. When I saw the orange triangle, the buggy, I was going too fast. I tried to swerve, tried to brake, but it was too late. I hit them."

"Ja." What could he do but agree? "Thank the gut Lord no one was badly hurt."

"It was my fault. I did it." Her eyes darkened with pain. "There was a family in that buggy. A mother holding her child." She held Gracie even closer. "I could have killed them. They must have been so afraid. How could I not remember that?"

"Maybe God knew that you needed time before you remembered," he said gently. "We can't understand His ways."

"I did that to them," she said again. "Afterward, when Leah tried to talk to me about it, all I found to say was that it wasn't so bad. That other people had done worse. How could I have dismissed it like that? What kind of person am I?"

"Anna, stop." He put his hands on her shoulders and turned her to face him. "If you see now that you did wrong, then that needs confessing and mending. But you're not that heedless girl anymore, are you?"

She took a breath, and it seemed to him that she steadied under his hands.

"No," she said softly. "I'm not."

"You're not," he agreed. "You're a woman grown, and you've had your share of pain. It's made you strong—strong enough to handle this, too."

Her eyes filled with tears, but they didn't spill over. She nodded.

His own heart was full, and he knew that he was past the point of choosing whether he had feelings for Anna. Wise or not, he did.

CHAPTER THIRTEEN

Anna could only be thankful that the trip to the medical clinic was by car, not by horse and buggy. Daad had arranged for Ben Morgan, an elderly Englischer who enjoyed driving the Amish, to take her and Myra today.

Not that she wouldn't eventually have to get back on the road in a buggy, but after what had happened the day before on the way home from the fair, she was glad it didn't have to be today.

How had that happened? She still didn't quite understand how she could suddenly remember so vividly after all that time had passed. It was as if a closed door in her mind opened, and the memories and emotions had come exploding out.

Samuel had been unfortunate enough to be in the way.

She had been the lucky one—lucky that he was there. For someone who didn't talk a great deal, Samuel had a gift for saying the right thing.

She glanced at Myra. Her sister-in-law sat quietly, hands folded in her lap, looking down. She was apprehensive, of course, about what awaited them at the clinic.

Doubt assailed her. Maybe Myra would be better off to have someone else with her. Leah had volunteered at the clinic, after all. She knew the people there, knew far more than Anna about genetic diseases.

But Myra had asked her, and so she was here, praying she could be what Myra needed today.

Praying even more fervently that all she'd have to do was help Myra celebrate good news.

Still, the very fact that Myra had to go in for an appointment seemed ominous to her. Good news might easily have come in a letter. It was usually bad news that had to be delivered in person.

"Here we are, ladies," Ben said, with a cheerfulness that didn't quite ring true. He'd undoubtedly figured out that this wasn't a routine visit. He drew the car up under a tree on the edge of the gravel parking lot. "I'll sit here in the shade. I brought my book, and I'm in no hurry at all."

"Denke, Ben." Anna slid out of the car and then realized that Myra hadn't moved. She sat frozen, staring at the front door of the clinic.

Anna's heart missed a beat. *Please, Father, guide me. Help her.*

She walked quickly around the car, opened the door, and took Myra's hand. "Komm, Myra. It's time for your appointment."

Myra just gazed at her for a moment, her eyes wide and frightened. Then she got out, moving as stiffly as a very old woman, and let Anna lead her up the front steps.

Once in the center hall, she guided Myra to a seat in the waiting room. The clinic, she knew, was on the right side of the building, while the labs and research facilities were on the left.

Leah had talked about the volunteer work she did for the researchers, helping to record the family trees of Amish families affected by genetic diseases. Would Joseph and Myra be joining that list?

"Sit down, Myra." Anna settled her on one of the plastic chairs that lined the wall. "I will tell them you're here."

The woman behind the reception desk heard the name and checked it off on the form. "If you'll have a seat, Dr. Brandenmyer will see you in a few minutes."

Anna nodded and returned to Myra, taking the seat next to her. She put her hand over Myra's clasped ones.

"It will be all right," she said softly. "You'll know soon."

Myra let out a soft moan. "If something is wrong with the baby, what will we do?"

If Anna closed her eyes, she could hear Jannie asking the same question. But it hadn't been the baby with a problem. It had been Jannie.

She took a shaky breath. She'd been worrying about how Myra would cope if the news was bad. Maybe she should be concerned about herself, too. Could she be strong in a similar situation yet again?

"Mrs. Beiler?" The door beside the reception desk had opened. The man who stood there was tall and lean, with graying hair and an eager, youthful smile. He approached them, holding out his hand. "I'm Dr. Brandenmyer. You're Leah Glick's sister-in-law, I understand."

"Ja." Myra seemed to thaw under his friendly smile. "This is Leah's sister, Anna Beiler."

The smile was turned on her. "It's so nice to meet you. We think very highly of Leah around here."

"It is good to meet you, Dr. Brandenmyer." That friendly smile had been accompanied by a look so piercing that it seemed he could see right through her.

"Just come along with me, will you please?" He went striding back through the door, and they had to hurry to keep up with him.

He led the way to a room that looked more like someone's private study than an exam room. He gestured them to a pair of padded chairs, picked up a folder from the desk, and then drew up a chair facing them.

He didn't put the desk between them,

she noticed. Some of Jannie's doctors had seemed to take refuge doing that.

"You've come here for the results of your amnio, so I won't keep you waiting." His hand rested on the manila folder on his lap, but he didn't open it.

Myra nodded. Her hand went out to clasp Anna's, and Anna held on tight.

"I'm sorry to have to tell you that it looks as if your baby has Down's syndrome."

Myra sucked in a strangled breath. "Are you sure?"

"We can't tell one hundred percent, of course, but yes, I'm sure. I'm very sorry."

"Denke," Myra whispered.

Anna put her arm around Myra's shoulders, pain like a knot in her chest. "I'm sorry," she murmured. "So sorry."

Myra nodded, her grip on Anna's hand wrenching.

"This is never good news, of course," Dr. Brandenmyer said. "We're more fortunate now than we used to be, because we're able to detect it early. It is a little unusual in a woman as young as you are."

Anna realized he was studying Myra's face as he talked, gauging how she was dealing with the news. He'd probably been in this situation more times than he could count, but there was no mistaking the compassion in his eyes.

"I have some reading material for you that will help you understand." He flipped open the folder and took out several small booklets, which he held out. Myra didn't move, so Anna took them.

"Thank you, Dr. Brandenmyer."

"It will be difficult to tell your husband, I know. I hope he's recovering all right from his accident?"

Myra nodded. "He is much better, ja."

"There is one thing you and he might want to discuss." His tone was cautious, as if he tiptoed into the subject. "A fairly high percentage of women who get this news decide to terminate the pregnancy. You can—"

"No." Myra seemed to come back to life. She put her hand protectively over her belly. "No, we will not do that. Our baby will be as God plans."

He reached out to pat her hand. "I didn't really expect anything else, but it's my job to tell you all your options. We know that about fifty percent of Down's syndrome babies also have heart defects, so that's another factor to consider."

Myra closed her eyes, as if she couldn't look at his sympathetic face any longer. Or as if she needed to hide.

"We understand," Anna said. She wasn't sure Myra could handle any more information right now.

Dr. Brandenmyer's gaze met Anna's, and she felt he understood all that she was thinking. He nodded.

"Maybe it will be as well if we leave it at that for now. Go home, talk with your husband, be sure you know what you want to do. You'll be seeing your regular doctor for appointments, but coming here for tests from time to time, so we'll talk again."

With her arm around Myra, Anna helped her to rise. She could understand now why Leah thought so highly of this man. No one could have been kinder.

But now she needed to get Myra home to Joseph. They'd have to figure out how to face this sorrow together.

"Is Myra doing any better today?"

Leah looked down at Anna from the

stool on which she stood, wiping down an already clean wall at Mahlon and Esther's house in preparation for worship services on Sunday. The work frolic was in full swing, with every available person from the family pressed into service.

"I'm not sure." Anna rinsed out the cloth she was using to wipe down the baseboards. "I thought so yesterday, but she really didn't want to come today, and I thought I shouldn't force her."

"She's helping by watching the kinder. The work goes faster without them, for sure."

"Ja, that's true enough. If we had your Rachel, plus Sarah and my Gracie and Barbara's two youngest running around, the house would be getting dirty instead of clean. Not that it isn't perfectly clean to start with," she added hastily. Esther's house had, as always, been spotless when they'd arrived this morning.

Leah chuckled. "For sure. I don't know how Rachel does it, but she can create more chaos in five minutes than the other children do all day."

"Maybe she takes after her naughty aunt." Anna said the words without thinking and then wished she hadn't. Her relationship with Leah was mending, but maybe it wasn't as strong as all that yet.

But Leah was smiling. "Ach, don't you talk that way about my baby sister. You weren't naughty, only spirited."

"And spoiled," Anna added.

"Maybe a little bit," Leah said. "But I'm as much to blame for that as anyone. Mammi and I were so happy for another girl after all those boys." She paused, looking down at Anna, her hand resting on the wall. "Maybe we made it harder for you in the long run. I'm sorry."

"Goodness, Leah, you've nothing to be sorry about." Anna blinked away the tears that had sprung to her eyes at her sister's words. "You were always the best big sister, even when I drove you crazy." She could think of a number of things her younger self had blurted out that she wished unsaid. "That's why I'm feeling that you'd be the better person for Myra to lean on now, not me."

Leah climbed down from the stool and moved it over, frowning a little. "I think you're wrong about that. Myra probably feels more connected to you. You're much closer in age, after all."

"Maybe that's so, but your work at the clinic makes you much better prepared than I am to help her."

The sense of helplessness she'd felt sitting with Myra in Dr. Brandenmyer's office swept over her again. Leah would know better what to say.

"Your friend must have gone through difficult times when she was pregnant, ain't so?"

"Ja, of course. But it's not the same. Jannie knew she was dying."

Leah's eyes clouded with pity. "Poor girl. But even though the cause was different, the grieving process is the same. Myra is grieving the loss of the child she expected to have, and she's adjusting to the one she will have."

Anna nodded, considering that. She'd read everything she could find on the stages of grief when Jannie had learned what she was facing. She just hadn't thought about how that applied to Myra.

"I see why everyone turns to Teacher Leah with their problems," she said. "Even if you're no longer the community's schoolteacher, you still have all the answers."

"Not all," Leah said, turning back to the

work. "After all, you're the one who went to college, ain't so?"

The edge in Leah's voice startled Anna so much that for a moment she just stood, staring at her sister. Then she put out her hand to stop Leah's brisk movements with the sponge.

"Leah? Does it make you angry that I took college classes?"

Leah kept her face averted. "Why would that make me angry? We'd best get to work, or Esther will think she has slackers for sisters-in-law."

Anna was tempted to let it go. But if she and Leah were going to repair their relationship, surely it was better to get all the sore spots out in the open.

"Talk to me, Leah. I can see that it bothers you. I know the church frowns on higher education, but I was living in the world then."

Leah stared down at the sponge in her hand. She turned slowly, still not quite facing Anna.

"I have a wise friend at the clinic," she said slowly. "An Amish woman who jumped the fence for the sake of an education. She told me once that people leave for all sorts of reasons—some for conveniences like electricity and airplanes, some for opportunities, like education. If I had ever left, it would have been for that. For learning."

"And I was the one who had that chance." Anna's mouth twisted with the irony of it. "I'm sorry, Leah. I didn't think. Do you still—"

"Ach, no," Leah said quickly, turning to her fully and clasping her hands. "I am in the right place for me. I know that for certain-sure. Our kinder are mine to teach and help, and I can learn all I want from reading. Sometimes I just wonder what college is like, that's all."

"And I was the one who got to find out, when I never cared a thing for learning. Your friend was right. I left for the freedom I thought I'd find there."

"Did you?"

Anna considered. Had she found the freedom she'd wanted so badly?

"Not so much as I imagined. I was still tied down, but by different things—the need for a job, for an education. And then by my love for Jannie and for Gracie."

"Would you change, if you could? The life you imagined for the one you have?"

"Never," she said instantly. "I have Gra-

cie. Loving her is more important than anything."

Leah smiled gently. "Then you know
how I feel, too."

Anna clasped Leah's hand and felt the
warmth of her sister's grip. They had crossed a bridge in the past few minutes, she
and her sister, and it was one that brought
them closer at last.

"You will have another sandwich, ja?" Esther passed the platter of cold meat sand-
wiches around the table again, determined
to feed her helpers.

That was part of the routine, almost a
ritual that Anna remembered from her earliest childhood. Whenever one family was
hosting church, all the women would gather
early in the morning to clean, then share
a simple lunch together before returning
home.

She'd never really thought about it before. As a small child, she'd found it a happy
break in the routine; as a teenager, she had
usually complained beforehand, no matter
how much she enjoyed the gathering once
she actually got there.

The work frolic was comforting in its own

way, a time for women's voices and women's work and women's laughter. If the men and the children had been here to share the meal, the talk wouldn't turn to matters of pregnancy, childbirth, and mothering.

"You're fortunate, you are, Esther." Barbara helped herself to a slab of applesauce cake. "When we host church, it must be in the barn. The way your living room and dining room join makes it easier to have it in the house already."

"I hope folks will not feel too crowded." Esther cast an anxious glance toward the front of the new house she and Mahlon had moved into in the spring. "We'll have to do the gathering with women in the kitchen and men on the front porch, I think."

"Ja, that will work best," Barbara agreed.

The gathering before the service allowed worshippers to file into the house in the traditional order . . . older women first, then younger, followed by children and teenage girls. Then the men, with the teenage boys bringing up the rear.

Anna found she was visualizing the silent procession, feeling the spirit of solemnity it added in preparation for worship. They didn't enter worship individually, chattering about the week's events or laughing with friends. Even if the place of worship was a barn, it was entered with reverence.

Esther poured coffee into thick white mugs. "I wish Myra had come today. Anna, you must take some applesauce cake home to her. Is she eating all right?"

"I don't think she's had much appetite the past couple of days, but she's making an effort."

"Gut, gut." Barbara heaved a sigh, her usually happy face solemn. Barbara had popped out five healthy kinder with little fuss and bother, and she was obviously hurting for Myra. "I wish we could do something. Leah, do you think this doctor can really be sure?"

As always, the family turned to Leah, the teacher, for answers.

"Not one hundred percent, as Dr. Brandenmyer told Myra, but the test she had is nearly always right. He's very gut at what he does. We're fortunate to have him in the area."

"The Amish are the reason he came here," Esther pointed out. "For the genetics, Mahlon tells me."

Anna had to contain a smile at hearing

her scatterbrained brother held up as an authority. She could tell that Leah had the same impulse, and it reminded her of all the times Leah had nudged her to keep an unwise word to herself, as if she saw the thought forming in a balloon over Anna's head.

"All we can do is give them our support and pray that the boppli is born healthy," Leah said.

"Dr. Brandenmyer said that fifty percent of Down's syndrome children have heart defects." Anna's heart ached as she said the words.

"Well, and that means fifty percent don't. We will pray for that, and for strength and wisdom for Myra and Joseph." Leah's tone was soft but firm. "Such children can sometimes go to school, like the Esch boy and Ezra Miller's two youngest."

"Ja, that's true."

Anna realized that Leah wanted to keep them focused on the positive, and she was right. Myra didn't need gloomy faces around her.

And Esther, who was still childless, didn't need to be frightened by a situation she might never have to deal with. Esther probably already worried about all the cases of Crigler-Najjar syndrome in the Miller family tree.

Esther's family included her distant cousins, who had been coming home from a visit to relatives when they'd had the misfortune to meet up with Anna Beiler behind the wheel of a car.

If she could find a chance to talk to Esther alone, she would ask about them. She'd never understood what the family had gone through until those moments coming home from the fair, when she'd held Gracie close to her body, terrified that she wouldn't be able to protect the baby if the worst happened.

She'd never be able to find peace until she could make amends. The thoughts she'd been having about staying—how could she do that if she were not forgiven?

The others began getting up from the table, gathering their belongings together, and she saw her chance.

"Let me help you clean up the kitchen, Esther." She seized a stack of plates and carried them to the sink. "I don't have to be home right away."

Esther protested, of course, but in a few

minutes the others were gone, and they were alone together in the kitchen.

Esther rinsed soap from a plate and handed it to her to dry. "You really didn't need to stay," she said.

"Actually, I wanted to talk with you."

"With me?" The whites of Esther's eyes showed, as if she were afraid of what Mahlon's fence-jumping sister might want of her.

"About your cousins who live out on the Fisherdale Road. Aaron Esch and his family." She sucked in a breath. "The people I hit with the car that night."

"Oh." Esther's apprehension didn't ease. "What about them?"

"I would like to go and see them." She chose her words carefully. "So that I can tell them how sorry I am. But I don't want to go there if they would rather I didn't."

That sounded as if she was trying to protect herself, wanting only to go if she could be assured of a welcome. Was that really what was behind her thoughts?

"Do you think they might be willing to talk with me?"

Esther washed a cup with unnecessary vigor. "I'm not sure that's a gut idea."

Anna felt as if she'd taken a punch to the stomach. "You mean they haven't forgiven me."

She hadn't truly anticipated that, she realized. Forgiveness was a basic tenet of Amish faith. She'd always thought, deep in her heart, that they would forgive.

"I don't know," Esther said, taking Anna's hand in her wet, soapy one. "Really, Anna, I don't. I mean, they wouldn't say much to me, being married to your brother. I just remember talk about how the little girl cried every time she had to get in a buggy afterward, and well . . ."

"I see." Where did she go from here? Anna wondered. If forgiveness wasn't possible, what then?

Chapter Fourteen

Samuel patted the big gelding, murmuring soothingly as he lifted the front hoof to finish the shoeing job. He had the animal in cross ties in the barn, but still, he was cautious, as always, working around a creature that outweighed him by so much.

Concentrating on the job at hand usually wasn't hard for him, but today too many other thoughts distracted him. Like Myra's unborn baby. Like Anna, and his feelings for her.

With Mamm gone, and Joseph's mamm passed as well, he'd thought maybe Myra would want their sister to come from Indiana at this difficult time, but she'd rejected that when he suggested it. She had her sisters-in-law, she'd said. She had Anna right here every day.

He began pulling off the old shoe. It had worn a bit unevenly, he noticed. He'd have to check the other shoes for that. A quiver went over the horse's skin, and he leaned against the animal's shoulder, comforting it.

Anna was here, ja, she was. He couldn't think about her without going right back to their trip to the fair. To what had happened on the way home.

The lack of knowledge that made a driver blow a horn in the horse's ears didn't surprise him—that sort of thing happened often enough that he didn't give it a second thought any longer, especially when he was driving an animal as well-mannered as Blackie. But Anna's reaction had startled him.

It had startled her, too, he figured. Her memories and grief had overwhelmed her without warning. She'd clutched Gracie as if she'd never let go.

As for him, he hadn't been much help to her in that crisis, now had he? Afterward, when it was too late, he'd thought of a dozen things he should have said to her. Maybe he really was as slow as Anna had always thought him.

Putting the hoof down, he straightened, stretching his back. Farriers who did this all day long often ended up bent over nearly double. He took the new horseshoe from the box.

"Komm now," he said, running his hand down the leg, pinching the cannon bone to get the animal to lift his hoof. "Almost done."

Ja, his day at the fair with Anna and Gracie had turned out different from what he'd expected. He'd thought they would have a pleasant day out, a chance for both of them to see how well they fit together, with no commitment on either side. Instead, a car full of careless teenagers had pushed them too far, too fast.

Well, him at least. He'd recognized, standing there feeling helpless when Anna needed him, that he'd gone beyond friendship, like it or not.

As for Anna—who knew what she felt? They hadn't been alone together since, so maybe that in itself was an answer.

He started to clinch the nails when the barn door rattled.

"Samuel?"

The gelding snorted, jerking against the cross ties. Off balance, Samuel tumbled backward.

"Samuel!" Anna arrived at his side a second later, before he could get himself up off the floor.

"I'm so sorry." She reached for him, her face filled with worry. "I shouldn't have come in without checking to see what you were doing."

She slid her arm around his waist to help him to his feet, and for a moment he let himself enjoy her embrace. Then he straightened.

"It's nothing. I am fine." He flexed his wrist, wincing a little. Maybe not so fine.

"You're hurt." Anna took his wrist in her hands, feeling it gently.

"It's nothing. Just a little bruise." He pushed away the temptation to let her keep fussing over him.

"I'll get some cold water." Before he could protest, she'd grabbed a bucket and hurried to the barn pump. She pumped furiously, filling the bucket.

In a moment she was back. She grabbed his hand and thrust his fist into the bucket. "This will help stop the swelling."

Suppressing a smile, he sat down on a straw bale, bucket and all. "Ja, Dr. Anna."

"Don't laugh," she protested, and he saw how seriously she was taking it. "I've caused enough trouble for people already. I don't want to add you to my list. Especially not now."

"It was Star's fault, not yours." He nodded to the gelding, now watching them as calm as he could be. "If I'd had my mind on my work, he wouldn't have gotten away with it."

Samuel certain-sure wasn't going to tell her why his mind had been straying, not with her sitting next to him on the straw bale, looking at him with such concern in those blue eyes.

He forced himself to stop drowning in those eyes and concentrated on what she'd said. "What did you mean, 'especially now'?"

"That's what I came to tell you. One of Bartlett's workers stopped by the house. Mr. Bartlett is coming this evening to see how the horse is coming along. If your wrist is bad, you won't be able to show him what you've done with Star." She sounded ready to weep at the thought.

"Ach, it's okay." He lifted his hand, dripping, from the water and flexed his fist. "See? And the gelding will do fine." He smiled. "As long as you promise not to scare him."

"Maybe I'd better stay far away." She gave a mock shudder. "I wouldn't want to jinx you."

"You couldn't do that." He saw the concern that lingered in her face, and he longed to wipe it away, longed to see her smile.

"I told Myra I would bring Bartlett's message over because I wanted to see you." She was looking down, so that all he could see of her face was the curve of her cheek. "I haven't properly thanked you for your kindness the other day."

"You do not need to thank me, Anna. You were hurting. I wish I could have found the right words to make it easier for you. But I'm not so gut at that."

"What you said was true, and I'd always rather hear truth than pleasant lies."

Who had told her pleasant lies? he

292 · MARTA PERRY

wondered. Someone out in the English world? A man she cared for?

"I'm sorry that you were frightened."

He didn't dare raise the question of who had told her pleasant lies. If he asked, if she answered, it would be yet another step deeper into a relationship he wasn't sure could work for either of them.

Anna shook her head. "Maybe what happened was for the best. It made me feel how much hurt I caused when I went away. If I'm going to stay here, I have to make amends for that."

If. The word chilled him. "Are you putting conditions on being here, Anna?"

She looked at him then. "I don't want to, but you're the one who said I must make amends."

"I don't think that's exactly what I said—"

She shook her head, cutting him off. "Close enough, and it's what I feel, too. Now that I know what that family went through because of me, I have to find a way to make things right with them."

"Your father already took care of the buggy. By this time, they will surely have forgotten about it."

Her eyes darkened. "Esther thinks they

wouldn't want to see me, so I've written them a letter, saying how sorry I am." She gave a shaky little laugh. "Who would guess it could take three hours to write a single page?"

"It's not easy to express what's in your heart."

Who knew that better than he did? Right now his own heart filled with caring for her, but he couldn't find the words to express any of it.

And even if he could, should he? Anna had the baby to consider. She couldn't take a chance on a man who might let her down.

Anna sat still a moment longer, looking at him as if waiting for something. Then she rose.

"Denke, Samuel. Thank you for listening. I should go. I hope it goes well with Mr. Bartlett."

He should stop her. He should tell her what he felt. But doubt kept him silent.

"I heard a truck," Myra said, glancing toward the side window that overlooked the lane and the ring where Samuel worked the horses. "It must be that Englischer, come to see Samuel about the horse."

Anna dried the dish she was holding and detoured past the window to put it away. "It is. He's standing by the fence, talking to Samuel."

She forced herself to move away again. It wouldn't help Samuel's confidence if he thought they were spying on him.

"Ach, I pray it will go well for him." Myra's voice filled with concern. "Samuel was so nervous he hardly touched his supper, did you notice?"

Anna nodded. She'd noticed. She'd seen his big hands crumbling his roll instead of lifting it to his mouth. She'd begun to notice too much about Samuel for her own peace of mind.

"Samuel has such a gift with the horses," Myra went on, apparently determined to talk about her brother. "I think it could be a business for him, don't you?"

Anna did, but she wasn't sure whether to say so or not. She glanced at the living room, where Joseph was sitting on the floor, playing with Sarah and Gracie.

"He wouldn't do that as long as Joseph needs him," she said, lowering her voice to speak under the clatter of dishes. "You know that."

"Ja, but Joseph is better." Myra was sounding more like her normally optimistic self tonight. "Look at him, playing in there with the little girls. He hasn't done that since the accident."

"We'll probably have to help him up off the floor when he's done."

Myra giggled. "You're right. And he won't like it, ain't so?"

That little giggle did Anna's heart good. "We'll make him behave, the two of us."

Myra nodded, her hand stilling on the cloth. "He's been so worried about me he's practically ferhoodled these days. But that must stop. I'm fine now."

Myra could hardly be fine, but if she was adjusting to the news, that was a relief. She'd seemed so quiet and stunned at first that they hadn't known what to do. "I'm glad you're feeling better."

"Ja." Myra ran her hand over her belly, smiling a little. "It's so foolish to worry. God will take care of our little boppli, I know."

Anna wasn't sure how to respond to that. Was Myra trying to convince herself that the test had been wrong? Surely not.

"I'm sure God will be with you and the boppli," she said finally.

Myra put another dish in the drainer, her lips still curving in a smile. "I love him already, you know. I feel as if my love protects him."

"Ja, I know."

This was bringing back memories. Jannie, convincing herself that all the tests were wrong, that she would be well and healthy, that Pete would give up his drugs, that they'd live happily ever after.

"You feel that way about your Gracie," Myra said. "At first I didn't know what to think when you told us she'd been born to your friend, but now I see that you love her just as much as if you'd carried her, like I am carrying my little boy."

"Did the doctor say the baby is a boy?" Anna didn't remember anyone saying the baby's sex. In fact, she'd thought Myra and Joseph didn't want to know.

"No, but I can tell." Myra caressed her stomach again. "I know."

Alarms went off in Anna's head. Myra's grief would be all the worse if she convinced herself of things that weren't true.

"You know, in those booklets the doctor gave us, it mentions a woman at the clinic who counsels patients." Now that Anna thought about it, that was probably the woman Leah had mentioned. "Maybe it would be a gut idea to go and talk with her a time or two."

"Ach, I don't need that. I have you to talk to, and Joseph. I'm fine."

"Myra . . ."

But Myra had walked over to the window. "Look, Anna. Samuel is working the horse now. Oh, he looks fine. You'd never know that gelding was the same skittish animal, would you?"

Anna joined Myra, standing back from the window so that Samuel would not catch their faces pressed against the glass. She could see Samuel perfectly well from here—his shoulders broad under his blue shirt, his black suspenders crossing them. He wore his straw hat, but even with the shade it cast she could see the intent look on his face as he worked the horse.

"He's done such a professional job with the gelding. I hope Mr. Bartlett appreciates it."

Myra clutched Anna's hand, as if that would make the watching easier. "I know

I'm prejudiced because he's my brother, but Samuel really is a fine-looking man, don't you think?"

Since that was just what she'd been thinking, she could hardly argue, so she nodded. "He has a lot of character in his face."

"Everyone sees that, I think. Everyone but him." Myra's eyes misted over. "When our father left, it seemed like he took all of Samuel's confidence with him. I'm afraid Samuel fears he's like Daadi. Unreliable."

Everything in Anna rose to deny that. "That's just nonsense. Everyone knows how responsible he is. Why, look how he's taking care of the business. He'll even give up working with the horses if Joseph needs him."

She was giving away feelings she hadn't even known she had, speaking so heatedly in Samuel's defense. But surely anyone who knew Samuel well would say the same.

Who was she kidding? She had feelings for him. If she were free to follow her instincts . . .

But she wasn't. She glanced into the living room. Gracie stood, a red ball in one

hand, attempting to throw it toward Joseph.
Instead it slipped from her grasp when she
flung her arm up, falling behind her. She spun
around, wobbling a little, looking at the ball
with round-eyed surprise.

Anna's heart clenched with love. She
couldn't follow her instincts where Samuel
or any other man was concerned, because
her daughter came first. Maybe she understood, better than she had thought at first,
Myra's frantic need to believe her baby was
all right. The love of mother for child was
elemental.

If she stayed, if Samuel was interested
and willing to commit . . . Well, those were
all huge ifs. How could she be sure that this
life was right for her baby? And how could
she be sure that her own rebellious spirit
wouldn't wake and demand freedom again?

As for Samuel, he seemed to have
backed away from the feelings he'd shown
the night he kissed her and from the intent she'd sensed when he'd asked her to
go to the fair. She'd thought then that he
was imagining them as a family. She'd
thought that a relationship was there if
she wanted it.

Since then, her sense had been that

he'd backed away. Even today, in the barn, she'd thought he was going to express his feelings, but he'd fallen silent.

Maybe he felt that was for the best. Maybe neither of them was ready for anything more than friendship.

Celebration seemed to hang in the evening air, mingled with the spicy scent of the marigolds planted along the edge of the back porch. Anna glanced at Joseph and Myra, sitting side by side on the porch swing. They looked . . . contented, that was the word. Despite all the trials of the past weeks, at the moment they were simply thinking of Samuel.

"So the Englischer, he was pleased," Myra prompted Samuel, sounding like a child who wants to hear a favorite story again.

Samuel leaned back against the porch post from his perch on the top step, setting aside the plate that had contained a slice of apple crumb pie. He glanced at Anna, as if inviting her to smile with him at Myra's moment of happiness.

"Ja, Myra, he was most pleased. He said he would recommend me to his friends."

"And he paid well," she prompted.

"He paid well." He grinned. "He paid well enough to make up for any customers I lost us in the shop while Joseph was out."

"Don't be ferhoodled," Joseph said. "You've done fine, you have."

"With Matthew's help, and your daad's. That boy has a gift for mechanics. He fixed that automated sander from the carpentry shop without advice from anyone. I'd have been asking Joseph, if it was me."

Anna leaned back in the rocker. She ought to gather up the dessert dishes and coffee cups, but she lingered, listening to the soft voices and watching the lightning bugs rise from the grass.

"Bartlett wants me to go along to the auction at New Holland with him. Help him pick out a young horse to train for driving. He has a fancy to get a buggy." Samuel paused, frowning a little. "I'm not sure if I should. It takes a lot of time to school a young horse."

Was he thinking again that he had to give up what he wanted for others? Surely not. "It must not take more than retraining one that's already been spoiled, like Star. You did wonderful gut with him," Myra said.

"That's right." Joseph jumped in on her words. "You'll take the time you need for it. It's important. And besides, I'm doing better every day, ain't so, Myra?"

She nodded, patting his knee. "You'll soon be all well."

It was what Myra would say to Sarah if she bumped her head, but Joseph didn't seem to notice. For that matter, Joseph and Samuel also didn't seem to notice that there was anything wrong with Myra's sudden cheerfulness. They both loved her and wanted so much to see her happy that they didn't look beyond the surface.

Anna would like to believe it, but she couldn't. She studied Myra, who was talking now with animation about something Sarah had said that day. All that easy chatter . . . that wasn't Myra.

Anna would have to do something. Talk to Joseph. Or maybe Samuel would be better. He was her brother, after all. Yes, Samuel was the one. She didn't want to worry Joseph if there was no need. Surely together she and Samuel would be able to convince Myra to talk to the counselor.

Joseph stretched, yawning. "I'm ready to go in, I think."

"I'll go with you," Myra said, standing. When Anna started to move, she waved her back to her seat. "Stay, no need to go in yet. Talk to Samuel."

Once the door closed behind them, Samuel gave a soft chuckle. "My sister, the matchmaker. Just ignore her. You don't have to stay out here if you have something else to do."

Anna shook her head. "It's a beautiful evening. I hate to go in."

"Ja." Samuel glanced out across the darkening fields. "We won't have too many more warm evenings like this to enjoy sitting out."

She tilted her head back to look up at the half-full moon. "It reminds me of when I was little. Everyone would gather on the back porch in the evening after chores, and I'd beg to be allowed to stay up later. 'Just five more minutes, Mammi.'"

"And she let you." His voice was warm, as if he had memories like those, too.

"Ja. I'd be so sure I could stay awake, but of course I couldn't. I'd drift off to sleep with their sweet voices in my ears."

She wasn't sure how it happened. One moment she was fine, and the next her voice choked and tears threatened to spill over.

Samuel swiveled toward her. Without saying anything, he reached out and took her hand. His was work-hardened and warm, but so very gentle. His fingers moved on the back of her hand, caressing it, sending waves of comfort through her.

"You are missing your mamm," he said finally. "I know. I feel that, too."

She nodded, not sure she could trust her voice to speak. She just held on to him, letting his strength and comfort flow through her, until the tightness in her throat eased and she could speak.

"She was so patient, always. She took such joy in every little moment with each of us."

He clasped her hand gently. "That's the kind of mother you want to be, ain't so? The life you want for your daughter, too."

"I guess so." What he said was true, wasn't it? Certainly that she wanted to be at least half the mother Mammi had been.

Exasperation with herself welled in her. Why couldn't she just decide, once and for all, that this was the life she wanted for herself and her daughter?

Samuel's fingers tightened on her hand. "Anna . . ." He hesitated, as if searching for words.

She had to stop him before he said something that would change things irrevocably between them. "Myra," she blurted out the name. "We have to talk about Myra."

She felt the surprise that went through him at the abrupt change. Felt him hold back for an instant and then accept.

"What about Myra? She seems better today, ja? I am so relieved that she's adjusting."

"Adjusting? She's not adjusting at all. Don't you see that?"

He let go of her hand then, frowning. "But she seems happier, more like her old self."

"That's just it." Anna leaned toward him, willing him to believe her. "That's not normal. She can't simply get over news like this all in a moment."

He mulled that over, not responding right away, his face in the dim light giving nothing away. Finally he shook his head.

"I don't know, Anna. Don't you think it's possible that she's prayed and has come to some peace about the boppli's condition?"

If only that were true. "But she hasn't. When we talked, she as gut as told me that the doctor is wrong. She said she's sure that the baby is a boy, and that he'll be fine."

She saw Samuel absorb the impact of her words. His face tightened, the skin seeming to draw against the bones. "Have you told Joseph?"

"Not yet." She shook her head. "I hate to upset him just when he's starting to improve. But I think she needs to talk to someone about it. There's a counselor at the clinic, a woman Leah knows. But Myra insists she doesn't need to see her."

Again he was silent. She expected herself to be impatient with him, but she wasn't. His lack of reaction didn't mean that he didn't understand or that he didn't care. It was simply Samuel's way.

"I'm not convinced you're right," he said slowly. "But I know we can't take a chance. We must all help her. Joseph, Leah, you, and me. But mostly you, I think."

"Me? Why me?" Did Samuel really want to trust his sister to her?

He took her hand again, holding it in a warm, insistent clasp. "You're the woman who is closest to her right now. She counts on you. I know you will help her. Ain't so?"

She nodded slowly, but somewhere deep inside a seed of doubt began to open. How could she help Myra face the truth? She had enough trouble doing that herself.

CHAPTER FIFTEEN

I'll let you get started on the dining room cleaning, first." Rosemary set a cleaning caddy filled with supplies on the oval table. "Just let me know if you need anything else."

Anna nodded, picking up a bottle of furniture polish. There had been a subtle change in Rosemary's manner since Anna had arrived as a household helper rather than a neighbor. Subtle, but there. Obviously they were now employer and employee.

That was fine. After working in a restaurant for three years, Anna knew it was best to just smile and get on with it. Whether a customer shouted at you for something that was the cook's mistake or stiffed you on the tip, that was just the way things were.

Besides, being Amish was good training in humility. She started polishing the mahogany breakfront. All that was really important was that she'd found a way to earn a little money.

And why is that important? the little voice at the back of her mind asked. *Because you're not really committed to staying here, that's why. Because you think someday you're going to want to run again, and the money will be needed.*

She'd saved up before she left the last time, squirreling away most of the money she'd earned working at Paula Schatz's bakery in town. But then the accident had happened, and she'd had to leave much more quickly than she'd intended.

The money hadn't gone far . . . just about enough for the bus that had taken her to Chicago, with very little left over.

Jarrod's mother had offered her money when she'd learned Anna was leaving. Anna had turned her down, of course. They'd done enough for her, hiring a lawyer to defend her against the driving charge. She couldn't take anything else from them.

In retrospect, Mrs. Wells had probably been so happy to see the Amish girl out of her son's life that she'd have gladly paid anything, not that Anna would have taken money for that.

Not very pleasant thoughts, she decided. She concentrated on the polishing, liking the way the liquid made the rich color of the wood come out.

Rosemary wandered back in while she was working on the table legs. "That looks great." She ran a finger along the top of the breakfront. "I just love this piece, don't you?"

"It's very nice," Anna said, starting on the chair legs while she was down on the floor.

Rosemary picked up the window cleaner and a paper towel. "I'll do the glass on the doors."

Anna glanced up, a little surprised. "You're paying me to do the work."

"I know." Rosemary grimaced slightly. "I was trying to be the boss, because that's what my husband told me to do. 'Tell the girl what to do and let her get on with it,' he said. But I'm not very good at that. I'd rather work along with you."

Anna had to laugh. So the change in Rosemary hadn't gone very deep. "I would like that better, too."

Rosemary sprayed the pane of glass and began polishing energetically. "It's pretty boring, doing the cleaning by myself. I guess it's different in an Amish family, with so many people around to help. You always have company."

"Ja, I guess so." Anna remembered what Myra had said about doing dishes with her sister when she'd first arrived. "Working together can be a time for talking and joking, too."

"That's the thing," Rosemary said. "Having someone to talk to."

Anna could hear the yearning for connection in Rosemary's voice. She knew the feeling. She'd certainly felt that way herself, when she first went to Chicago. She'd been out of place there, and apparently Rosemary felt out of place here.

"I was often lonely when I went out in the English world," she confessed, wondering if it would help. "I was independent, but lonely."

"I'm not . . ." Rosemary stopped, shrugged. "Well, I guess I do get lonely, with my husband gone so much of the time."

"Why did you move here? I'd think you'd be happier in town, where you'd have near neighbors." Joseph and Myra's place was the closest house, and that was a good half mile down the road.

"Oh, we thought it would be fun. Picking out the land, deciding on the house plans, and then decorating the place." Rosemary stood back from the breakfront to see the effect of the shiny glass doors. "I did enjoy that. I picked out everything in the house myself, and Richard gave me free rein. Whatever I wanted, I could have."

"Generous," Anna said. Richard must do very well if he could afford that.

"Richard is always generous. He's just not here very much to enjoy the place now that we have it." Rosemary leaned on the back of a chair, the paper towel idle in her hand. "Once the house was finished, I realized there wasn't much to do here."

"What did you do before you got married?" Anna reminded herself that Rosemary was paying her well for her time. If she wanted to use that time to talk, she'd listen.

"I was a secretary. Richard's secretary, to be exact. I worked my way up from receptionist to the boss's secretary." She made a little face. "That's a pretty tacky story, isn't it? But I do love him."

"I can see that." There was a softness in Rosemary's eyes whenever she mentioned her husband. "It's a shame you can't have more time together."

"I guess it's not like that for you Amish. Myra and Joseph are together all the time, I see."

"Just about. That's the Amish way. They started out being farmers, with the whole family working together to run the farm. But it's hard to find enough good farmland, even here in the valley, so people have to turn to something else. They still try to keep the work as close to home as possible."

"Joseph could probably make a lot more money if he went to work in a factory."

"That isn't the most important thing to us."

Us, she'd said. But here was another

place where she felt like two different people. The Annie who'd worked for tips in the restaurant so she could take college classes—that Annie would have done almost anything to make more money. She had known only too well that it meant the difference between having a decent place to live and being out on the street.

And she was still doing it, in a way. Hedging her bets. Working for Rosemary to have the money she'd need if she left.

"Do you miss it?" Rosemary asked. "Your life in Chicago, I mean."

"Sometimes," Anna said, trying to be honest.

"Gracie's real mother—birth mother, I mean. She wasn't Amish, was she?"

The question startled Anna. "No, she wasn't."

Jannie hadn't been anything definite, it seemed. Just another of the lost kids who ended up in one big city or another.

"It makes me wonder." Rosemary tilted her head to the side, watching Anna's face. "I wonder if you're doing the right thing, trying to bring up an English child in the Amish world."

For a moment Anna couldn't speak. The blow had been unexpected. Finally, she fell back on words that weren't her own.

"Her mother wanted me to raise her right. That's what I'm trying to do."

"Sure, I know you have Gracie's best interest at heart. I just wonder if bringing her up Amish is what her mother had in mind."

Anna took a breath, tamping down her anger. Rosemary seemed to be one of those people who blurted out what was in her head, even when it wasn't really any of her business.

"Gracie is my child," Anna said. "I must make the decision about what is the right life for her."

It was what she believed with all her heart. She just wasn't sure she knew what that right life was.

Anna shook out the damp sheet and pinned the corner to the clothesline Joseph had put up for Myra in the backyard. The breeze caught the sheet, billowing it out like a sail. Anna lifted her face.

It felt like fall suddenly, with a crispness

in the wind that hadn't been there the previous day. The calendar was turning to October, and this long September warm spell was coming to an end.

Anna clipped the sheet to the line, trying to concentrate on the simple task. Trying not to let her mind spin back to that conversation with Rosemary yesterday.

Was it right, to consider bringing Gracie up as Amish? Was that what Jannie would have wanted?

When she and Gracie had arrived, all she'd been able to think about was safety. Like a rabbit diving into its hole at the approach of the fox, she'd bolted home, knowing they'd take her in.

Knowing, too, that she could disappear into the community. The outside world would look only at the dress and think Amish, without peering any more closely at the individual behind the prayer kapp.

The panic that had driven Anna had vanished quickly, but it had taken weeks to make her feel safe. Now she did. Now she seriously considered staying.

And that brought her full circle back to the question she would like to avoid. Was it right to bring Gracie up here?

She reached automatically for the basket to pick up the next piece of laundry and found it empty. She'd hung the entire line full with sheets and pillowcases without even noticing.

She stood for a moment, frowning as she watched them flap in the breeze. She wanted to talk to someone. If she could lay out all her doubts, maybe her course would become clear.

As a child, she'd always turned to Leah, the big sister who could solve every problem, but she couldn't talk to Leah, of all people, now. She would be so hurt if she knew Anna had doubts.

All of them would, if they knew. The whole family had enough to worry about, what with Joseph's slow recovery and Myra's cheerful pretense that nothing was wrong.

As Anna picked up the basket, she saw movement out by the barn. It was Samuel, leading one of the horses. Over his shoulder was the chain he'd used to move her car that first day.

Anna dropped the basket and scurried toward him, telling herself it was none of her business what he was doing, but compelled to go anyway.

By the time she reached the barn, he'd already disappeared inside. She hurried in. Samuel was harnessing the horse to her car.

"What are you doing?" she said.

Samuel looked up. He was probably startled, but his stolid face didn't reveal it. He patted the horse's shoulder.

"I asked you that the day you came back, when I found you in here harnessing up Joseph's buggy horse."

"I know. I remember." She crossed the barn floor toward him. "What's going on, Samuel? Where are you taking my car?"

His eyebrows lifted slightly. "Your daad sent word over by Matthew. He's arranged for the junkyard man to come for it today. He asked if I'd haul it out of the barn for them, not wanting the tow truck to come in here."

"Today." She'd been expecting it, but still it seemed to catch her by surprise.

"Ja, today. You did tell him to get rid of the car, ain't so?"

"I did." She hesitated, but after everything else she'd said to Samuel, she could say this. "I just didn't think it would bother me so much when the time came." She moved closer, patting the dusty fender much as Samuel had patted the horse. "This was Jannie's car. I couldn't afford one. As you can see, she couldn't afford much of a car."

The tension in his expression eased. "Your friend left it to you."

"I hadn't driven since the accident, just used public transportation, but she insisted I had to try. In case I needed to get the baby to the hospital or anything."

"So she cared about the baby's future, even knowing she wouldn't be there."

Anna ran her finger along the side mirror, her thoughts drifting into the past. "We drove out of the city one day, when she felt well enough. She wanted to see the country, she said. To see trees and grass again before she . . ." Her voice failed her.

"I'm sorry." His voice was a low rumble. "It's brought up sad memories."

Anna shook her head. "Bittersweet, maybe. Not entirely sad. She was happy that day."

"If you don't want to get rid of the car, you can tell your daad why. He'd understand."

"No point in that. It's so far gone it's of no use anyway, I guess."

For a moment Samuel stared at her, as if absorbing her words. Then something flared in his eyes. "Were you planning to make a quick getaway, Anna?"

The edge of anger in his voice caught her on the raw, startling her. Samuel, who never lost his temper, was furious with her.

Her own temper rose in an instant. "If you're thinking I'd run off and leave Myra when she needs me, you don't understand me as well as you think, Samuel Fisher."

He seemed taken aback by the direct attack. He took a step toward her, the anger fading from his face, and something solemn taking its place.

"If you left, I would be sorry on my own account, not just on my sister's. I would be disappointed in you, as well."

The mood had changed so quickly she felt oddly off balance. Everything that might be between them seemed to hover in the air, unspoken. She wanted to touch him, to assure him that she was here forever, that it was safe for them to love each other. But how could she? The doubts still clung.

She shook her head, trying to swallow

the lump that had formed in her throat. "I don't want to disappoint you. Or anyone else. I just . . ."

It was hopeless. He wouldn't understand. He'd have only the simple answer that she belonged here, so her child did, too.

"Tell me." He caught her hand in his. "What is troubling you so?"

Anna couldn't seem to turn away from his intent gaze. Finally she shook her head.

"It's foolish to let it trouble me, maybe. But when I was working at Rosemary's yesterday, she said something that . . . well, it raised a question in my mind." She stopped, not sure she should continue.

"What did she ask?" Samuel obviously wouldn't let it go.

Anna took a breath. "She asked whether it was right, to raise a child born English as Amish."

Samuel was quiet for a long moment. She had the sense that beneath his calm surface, tension roiled.

"I shouldn't have said anything," she said quickly. "Just forget it." She tried to smile, but it probably wasn't very convincing. "I've gotten into the habit of confiding in you, and that isn't fair."

His hand tightened on hers. "We are friends. We should be able to say the difficult words, ja?"

She nodded, her throat tight.

"So tell me what it was your friend Jannie expected from you."

She took a shaky breath. "At first, she counted on me as you would on any friend. She thought she was going to be all right. She floated along on that belief for months, it seemed, ignoring what the doctors told her."

Her throat thickened still more, so that it was an effort to get the words out.

"When she finally accepted that she wasn't going to survive, all her strength went to the baby."

"It's what a mother does," he said quietly.

She nodded, tears pricking her eyes. "Jannie had always been so timid. Malleable. She never seemed to have a thought of her own, just went along with what everyone else wanted. Suddenly she was a mother lion. She decided what she wanted to do and pushed everyone into line. Got the lawyer, got Pete to sign the papers, arranged for me to adopt. The lawyer was doubtful about me. He tried to get her to give the baby to an agency for adoption, but she was determined that I would be Gracie's mother."

"Did she tell you why?"

"She said she could count on me to raise Jannie right."

"If she thought that, it was because of the person you are, ja?" His voice was gentle.

"Of course."

"And you are who you are because of how you were raised. How could she trust you with her baby without trusting what you come from?"

His words seemed to sink into a place deep in her heart, easing and soothing. They rang true, and she knew he was right about what Jannie had intended.

"Jannie knew I was Amish," she said slowly. "She was the only one out there who did know. She must have realized, must have thought all along that coming home was what I would do."

"That is what I would think, from what you've said about her."

"Denke, Samuel." She looked into his face, gratitude welling in her. "Thank you."

"There is something else I must say. Something you might not want to hear." His voice was very grave. "Your friendship with the English woman . . . I don't think it is a gut thing."

She could only stare at him. "Rosemary? Why would you say that? True, she did raise doubts in my mind, but that's just because she didn't understand. I'm sure she meant well."

"When you are with her, you start to think like an Englischer again, ain't so?"

Think like an Englischer. The words echoed. Maybe they were true. Maybe that's why they stung so much.

She straightened. Grateful as she was to Samuel, she wouldn't let him dictate who her friends were.

She managed a smile. "I appreciate your help. Now I had better let you get back to your work, and I'll get back to mine."

She turned and walked quickly out of the barn.

. . .

"Komm, komm." Myra's hands fluttered as she gestured Samuel toward the bedroom. "The boppli's crib must go in the corner of our room, where I can get to it easily."

Samuel carried the crib mattress through the doorway, his misgivings growing. "Myra, you have months to get the crib ready for the boppli. Why must we do it today?"

"Over here." Myra ignored his question. "The crib must be here." She sketched the shape of the crib with her hands against the wall.

He set the mattress down. "I will go and get the tools and the other pieces."

"Ja, ja," Myra said absently. She stared at the spot where the crib would go, smiling.

He hurried out of the room and back down the stairs, wishing he knew what was going on in his sister's mind. She had taken a sudden fancy to set up the crib she had borrowed from Barbara, since little Gracie now occupied the one that had been Sarah's. She didn't want Joseph doing all that bending, so she'd decided that Samuel must do it.

He glanced into the living room, where

Joseph was keeping the two little girls occupied. Joseph met his eyes and gave a helpless shrug. He didn't know what to do, either.

If Anna were here, she might be better equipped to handle Myra's sudden whim, but Anna had gone over to Leah's house this morning to help her prepare for a party at the school.

Anna was never far from his thoughts these days. He sorted through the crib components, which Levi had stacked on the back porch, making sure all the bolts and nuts were there.

He'd gone over and over the conversation he and Anna had had in the barn yesterday, trying to assure himself that he'd said the right words. He could understand her worries about what the English woman had said. It was no simple matter, bringing up an English child to be Amish.

But Gracie had been Anna's child since she was born, and Anna had never stopped being Amish, despite her attempt to live in the English world. He believed with all his heart that what he'd told Anna was true. Her friend must have known that the way

Anna was raised made her the person she was.

He carried an armload of crib bars up the stairs and into the bedroom. Myra still stood where he'd left her, looking with dreamy eyes at the place where the crib would go. Concern edged its way to worry.

"I'll get the rest of it," he said, and escaped.

Coward, he accused himself as he hurried down the steps. If Anna were here, she'd know what to do. He felt a flare of resentment that he knew was totally unreasonable. Anna had every right to go to Leah's or anywhere else this morning. He should just be relieved she wasn't back at Rosemary's again.

He wasn't wrong, was he, thinking that the Englischer's friendship wasn't best for Anna right now? Most Amish had some English friends, but for Anna, so recently returned, he feared the lure of that other life might be too great.

Anna hadn't liked it when he'd said so. He'd seen the flare of resentment, quickly suppressed, in her eyes.

In the old days, Anna wouldn't have

bothered to suppress it. Maybe that wouldn't have been so bad. At least then she wouldn't have been treating him with such cool politeness.

That bothered him more than he'd like to admit. Worse, it made him wonder whether his concern over that friendship was for Anna, or for himself.

He carted the rest of the crib pieces upstairs. He'd best concentrate on the job at hand. Worrying about Anna didn't get him any further, did it?

But he couldn't shake her from his mind so easily. He squatted, pulling the crib pieces together under Myra's watchful eyes.

"I will put Sarah's quilt on it for now," she said. "But I'm going to make a new one, just for him. He'll like that, don't you think?"

"Ja." Samuel's voice sounded strangled, and he cleared his throat. "When do you think Anna will be back?"

"Sometime this afternoon." The faraway look faded from Myra's face, thank the gut Lord. She smiled. "You like our Anna, don't you?"

"I like her fine. Don't you go matchmaking, now."

"Why not? Who else will say it to you, if

not your own sister? You and Anna would make a fine pair."

"Why?" He attached the side rail to the headboard. "Just because Anna needs a daadi for Gracie and I'm past the age of courting a teenager doesn't mean we're right for each other."

"Don't be ferhoodled. Because you two fit together perfectly, that's why. I wouldn't have thought that three years ago, but you've both changed. You've grown into yourselves, in a way."

"Maybe. Anna has grown and changed, that's certain-sure." He stared at the screwdriver in his hand, wondering why he'd picked it up. "But I don't think the changes in me have made me any more suited to marriage. Maybe less, if anything."

"Ach, Samuel, you must not think that." Myra dropped to her knees next to him, startling him. "This is because of Daad, ja?"

He shrugged. "Maybe." He tried not to say more, but the words seemed to press at his lips, wanting to come out. "You know what it did to us, him leaving like he did. What if I did that?"

"You wouldn't."

The total confidence in her voice comforted him, but he couldn't let go of his fears so easily.

"Nobody would have thought that about Daad, either, but he did."

Myra was silent for a moment. "Didn't anyone?"

That brought Samuel's startled glance to hers. "What do you mean?"

Her gaze slid away from his. "I . . . nothing. I shouldn't have said that."

He took her chin in his hand, turning her face toward his. "Tell me. Did you know Daad was thinking about leaving?" It seemed incredible that little Myra would know something like that.

"Not know, exactly." Her eyes darkened with the memory. "But sometimes when he was away from home working with the carpentry crews . . . well, when he came back, he talked differently. Like that other place out there was his real home." She shook her head, as if bothered by her inability to explain it all. "And he wasn't so very gut at keeping his word, Samuel. We all knew that, even you."

He opened his mouth to speak and

closed it again. He didn't know what surprised him more, the fact that such words were coming from little Myra or that they rang so true.

"Daadi . . . maybe it's true that he didn't always do what he said he would." His memory provided him with too many examples of that. "But there was always a gut reason. And he'd make it up afterward."

Just saying the words made him see how lame they were. Could a man ever make up for not keeping his word?

"You see," Myra said, as if she knew what he was thinking. "I loved Daadi, but I guess I always knew I couldn't count on him." She put her hand on Samuel's arm. "It's harder for you. You were his favorite, and you'd have done anything to please him."

Samuel wanted to deny it, but he couldn't. "If that's true . . ." His voice sounded like someone else's. He cleared his throat. "If that's true, it makes it even worse. I always wanted to be like him. What if I am?"

"Ach, don't be so foolish." Her tone scolded lovingly. "Look at yourself. You've never broken your word one single time in your whole life. Everyone knows that about you, except maybe you."

He shook his head. He couldn't sort it out. He needed time to get his mind around it.

"I'm not telling you what to do." Myra patted his arm. "I just want you to be as happy as I am." She reached out to touch the crib with a gentle caress. "I have Joseph, and Sarah, and a fine home. And now the new baby. My perfect little boy."

Her words stabbed Samuel, chasing away every other preoccupation. "Myra, the doctor said—"

"Ach, don't even think about that. The doctor was wrong, that's all. I'm sure of it."

"But Myra . . ."

She rose, hand cradling her belly. "Komm, get working on that crib so I can see how it looks. I will get the bedding for it." She hurried from the room before he could say another word.

He sat down on the floor, feeling as if gentle Myra had just taken his heart and shaken it. First the revelation about his father, and now this . . .

He'd misjudged the situation with Myra,

dismissing Anna's concerns. He should have listened to her. She'd been right.

They had to persuade Myra to get help, but how? His heart quailed at the thought of arguing with her about her baby.

He had to talk to Anna the minute she got back. Anna would know what to do.

CHAPTER SIXTEEN

Anna clucked at Myra's buggy horse, and the animal obediently picked up speed along the narrow road. It was surprising, really, how quickly she'd felt familiar with the horse and buggy again. After not driving a buggy in three years, the lines had felt odd in her hands at first, but now it was as if she'd never been away from it. The tension she'd felt after the near-miss coming home from the fair was still there, but it was under control.

She had to admit there was at least one advantage to driving a horse instead of a car. The horse had instincts a car never could. Myra's buggy horse was on her way home, and if she didn't stop her, the mare would keep going until she got there.

She had a stop to make, now that she'd delivered the baked goods to Leah for the school sale. She'd picked up a phone card the last time she went to the grocery store for Myra, so she could finally make a long distance call to Liz in Chicago.

A phone shanty stood at the intersection of two farm fields. She checked the horse and turned into the dirt lane that led to the shanty.

The idea of putting a telephone in a shed far from the house was so foreign to the English world that she was glad she didn't have to try to explain it to anyone. People out there made being constantly connected a necessity, as if they couldn't survive for even a few hours without cell phones and e-mail. She'd seen people in the restaurant trying to eat and talk on the phone at the same time, and ignoring the human being sitting across the table, like as not.

To the Amish, a telephone in the house would encourage idle chatter with others instead of concentration on the family. Still, they recognized that a telephone was necessary for emergencies and sometimes for businesses. So the answer was simple—put the phone far enough away from the house so that one wouldn't be tempted to idle talk but near enough to be reached when needed.

Betsy, apparently deciding that the phone shanty was Anna's only possible destination, came to a stop next to it without being asked. Anna got down quickly, pulling the phone card from her pocket.

At last she could talk to Liz. Maybe hearing her friend's voice would erase the unsettled feeling that had haunted her lately.

Not lately. She ought to be honest with herself, at least. She'd been unsettled since the car had been hauled away, to be exact. It had taken her last illusion, irrational as it had been, that she still controlled her ability to come and go. And that conversation with Samuel certainly hadn't helped, either.

He had been so kind, so reassuring when she told him about what Rosemary had said. His calm, reasonable approach had comforted her. More, it had restored her faith in her own judgment.

Then he'd as much as told her she should drop her friendship with Rosemary, as if

Anna were a child who needed his guidance. Or more likely from his viewpoint, a slightly defective Amish woman who couldn't be trusted to have an English friend without being lured back to that world.

Anna had thought they understood each other. She'd thought he was the one person she could count on for support. Well, she'd been wrong.

Irritation made her yank open the door to the phone shanty. She stepped inside. A plain black phone sat on a rough wooden shelf, a basic answering machine next to it. A blinking light suggested that the owner hadn't been by to check messages recently.

There was not even a stool to encourage anyone to stay and chat. She put the plastic card on the shelf next to the phone and breathed a silent prayer.

Please, let Liz be there. I need to talk to someone who will understand.

The good Lord must have been listening, because Liz picked up on the second ring. Longing swept through Anna at the sound of her voice. If she could see her right now, sit and talk . . .

"Liz. It's Annie. I'm so glad you're home."

Just saying the words made her feel like Annie again.

"Annie, thank goodness." Liz's voice fairly leaped through the telephone receiver. "I've been going crazy wanting to talk to you. Why haven't you called?"

Anna skipped over the question, knowing she couldn't answer it in any way that Liz could understand. "What is it? What's wrong?" Her heart seemed to pick up speed at the urgency in Liz's words.

"It's Pete." Liz's voice was controlled, but an effort. "He's been around again, trying to find out about you and the baby."

Anna's heart thudded to her shoes. "Did you talk to him? What has he done?"

"Don't get excited. Honestly, I thought by this time he'd be long gone, but it hasn't worked out that way."

"Liz, I'm so sorry—"

"Now you stop that." Liz was brisk. "It's not your fault that idiot has slid over the edge into crazy. If he'd stop pickling his brain with drugs, maybe he could see sense for once."

Anna found she was pushing the receiver against her head so hard that it hurt. "Did you talk to him? Did he threaten you?"

Liz snorted. "He tried. I'm not scared of a nutcase like him."

Anna took a breath, trying to focus. Liz wasn't letting Pete scare her, and she couldn't either. "What exactly did he say?"

"Just the same as before. He kept saying Gracie was his baby and he wanted her." Liz snorted again, expressing her opinion of Pete. "I told him he didn't know a thing about bringing up a baby and never would. I told him he didn't have a legal leg to stand on."

"What did he say to that?" The walls of the shanty seemed to be closing in on her, and Anna had to force herself to breathe.

"That he wasn't counting on the law to get her back. That's why I had to talk to you, Annie. I had to tell you. I'm afraid that if he finds that baby, he's going to grab her and take off."

"He's not going to find her." Anna had to be sure of that. She had to. She closed her eyes, searching for the calm that eluded her.

"Annie, listen. When Pete realized he wasn't going to get anything out of me, he said he didn't need me anyway. That he'd figured out how to find you without help from anybody."

An icy hand closed around Anna's heart. For a moment she couldn't speak. Gracie . . . She wanted to drop the phone, race home, grab the baby. Run. Run.

She couldn't. What good would that do, to run mindlessly? *Please, Lord. Help me to think.*

"Annie? Are you there? I tried to get him to tell me what he meant, but he wouldn't."

"Yes. I'm here." She took a breath. "He was bluffing. He had to be. There's no possible way he could guess where I am."

No one in Chicago knew about her past. She'd told no one, just Jannie. Jannie wouldn't have said anything. If she had told Pete where Anna was from, surely he'd have come after her before this.

"Well, that's good. But regardless, you need to go to the cops."

"I don't think . . ."

"Never mind thinking, just listen to me. Pete's a convicted felon who signed away his rights to the baby before she was even born. The police will help you. They'll give you some protection."

Anna tried to imagine the reaction should an Amish woman go walking into the local police station. This wasn't an ordinary situation, but if she went to the police, she'd have to tell them everything about Jannie and Pete.

Anna had the legal papers. She could convince them, eventually, but how long would that take? If they made inquiries in Chicago, which they were bound to, her location might slip out.

And sooner or later it would leak out here. How could that help but happen? And her family would know all that she hadn't told them.

"I can't." The words burst out. "I mean, it would just make things worse if people knew. Besides, I'm sure Pete couldn't know how to find me. We're safe here."

Please, Lord, let me be right.

"I still think the cops—"

"I can't, really."

Liz was silent for a long moment. Then she sighed. "Well, as long as Pete is wandering around the neighborhood here bothering people, we know he can't be coming after you. I can try to keep tabs on him, so we'll know if he sets out on any long trips. But you've got to give me a phone number where I can call you if anything happens."

That was the one thing Anna couldn't do. "I can't. I mean, I don't have a phone."

"Come on, Annie." Liz's voice was laden with disbelief. "What are you doing, living in the dark ages? Everyone has a phone."

"I don't. I'm sorry." She rubbed her temple with the heel of her hand, trying to think.

"You don't want to give me an address, I suppose. But what about a neighbor? There must be somebody who could pass along a message to you. Don't you have a landlady or a super?"

There was Rosemary. She could give Liz Rosemary's number. But if she did, she'd have to tell Rosemary at least something of the truth.

For a second, Samuel's face formed in Anna's mind. What did it say about their relationship, if she confided in Rosemary and not in him? Maybe it said he was right in what he feared about her.

Gracie. She had to keep her mind on Gracie, no one else. She took a breath.

"I'll give you the number of a neighbor. You can trust her with a message for me."

The ban on telephones, annoying enough when she was a teenager and longed to be in touch with her friends, now seemed monumental. Anna turned the buggy into Joseph's lane. The horse, knowing the terrain as well as she did, picked up speed as she sensed her barn.

If Anna had called Liz sooner . . .

Still, what good would that have done? It wouldn't change the facts. Whatever was going on in the recesses of Pete's mind, he'd apparently become obsessed with the baby he'd never wanted.

Anna had had to give Liz Rosemary's number, no matter what Samuel thought of her relationship with the neighbor. Rosemary's telephone represented her only lifeline to Liz. If Pete really did know something about where Anna was, she had to have warning.

She'd intended to stop at Rosemary's on her way home, but Rosemary hadn't been there. It was unreasonable to feel so annoyed over that fact. Rosemary couldn't have known that Anna would need her.

Her hands were cold on the lines, despite the warmth of the day. What had she been thinking, trying to hide Gracie in a place where she couldn't even call for help in an emergency?

The horse slowed as the buggy neared the end of the lane. Samuel and Matthew appeared in the shop door. The boy ran to the horse's head while Samuel approached the buggy, looking up at Anna, his face tight.

"Matthew will take care of the horse and buggy for you." His tone was abrupt. "Komm, please. I need to talk with you." He held out a hand to help her down.

She had to yank her thoughts away from Gracie to concentrate on his words.

"In a bit, ja? I must go and check on Gracie first." She needed to hold her daughter in her arms and feel that she was safe. The need was a physical ache.

"Gracie is napping." He took her arm, urging her toward the shop. "Myra put her down not half an hour ago. This is important."

Important. Her mind skittered from one thought to another as she let him lead her to the shop. What would Samuel consider important at this point? Had he glimpsed her buggy approaching Rosemary's house and decided to lecture her again?

The shop was dim after the bright sunshine outside. Before her eyes could adjust, Samuel turned to her, his figure no more than a dark bulk against the rectangle of light from the doorway.

She took a quick breath. If he thought he could dictate who she saw, he'd better think again.

"It's Myra." His voice roughened with emotion. "Anna, you were right about her. We must do something."

Now Anna saw what was in his face. *Fear.* He was afraid for Myra.

She reached out, touching his arm. It was like iron under her fingers. His control was holding, but she had a sense that it wasn't going to last for long.

"All right, tell me. Tell me what happened."

He sucked in a breath. "She wanted me to put up that crib for her, so I was doing it."

"Already?" Levi had brought the crib yesterday, but what was the hurry?

"She insisted. She started talking about the baby." His eyes were dark with misery, and the look tugged at her heart. "Anna, I should have listened to you. I didn't. I thought I knew better."

"That doesn't matter." She shoved her

own worries to the back of her mind. "Tell me what she said. She didn't try to hurt herself, did she?"

His face went white. "No!" A shudder went through him. "You don't think she would do that!"

"I don't, but we have to think of every possibility."

"There was nothing like that. She seemed happy. Too happy, I thought. And then she started talking about how the doctor was wrong. How she was going to have a perfect baby boy."

"Ja," Anna said, her heart sinking. "I was afraid that's what she was thinking."

"She's not accepting it. I thought she was coming to see that whatever happened, it was God's will. I thought that was why she seemed so calm now." He sounded as miserable as Anna had ever heard him. "And all the while she was just convincing herself that it wasn't real."

"Samuel, you have to understand. This news is just too hard to accept, so she has to make herself believe it isn't true." Again Anna thought of Jannie's pretense that everything was all right.

Samuel shoved his hand through his

hair and rubbed the back of his neck. "I should have seen it. I know Myra better than anyone. Why didn't I see it?"

"You can't blame yourself."

She'd wanted him to understand, but she hated seeing the pain in his face, hearing the blame in his voice. Samuel would fault himself—that was inevitable. He always held himself to a higher standard than anyone else.

"If I had listened to you . . ."

"It wouldn't have made a bit of difference as far as I can see." She forced herself to sound brisk. "We have to get Myra to agree to see the counselor. Ja?"

Her attitude seemed to steady him. He took a deep breath, his gaze focusing on her face. "Are you sure this woman can help her?"

"I don't know, but if she can't, she'll work with the doctor to find the answers for Myra. Leah knows this woman. She has every confidence in her."

"Ja, that's gut." The haunted look slid off his face. Given practical steps to take, Samuel would have the strength for it.

"Did you talk to Joseph about what Myra said?"

He shook his head. "He did seem to think something was wrong with her insisting on putting up the crib right away. As for the rest, I waited for you. I thought . . . well, you were the one who saw it first. I thought you would know what to do."

She nodded, trying to focus on how to handle the situation. "Maybe it would be best if you talked to Joseph about what Myra said to you. I'll check on her. Then I think I should tell Leah. She might come over and speak to Myra."

If Anna went to get Leah, she could stop and see Rosemary on the way. That sounded so selfish, but she had to deal with the pressure of her problems, too. The sooner she made arrangements about Liz calling, the better.

"That is the right plan. I'll see what Joseph thinks. Surely, if we all show Myra how worried we are, she'll go to see the counselor, even if she thinks she doesn't need it for herself."

"Ja. Myra would do anything to keep the people she loves from worrying."

That was true, wasn't it? Anna's thoughts jumped back to her own worries. Not even Myra's love and caring could help with that.

Fear rushed through her again. Pete. She had to keep Gracie safe. She realized that her fingers were digging into Samuel's arm.

She let go quickly, pressing her hands together. She had to concentrate on the problem at hand. One thing at a time.

"This is going to be all right, Samuel. Have faith." She started to turn away.

Samuel took both her hands in a warm, firm grip, preventing her from moving. "Something else is troubling you, Anna. Was ist letz? How can I help?"

"I . . . It is nothing." Tears stung her eyes. She wouldn't cry.

His hands enclosed hers, not letting go, and his intent gaze held hers. "It is not nothing, I think. You were already upset when you got home, but I was too caught up in my own worries to see it. Did something happen while you were out?"

"Not exactly." Her lips were trembling. She clamped them together. She couldn't break down, not now, not in front of Samuel. "It's nothing." She should pull her hands away from his, but she couldn't. She found too much comfort in his grip.

He lifted her hands, holding them close

against his chest. She could feel the beating of his heart.

"I know better, Anna." He shook his head, his eyes never leaving hers. "Maybe neither of us was ready for this to happen, but it has. We are too close now for you to lie to me. Tell me what is wrong. Let me help you."

Tears welled in her eyes. "I want to, but I can't," she whispered.

"Ja, you can. Whatever it is, I will try to understand."

The need to speak flooded through her. "I can't . . ."

He waited. Just waited, his hands pressing hers against his solid chest.

She choked back the tears. "You can't help. No one can." She sucked in a ragged breath. "It's Gracie's father. He's looking for us. He wants to take her away from me."

Samuel stood motionless as he struggled to accept and understand Anna's words. He should respond quickly, but he couldn't. That was not his way.

He focused on her face, seeing the mixture of torment and rebellion in her eyes. "I don't understand. You told us the father didn't want the baby."

"He didn't." She almost spat out the words. "He couldn't wait to sign the papers giving up his rights. She wasn't even born yet, and he already knew he didn't want her."

"Then what has happened?" Samuel felt the impatience running through her, and he held her hands firmly in his, sensing that if he didn't, she would run away. "Help me to understand."

"How can I, when I don't understand it myself? He didn't contact Jannie when the baby was born. He didn't come to Jannie's funeral. Then he turned up a year later, suddenly deciding he wanted the baby." The anger in her voice slid away to a tremor. "It was as if Gracie was a toy he'd forgotten about for a while and then remembered."

"I'm sorry. So sorry." Whatever the right or wrong of it, Anna was hurting, and Samuel longed to make that better. "What kind of man could not want his own child?"

But even as he said the words they were bitter on his tongue. His own father had been able to walk away from his children without a backward glance.

Anna turned away from him, as if he'd

said the wrong thing, rubbing her hands on her arms as if she were cold. "I'm sure there are plenty of men who don't want to be fathers. And Pete has been scrambling his brains with drugs for years. I doubt he could form a thought about what it means to be a father."

"Poor man."

She spun, anger flaring in her eyes. "Poor man? What about all the people he's hurt? He doesn't just use drugs himself. He sells them. He knocked Jannie around for as long as they were together. The night he came and tried to take Gracie—" She stopped abruptly, wrapping her arms around herself.

"He tried to take her away from you?" Samuel's blood chilled at the thought. "Anna, what happened? You weren't hurt?"

She took an audible breath, pressing her fingers tight against her arms. "I didn't have any warning. Just opened the door and there he was. He barged in before I could react, yelling, demanding that I produce the baby. Thank heaven she was asleep." Her voice trembled a little on the words.

"You had no one to help you?" His heart

pained him at the thought of her facing that alone.

She shook her head. "I tried to talk sense to him, reminding him that he'd signed away his rights to her, but I don't think he even heard me. He was high on something, his eyes wild. When I wouldn't produce Gracie, he tried to go after her. We struggled. He hit me, knocked me down." She spread her fingers against her ribs, as if remembering the pain. "I couldn't have stopped him."

Samuel's own hands clenched into fists. He couldn't raise them against another human being, but for the first time in his life, he wanted to. *Forgive me, Father.*

"What happened? How did you get away?"

"The neighbors heard what was going on. They rushed in, hustled him out. They called the police." A tremor went through her. "They said I should go in the next day and file a complaint against him, but I didn't. I packed our things and ran."

"You came home," he said. That, at least, he understood, that longing to be home.

"I came home. But he's still after us."

She pressed her fingers to her temples, turning to face him. "I was so sure he'd forget about it. Either that, or be arrested again for dealing. But Liz says—"

"Liz. That is the friend you called, that day at the hospital."

"I talked to her then and again today." Her breath seemed to catch, and her blue eyes grew dark. "She said he hasn't given up. He's questioning my friends about me. He even told her that he had a way of finding me without her help."

"Anna, I'm sorry. If I had known . . ."

If he had, would it have changed anything between them? The longing to protect her was stronger than Samuel could have imagined possible.

"You couldn't have done anything," Anna said. "I have to see Rosemary. Liz will call her if anything changes."

For a moment Samuel tried to reason away the hurt that brought. "You would trust a stranger when you won't trust your family?" *Or me.* That was what he really wanted to say. "Anna, you must talk with your father about this."

"I can't. Don't you see that?" She turned on him, anger bringing a flush to her cheeks.

"You heard what he said that day at Barbara's picnic. You know how fair he always is. If he thought the father wanted Gracie, what would he do?"

"Anna, listen. If your father understood all of it, if he knew everything you've told me, I'm sure he would stand by you."

"And what if he didn't? What if he said that a legal paper doesn't make Gracie mine? I can't risk it. I can't tell him. Once it's said, it can't be unsaid."

"But—" Samuel thought she was wrong, but her quick mind ran circles around his. He couldn't find the argument that would convince her.

"Samuel, you can't tell anyone." Fear made her voice urgent. "You must promise me that you won't tell anyone what I've told you." She grabbed his arms, her grip fierce. "Promise me."

"Ja, Anna, I promise." Whether it was right or wrong, he could do nothing else. "I won't tell. And I will help you."

She let go of him, stepping back, her face changing as if she had turned into someone he didn't know.

"Help? If Pete came and tried to take the baby, what could you do? You wouldn't take up a weapon against him. You wouldn't call the police."

"Anna—"

She shook her head, eyes filling with tears. "Don't you see? I can't keep Gracie safe here. I should never have come home."

CHAPTER SEVENTEEN

Anna's throat was still tight with unshed tears from that painful scene with Samuel when she reached Leah's house. No matter how frightened she was about Pete, Myra's problems were more immediate.

Reason told her that chances were very small Pete could find her, even if he'd somehow learned where she came from. Amish society was one of the few places in America that was off the communication network. No search of phone records or Internet sites would tell him anything.

"Ach, Anna, it's wonderful gut to see you." Leah turned away from the kitchen sink, drying her hands as she hurried to embrace Anna. "I didn't expect you to come back again today, or I wouldn't be in the midst of doing the dishes."

That was the flip side to Amish isolation. She hadn't been able to call and tell Leah about the trouble. She'd had to come and hope Leah was here.

"It doesn't matter at all," she said quickly. The stacks of baked goods Leah had been collecting this morning must all have been delivered. With its warm wood cabinets and sparkling countertops, Leah's kitchen looked like any English kitchen, except that the appliances ran on propane and there was a gas lamp over the pine table.

"I had to talk to you—"

Anna's words were arrested when two-year-old Rachel came rushing across the kitchen to throw herself at Anna's legs. "Gently, Rachel," Leah chided.

Anna scooped the little girl up in her arms to plant a kiss on her chubby cheek.

"Gracie," Rachel demanded, patting Anna's face.

"Gracie couldn't come this time. Next time, all right?"

Losing interest since her cousin wasn't there, Rachel wiggled. "Down."

Anna couldn't help but chuckle as she lowered her niece to the floor. "She does know what she wants, doesn't she?"

"She's spoiled, that's what, with Daniel and the older children fussing over her since the day she was born."

Given the indulgent smile on Leah's face, Anna thought they weren't the only ones doing the spoiling. Rachel was the boppli Leah had never expected to have, until Daniel came to the valley.

And if Rachel was a little indulged, was that so bad? She was also greatly loved, not just by her parents but by her extended family, indeed, her whole community.

Anna's heart clenched. If she had to leave, Gracie would never know that love.

"Sit, now, and I'll fix some tea." Leah waved her dish towel toward the nearest chair.

"Not now, denke." She had to get to her reason for coming. The memory of Myra's bright, unnerving smile pushed at her. "I have to talk to you about Myra."

Leah's eyes filled with concern. "What has happened?"

"She's not adjusting at all to the situation. She's convinced herself that the doctor is wrong. I'm afraid, when the reality finally hits, it will devastate her."

"Ach, I was afraid of that."

"I hoped we could get her to meet with your friend at the clinic, but I'm afraid she won't agree."

"Lydia Weaver. Lydia is just the person to help her. I've never met anyone more compassionate." Leah's own face shone with caring.

She tossed the dishtowel she was holding onto the rack and went to the door. "Elizabeth?" she called up the stairs.

"Ja, Mammi." Footsteps thudded on the steps, and Leah's stepdaughter appeared. "Aunt Anna." She smiled. "It is gut to see you."

"Elizabeth, I need you to watch Rachel. Aunt Anna and I must go out for a few minutes."

Curiosity filled Elizabeth's eyes, but she didn't ask questions. She just nodded and went quickly to the living room where Rachel was playing.

"Now." Leah took Anna's hand in a firm grip. "We will go to the telephone shanty to make an appointment for Myra right away."

Anna felt the burden she'd been carrying grow suddenly lighter as they hurried out to the buggy. Leah could be counted on.

She climbed up, and Leah got quickly into the seat next to her.

"The closest phone is just across the field, but we can go by the lane." Leah pointed out the route. "Daniel had the phone shanty put in after little Rachel arrived so soon and Rachel Brand had to deliver her."

"I'm sorry." Anna's words came without planning. "I wish I'd been here."

"I know." Leah clasped her hand.

"If I hadn't stopped writing, it wouldn't have been so hard for you to find me."

"When you left, you promised you'd stay in touch." Leah said the words slowly, as if they were heavy. "Why, Anna? Why didn't you?"

Tears blinded her eyes. "I thought it would all be easy." She looked back in wonderment at the foolish girl she'd been. "When it wasn't, when it was a struggle just to survive, I felt I couldn't tell you that. And I couldn't lie, so I just stopped writing."

Leah clasped her hand firmly for a moment. "You can tell me anything."

Anything? Pain struck Anna's heart.

She'd thought that once she told Samuel about the troubles with Pete, she'd be free of the compulsion to tell someone, but instead the need was even stronger. She longed to spill out the whole story to Leah. Leah, more familiar with the world than most Amish through her work at the clinic, would probably understand.

But what if she told Daadi, and what if he thought Pete should be given a chance? How could she risk it?

She couldn't. Anna wiped away a tear with the back of her hand and saw that tears filled Leah's eyes, too. "Look at us, riding along and crying. What would people think if they saw us?

"They might think it is gut that I have my sister back," Leah said.

Anna's heart clenched, and again she felt the pressure to tell Leah. But she couldn't.

"What if Myra refuses to go?" She asked it abruptly, because it seemed easier to focus on that.

Leah patted her shoulder. "I think when

the two Beiler sisters are determined, no one will stand in their way for long. We'll get her there."

"Samuel will help. We talked about it, and he'll convince Joseph."

"Ja, that's gut. Myra needs everyone in agreement on this."

Leah gestured toward the grassy lane that led to the shed, and Anna turned in. Betsy probably wondered why she was making two trips to a phone shanty in one day, but she plodded along obediently.

"So you and Samuel are getting close, ain't so?" Leah said.

A few days ago Anna would have been able to turn the question away with a laughing response. Now she couldn't. Now her throat clogged with tears at the thought of how she'd left things with Samuel.

If she could change what she'd said to him—no, she probably wouldn't if she could. What she'd said was true. She dare not risk doing what he wanted. And if Pete came . . .

If Pete came, all she could do was what she'd done before. Run. As far and as fast as she could.

. . .

Joseph was getting stronger—there was no doubt about that in Samuel's mind. He'd come out to the shop when Anna left for Leah's again, obviously curious.

Not having figured out how to tell him about Myra, Samuel had taken the cowardly way and shown him the machine he was working on. The result was predictable. At the moment, Joseph was seated on a chair next to the workbench, tinkering with the portable generator that had been acting up.

Joseph's improvement was a relief to Samuel's mind, but in a way he almost wished it weren't so, since that might give him an excuse not to have the conversation he knew he must have.

He'd promised Anna he'd talk with Joseph, and so he would, as soon as he finished welding the broken harrow. He slid his goggles into place and started the torch.

Unfortunately, even that didn't keep him from thinking of what Anna had said, standing in this very spot.

She'd been upset, that was all. She hadn't meant it about leaving.

But he was afraid she did, and after hearing her story, he couldn't bring himself to blame her for anything she'd said. Thinking of her confronting a dangerous addict on her own tied his stomach in knots. He could only thank God she hadn't been hurt.

Still, she'd lied. She continued to lie to her family by what she didn't say, and now she'd brought him into the lie, too.

If she let her fear of that man push her into running again, what chance was there that they'd ever see her again?

She'd leave pain behind for all of them, but he couldn't pretend he was thinking of the others. It was the possibility of his own loss that tortured him. He loved her.

He'd never intended to let that happen. Hadn't thought it could. But it had. And now, just when he'd begun to believe he could trust himself to love someone, she might disappear.

He switched off the torch and bent to have a look at the harrow. Anna wouldn't leave. She and Gracie were happy here. He had to believe that.

Satisfied that his work, at least, was under control, he tossed the goggles aside. Enough of these thoughts. He had to talk to Joseph, and the sooner the better.

Joseph looked up at his approach and put down his screwdriver, stretching cautiously. "I'm thinking maybe that's enough for today. I should go in and make sure Myra's all right. Did you know Anna went off to see Leah again this afternoon?"

Samuel didn't miss the critical note in Joseph's voice. He leaned against the end of the workbench, trying to decide how to respond. Ordinarily Joseph was the most easygoing of men, but his slow recovery had put an edge on his temper.

"It's gut to see Anna and Leah being friends again, ain't so?" he said mildly.

Joseph pressed one hand on his ribs as he levered himself to stand. "That's fine enough, but Anna left Gracie for Myra to mind. She should be helping Myra, not giving her extra work to do."

Samuel had the sense that Joseph was probably talking out of his own frustration at not being able to do what he should. Still, Samuel couldn't let a rift start between Joseph and Anna if he could help it.

"Anna went to see Leah today because she's worried about Myra. As I am. We hope that Leah will be able to help."

"What do you mean? Worried about what?" Joseph straightened to his full height, supporting himself with a hand on the bench. "Myra's fine and healthy. The doctor said so."

Did Joseph really not suspect anything? "Ja, her body is all right. But her mind—"

"There's nothing wrong with my Myra's mind. I am her husband. If something was wrong, I would know."

"Joseph, have you heard the way she talks about the baby? It's like she didn't hear anything the doctor said. Anna thinks—"

"Ach, Anna. I love my sister, but she always brings too much drama to everything. You know what she was like when she was a teenager. She's making a mountain out of a molehill, that's all."

"Anna isn't the person she was when she went away. She's a grown woman now, and she's worried about Myra. So am I. It is not gut for Myra to refuse to accept the truth."

"There is nothing wrong with Myra." Joseph's face reddened. "It is a difficult time for her. You should be supporting her, not criticizing her."

Samuel had gone about this all wrong, it seemed. "I am not criticizing. I just want her to get the help she needs."

"Myra is fine." Joseph turned away, probably too fast, because he sucked in a breath and put his hand to his ribs. "Just leave it alone. Both of you leave it alone."

He walked stiffly out of the shop. Usually Samuel would have given him an arm to help him into the house, but he didn't think Joseph would appreciate that right now.

Samuel ran a hand through his hair. Anna had trusted him to gain Joseph's support, and he'd failed.

Anna checked the chicken potpie that simmered on the stove. Almost done. Maybe supper would improve the atmosphere in the house. Everyone, even Sarah and Gracie, seemed a bit out of sorts since she got home.

Her own thoughts had been chaotic. Leah's call to her friend at the clinic had resulted in an appointment for Myra tomorrow. Now, somehow, they had to convince her to keep it.

And Anna had stopped at Rosemary's on the way home. She'd tried to explain as little as possible, but Rosemary had jumped to so many conclusions that maybe it would have been better to tell her everything.

Rosemary had agreed to come right over if Liz called. That was the important thing. But she'd gone further than that. She'd offered Anna a loan to leave now— today, in fact.

Anna ladled potpie, made the traditional Amish way with square, puffy noodles, into Myra's biggest earthenware bowl. She didn't want to take Rosemary's money. She didn't want to leave now, maybe not ever. But it might be better, at that. If she were to leave, the longer she put it off, the harder it became on everyone, including herself. At least now she knew someone would support her, if it came to that.

She'd told Samuel she wouldn't leave while Myra needed her. The promise stuck in her heart.

She headed for the door to call everyone for supper, only to find them already coming in from the backyard, Myra holding

Sarah's hand, while Samuel carried a wiggling Gracie.

"Supper is on."

"Ja, we smelled it." Samuel's smile seemed a bit strained.

Anna pulled the highchair close to the table. The bustle of getting everyone settled created a cover for her question to Samuel. "How did it go?" she murmured.

"Not gut." Concern darkened his eyes.

There wasn't time for more, but she thought she could guess the rest. Joseph was refusing to face the truth.

She slid into her seat, clasping her hands for the silent prayer that began the meal.

Dear Father, help us. Are we doing the right thing? Help Myra.

She sent a covert glance at Gracie, to find her sitting quietly, small hands linked as she concentrated on mimicking the others. Anna's heart seemed to turn over. Gracie was at home here. How could she think of taking her away?

Joseph nodded to Samuel, who lifted the heavy bowl of potpie and started it around the table. What had happened between the two of them, then? Samuel had said it was not gut.

Anna tried to concentrate on cutting up the puffy square of potpie dough for Gracie, who was already making a fine mess with her applesauce.

"Gracie, not with your fingers." She put a spoon into her daughter's hand. "Use the spoon."

"Sarah would still rather use her fingers than a spoon," Myra said. "I must work on that before the boppli comes."

Anna nodded. If Myra was talking naturally about the baby, that was what they wanted, wasn't it?

Myra ran her hand across her belly, lips curving. "I will feel him kicking soon, ja? I remember from Sarah. That is such a joy, to feel that. Remember the first time you felt that, Joseph? Remember?"

Anna's heart sank. Myra was talking too fast, her eyes too bright, her cheeks flushed like someone with a fever.

"I'm sure you will," she said, hoping to soothe her.

Joseph clasped Myra's hand in his. "I remember. We are all right about this boppli."

He shot a glance at Samuel. "Myra and me, we accept God's will for this child. We will love and care for it, no matter what."

"He." Myra's voice emphasized the word, and she snatched her hand away. "Our baby is a little boy, I know it. He is our perfect little son."

"I know you would like a son this time." Joseph spoke carefully, as if any word might cause hurt.

"It is a boy. I know it. I don't need any tests to tell me. The boppli feels different this time, and everyone says that's a sure sign."

Alarm shivered through Anna. She had to find something to say to defuse the situation. Myra seemed to be teetering on the edge of an explosion.

"We could start a crib quilt for the boppli," she said. "Wouldn't that be nice?"

The words, meant to comfort, seemed to have the opposite effect.

"Don't talk as if I were a child myself." Myra's voice rose. "You think there is something wrong. There's not! Nothing is wrong with my baby!"

They were all stunned into silence, to

hear gentle Myra shout at them. Then Sarah, never having heard that tone from her mother, burst into tears. Gracie's face puckered, and in an instant she was crying, too.

Myra's chair scraped as she shoved it back. Anna expected her to go to Sarah. Instead, she turned and hurried from the room, shoulders stiff. They heard the thump of her feet on the stairs, followed by the slam of the bedroom door.

Anna leaned over Gracie, trying to comfort her. "Hush, hush, little one. It's all right."

Moving stiffly, Joseph lifted Sarah from her chair, cuddling her in his lap. He looked at Samuel, his eyes dark with misery.

"I'm sorry. You tried to tell me, but I wouldn't listen. I'm sorry." He glanced at Anna, as if to include her in the apology.

"It's forgotten," Samuel said quickly. "Myra is all that's important now."

Joseph nodded, his eyes suspiciously bright. "Ja." He cleared his throat. "Anna, you and Leah, you will help, ja?"

"Of course we will." Pain clenched her heart to see her big brother look so hurt and bewildered. She would do anything she could to make this better.

And what if she had to leave? What would she do then?

CHAPTER EIGHTEEN

After nicking himself with the screwdriver twice in ten minutes and coming within an inch of slicing Matthew's hand, Samuel had decided that he was a danger in the shop. Leaving Matthew to carry on, he'd brought Mr. Bartlett's new young horse to the ring to work him for a bit. That, at least, he could do without danger to anyone else.

His problem wasn't hard to figure out. His heart was with Myra at the clinic, and his mind busy with prayers for her.

Be with her now, dear Lord. Open her to hear the counselor's words.

The two-year-old gelding, apparently sensing his lack of concentration, dropped to a walk. Samuel flicked the lunge whip in his general direction to get him moving again.

After Myra's outburst at supper last night, he'd thought it would be impossible to get her to the appointment, but it hadn't turned out that way. Maybe she'd actually frightened herself as much as she had them.

In any event, when Joseph had gone up to the bedroom to talk to her once the children were settled, she'd been so passive that that seemed to frighten him, too. Convinced this was for the best, bolstered by Anna's conviction, he'd finally gotten her agreement to see the counselor.

This morning she'd clung to Anna, so it had been decided that Anna would go with Joseph and Myra while Leah stayed with the children. Samuel didn't doubt that Leah had spent the time praying, just as he had.

When he spotted the car turning into the lane, he slowed the horse, bringing him in smaller and smaller circles until the animal stood next to him. He stroked the strong neck, murmuring quietly for a few minutes before turning the colt into the adjacent pasture.

Common sense told him that they could hardly expect a miracle from one session. Even so, he wanted to rush into the house, needing assurance that his little sister was better.

He contented himself with strolling toward the back porch, wondering whether it would be too obvious if he went inside for a drink of water. Maybe so. Instead he used the pump by the porch, lingering over filling the tin cup, pushing his straw hat back on his head, drinking. He was about ready to repeat the process when Anna came out of the house.

He waited until she neared him, reading the tension in the fine lines around her eyes. "How did it go?"

"Not here."

Anna took a quick glance around. She nodded toward the grape arbor and led him quickly to the slight privacy it provided. Then she turned toward him, and what she saw in his face must have telegraphed how worried he was.

"I'm sorry, I didn't mean to alarm you. It's nothing bad. The counselor was very encouraging."

"But you're still concerned." He could read her feelings so easily, even as relief flooded through him at the counselor's confidence.

"I'm just not sure." She bit her lip for an instant. "Myra was so quiet when she came out of the office. I thought— I hoped and prayed we'd see . . . well, some sign that she's coming to grips with the situation." Anna looked up at his face. "I pushed this, I know. Have we done the right thing? What if . . ."

"Now stop." He took hold of her arms, feeling the tension in her. "Anna, you must not think that way. You saw how Myra was last night. You know we had to make this decision for her, out of love."

"It's so difficult. I keep thinking of Jannie, of how I questioned myself every day. Was I doing the right thing for her? I'd never been responsible for anyone before. Never wanted to, never thought I could be."

Her uncertainty took hold of Samuel's heart and squeezed. "Was that why you ran away from us?"

"I don't know. Maybe." She shook her head. "It didn't work, if that was why. I took responsibility for Jannie and then Gracie. And now Myra." Her voice trembled. "What if I'm wrong?"

"I told you. You're not wrong." He drew her closer, uncertain if this was what she needed, but longing to comfort her.

With a sigh, Anna leaned against his chest. He wrapped his arms around her. *Comforting,* he told himself. *That's all she needs right now.*

"This time you're not alone." He said the words softly, his breath stirring the hair at her temples. "We're all taking responsibility for our Myra. We all love her, and the boppli."

Anna nodded, and he felt the movement. His heart was so full it seemed it would burst out of his chest. He longed to tell her what he felt, but this . . . this was like walking on ice. The smallest misstep could send him plunging to the depths.

So he stood, holding her, sensing the tension ebb slowly from her body. Loving her.

How foolish he had been, to think he couldn't love anyone for fear he was like his father. When true love came, it wiped away every doubt. If he told her . . .

No, not now. Not when she was so worried. He rested his cheek against her hair and was content.

"Anna?" Leah's voice accompanied the slam of the screen door. "Are you out here?"

Anna pulled back, wiping her face with her palms. "I'm here." She walked quickly out of the arbor, and Samuel followed.

Leah stood at the bottom of the porch steps, looking a little flushed when she saw them. "I'm sorry. I didn't know—"

"I was just filling Samuel in on what happened," Anna said quietly.

"Gut." If Leah thought anything else, she was wise enough not to say. "I'm heading home now. I'll stop over sometime tomorrow."

"That would be a help," Samuel said. "You understand this better than we do."

Leah shook her head. "You're both doing fine." She patted his hand, and then seemed to realize that she was holding an envelope. "I nearly forgot. Matthew brought the mail in. There was a letter for you."

She handed the envelope to Anna and hugged her. "Don't worry too much, the pair of you. Myra will be well."

Anna gave her a quick squeeze. "Denke, Leah. Da Herr sie mit du."

May God be with you. It was the first time Samuel had heard Anna use the loving response since her return. Leah's eyes sparkled, and she walked quickly toward the buggy as Matthew drove it up.

Anna stood for a moment, holding the envelope in her hand. She looked a bit frightened. "Samuel, it is from Aaron Esch. The family . . ."

"Ja, I know." The family whose buggy she had hit. "Aren't you going to open it?"

She took a deep breath and then ripped the envelope open. A single sheet of paper fell out. "It is from Aaron's wife."

She bent her head to the words, and he murmured a quick, silent prayer. Anna was dealing with enough just now. Let the letter not make things worse.

She looked up at him, pressing her lips together as if to keep them from trembling. "She says they will see me, if that is what I want."

"Is it?"

She hesitated for a moment, then nodded. "I think so. It's time I took responsibility for what I did."

"It's a long drive to the Esch farm. I will take you there, if you like."

Her fingers closed over his. "Denke, Samuel."

Giggling, Sarah sent a spray of bathwater onto Gracie's round tummy. Gracie responded by waving both hands, splashing herself in the face and dampening the front of Anna's dress. She looked so startled at what she'd done that Anna was surprised into a laugh.

"Two little fishes swimming in the creek." Anna grabbed the towels she had waiting. "The big bird swoops down and snatches them up."

She scooped Gracie up with one towel and then quickly grabbed Sarah with the other, leaving no time for wails about leaving the bath.

"Bird, bird," Sarah cried, entranced with the new game. "Dry me, bird."

"I will, I will." Anna pulled them both into her arms, rubbing their pink bodies with the towels. She was getting herself nearly as wet as they were, but holding them so close made it worthwhile. Their innocent laughter was an antidote to the day's worries.

They were probably making more noise than they should, since Myra was supposedly asleep in the bedroom across the hall. Myra had spent the afternoon there, come down and picked at her supper without speaking, then gone back up again, saying she was tired.

It was so unusual for Myra to sleep during the day that Joseph's stress had shot up again. Maybe it would have been better to let Myra come to terms with the baby's problems on her own. Maybe . . .

Since Anna had the same worries, she could hardly argue. She'd chased him and Samuel off to keep Sarah and Gracie occupied while she did the dishes. A half hour in Samuel's calm, steady presence would be better for Joseph than a half hour of asking questions to which they had no answers.

Anna popped nightgowns on the two squirming children, thinking that she could have used a quiet half hour with Samuel herself. For an instant she was back in his arms again, feeling the steady beat of his heart against her cheek.

Gracie wiggled free of her and made a dash for the bath, clearly intending to climb back in.

"No, you don't." Anna snatched her up, nuzzling her soft, damp cheek until Gracie giggled. "Time for two little girls to have their stories."

"Sarah pick," Sarah declared, and darted for the bedroom.

Gracie twisted to join her cousin, so Anna put her down and followed the two of them into their bedroom. Gracie grabbed a book as well, and Anna sat on Sarah's bed, drawing Gracie onto her lap and snuggling Sarah against her.

The orange reflection of the setting sun suffused the room with a gentle glow, and the soft sounds of evening filtered in—the whoo of an owl, the distant clop of a horse's hoof, the continuous cricket chirping.

Anna pressed a kiss on Gracie's damp curls as she opened the book of nursery rhymes. If they left, Gracie would lose this peaceful setting, the stable upbringing, the love of a large family.

But if they stayed, she would lose everything the world valued—higher education, the latest technology, clothes and cars and all the rest of it.

The choice might not be Anna's to make. The thought lay under the tale of Jack and Jill as she read.

There had been no news from Liz. She clung to that as she read a Bible story, said prayers, and tucked them into their beds with hugs and kisses. Gracie was already half-asleep, and she curled under her blanket without a fuss.

Sarah took a few minutes to arrange her rag doll just so, but her eyes were drooping, too. With a last kiss, Anna went quietly out.

Myra stood in the hallway, looking heavy-eyed. "I fell asleep." She sounded surprised. "Did you put Sarah to bed already? I should have."

"You needed the rest. She went down fine for me, but she's not asleep yet. Why don't you go in and snuggle with her for a minute?"

Myra brushed her forehead with her hand, as if wiping away the wisps of sleep, and tiptoed into the room.

Through the half-open door, Anna could see that Gracie didn't stir. Sarah sat up, holding out her arms to her mother, and Myra sank down on the bed, hugging her. Myra's shoulders shook, and Anna tensed. Maybe it hadn't been such a good idea for Myra to go in, not if she was going to let Sarah see her crying.

Perhaps Myra thought the same, because she straightened, talking softly to her daughter. She kissed her, tucking her in, and came out quickly.

"All right?" Anna closed the door.

"Ja." Myra blinked, as if trying to focus. "I was just—" She stopped, hand on the door, and then leaned her head against it.

"Myra—" Anna wasn't sure what to say. If only Mamm were here. Mammi would know what to say. The thought was like a sharp stone in her chest.

"Remember what it is like when they're tiny babies?" Myra said, drawing away, still touching the door with her fingertips. "Remember how you could never stop worrying about the baby, even when she was sleeping, so you'd keep checking on her?"

"I remember." Anna put her arm around

Myra's waist, urging her gently toward the stairs. "Sometimes I couldn't hear her breathing, so I'd put my hand on her, just to feel the movement of her chest. It's a wonder I didn't wake her up every ten minutes, doing that."

She could laugh at herself, looking back at it now, but at the time it had been terrifying to have that small life in her care.

Myra actually smiled. "Ach, I was the same. Maybe every mother is."

Myra's response sent a wave of relief through Anna. It was Myra's own sweet smile. "Maybe so, but I didn't have anyone to ask."

"I'll know better this time." To Anna's dismay, Myra's face assumed that mask that declared everything was fine, but she thought she detected a few cracks in the facade.

"I think maybe we'd be a bit that way with every boppli, no matter how many we have," Anna said carefully. "Loving each one as if he or she is the only one, a little like God loves us."

"Of course we do. I will. My boppli is fine, he's fine, he . . ." She stopped short, her lips trembling. "I can't." Her voice choked, and tears flowed down her face like a sudden downpour.

"It's all right," Anna murmured, and then was disgusted with herself. It wasn't all right. Why couldn't she think of something useful to say?

"What if I can't do it?" Myra spoke through the tears, and the mask was gone for sure now. "What if I can't take care of the boppli? What if I can't love this one like I love Sarah?"

There it was, Anna realized as she put her arms around Myra. That was the fear at the center, the one Myra hadn't been able to express.

"You will," she murmured. "Some days you might feel as if you can't, but when that happens, we'll be there to help you. The family won't let you down. God won't let you down. You're not alone. You know that, don't you?"

For a long moment Myra didn't respond. She just clung to Anna. Then, slowly, she nodded. "Ja," she whispered, and the fierce grip of her hands eased. "Ja. I know that."

The tension in Anna ebbed as well. Myra had taken the first step on a long, difficult road.

· · ·

The closer the buggy got to the Esch home, the more Anna wanted to run in the other direction. Coward, she chided herself, but it didn't seem to do much good.

She glanced at Samuel. His strong face was shielded by the brim of his straw hat so that she couldn't see his eyes, but she imagined that his tension had increased as well.

They had talked during the long ride, mostly about how Myra had been over the past few days. She had seen the counselor again yesterday, and again had come home quiet and withdrawn, but overall she seemed better. She talked rationally now about the baby, without the frantic optimism she'd displayed before, and she'd expressed a desire to talk to Bishop Mose.

Anna found she was watching Samuel's sure hands on the lines. Other than expressing his deep concern for Myra, he'd kept their conversation casual, a far cry from the moments they'd shared that day in the arbor. Either Samuel didn't feel comfortable pushing too close when she was preoccupied with this visit, or he regretted what had happened between them.

Either way, she should be glad of his retreat. She'd grown to care for Samuel, and she recognized the desire to let that caring ripen into something stronger. But she couldn't do that, not when the future was so uncertain.

Samuel slowed the horse and made the turn into a farm lane. Her throat tightened, and she gripped the seat with both hands.

"Is it too late to change my mind about this?" She was only half-joking.

His gaze assessed her. "It's natural to be nervous."

"What if they don't forgive me?" She asked the question, but she was afraid to hear the answer.

"If they refuse forgiveness, then the burden of that failure is on them." He said the words as if no doubt existed in his mind.

"Don't you think that quick forgiveness lets the sinner off too easily?"

"Easily?" He came to a stop some distance from the front porch but didn't move immediately, seeming to ponder the word. "You have suffered for what you did, I think. Maybe you will continue to suffer. It is up to God. All we can do is follow His direction. Forgive, if we wish to be forgiven." He jumped down and held out his hand to her. "Komm. They're waiting for us."

He was right—a man and woman stood on the porch.

"Aaron, Elizabeth." Samuel took over, nodding gravely to them. "This is Anna Beiler."

Anna's voice seemed to have disappeared. She nodded, taking in the expressions on their faces. The man, his dark hair cut short in a bowl style, his beard wiry, looked at her with what seemed to be curiosity. But the woman—when Anna met her gaze, she felt as if she'd received a blow.

"Komm." Aaron Esch spoke as he opened the door. "Wilkom to our home."

They filed into the living room and took seats as solemnly as if they were going to church. And waited. Obviously Anna was supposed to speak first.

She cleared her throat. "Denke." Her mouth was dry, so dry she didn't know how she was going to get the words out. "I asked to come because I wanted to see you in person to ask for your forgiveness. I regret, so much, that my actions harmed your family."

They looked back at her, their faces

impassive. It was only now, when she thought it might not be granted, that she realized how important their forgiveness had become to her.

Finally Aaron nodded with deliberation. "It is gut that you feel so, but not necessary to ask. We forgave you long ago, as Christ commands."

Something flickered in the woman's eyes as he said the words, something hidden so quickly that Anna almost missed it. Maybe she only saw the feeling because she was sensitive to everything they did and said. And so she knew. Aaron might have forgiven her, as he said, but Elizabeth had not.

Anna's heart seemed to wince. Was that so surprising? Would she forgive so easily if someone put Gracie in danger?

"Denke. I . . ."

A little girl ran into the room and stopped, obviously taken aback at the presence of strangers. She must have been about five or six, with big brown eyes that studied them curiously.

"Mary, komm, schnell." The woman rapped out the words and reached for the child. The little girl's face puckered, and she ran to her mother, burying her face in her mamm's apron.

Another blow to her heart. That Elizabeth felt the need to protect her child from Anna—it was almost too painful to bear.

But she had to. That was why she was here.

"I have a daughter of my own now." She centered her heart on Gracie, searching for the strength to go on. "I didn't understand until I was a mother how terrifying it is when your child is in danger." Her voice choked in her throat. Tears welled in her eyes. "I know now. You would suffer anything to spare your child."

She wanted to say more, but the words failed her. She put up a shaking hand to wipe away her tears. Tried to speak again, but could only shake her head, covering her face with her hands.

"Don't be sad."

Anna was so sunk in her own guilt that she didn't realize at first that it was the little girl who spoke. The child tugged at Anna's hands, pulling them away from her face.

"Don't cry. It'll be all right. My mammi can make it better."

Anna looked from the child's sweet face to the mother, to see Elizabeth's face crumple. Elizabeth held out her hand, and Anna took it.

CHAPTER NINETEEN

Anna walked down Main Street, remembering to adjust her stride to the casual stroll of an Amish woman instead of the fast pace of a city dweller. Samuel had wanted to pick up something from the hardware store on their way home, so they'd made a stop in town. Remembering that she was nearly out of Gracie's vitamins, she'd decided to walk the two blocks to the pharmacy.

The maples that lined the town square were already changing color, and a crispness in the air declared that fall was really coming.

Despite her concerns about Myra and

her fears of Pete's actions, at this moment she felt only a strong sense of relief. It surprised her, in a way. She hadn't fully realized how much her unpaid debt to the Esch family had weighed on her.

Had Bishop Mose understood that when she'd first come back? Maybe that had been behind his reluctance to let her kneel before the congregation to confess.

If she had confessed then, she'd have been faking it; she knew that now. She'd thought that would be the utmost in humiliation, but really, she'd have been trying to take the easy way out. Bishop Mose hadn't let her go through the motions, and whatever happened to her in the future, she'd be forever grateful.

She pushed open the glass door of the pharmacy, catching a glimpse of herself as she did. To dress Amish meant to be stared at when you went into the English world, but it also gave her a pleasant sense of anonymity. She was any Amish woman, her hair and face half-hidden by the bonnet.

She dawdled in the baby supplies aisle, knowing she didn't have to hurry. Samuel would dally over his transaction, getting all the news of town while he was at the hardware store.

Thinking about him gave her an odd little flutter in the region of her heart. He had understood, without question, her need to see the Esch family. He'd been confident she could do it—more confident in her than she'd been in herself. She wasn't sure how it had happened, but he'd become so important in her life that it was hard to imagine doing without him.

She carried the vitamins to the counter, exchanging the usual comments about the weather with the clerk as she paid. She would go back to where they'd left the buggy, and Samuel would be waiting. They'd have another half hour or so alone together on the way home. Maybe she could find the words to tell him how much she appreciated his support.

She walked toward the door. Just as she reached it, a rack of newspapers caught her eye. She turned aside to read the headlines, and then glanced through the plate glass window at the street beyond.

Her breath stuck in her throat. Pete—

that was Pete, walking across the street toward the square, peering around as if looking for someone. Looking for her.

She recoiled, grabbing the paper rack to steady herself. He couldn't see her, surely he couldn't. She stood safely away from the window. But if she hadn't stopped at the last moment to look at the papers, she'd have walked out onto the street within twenty feet of him. Her heart thudded in her ears, nearly deafening her.

How could he be here? She moved carefully to the other side of the rack, peering toward the small park at the heart of the square. Pete sat down on one of the green benches, glancing up and down the street. He'd picked the perfect location to watch for her, able to see anyone going into or out of the Main Street shops.

Calm down. Think. He wouldn't be doing that if he knew exactly where she was. That gave her a chance.

But why hadn't Liz called? Her mind skittered off in that direction. Liz must not have realized he'd left Chicago. She'd find out, probably, but by then it would be too late.

Please, Lord, help me think this

through. Help me to make the right decision. If I don't—

No, she wouldn't let herself veer down that road. If she let panic take over, she'd lose. She pressed her fingers to her temple, a wordless prayer rising in her heart.

She had to get home, grab Gracie, and get out of here before Pete started working his way through the Beilers in the community. At least he wouldn't find them conveniently listed in the telephone book. That would delay him for a while.

She could go to Rosemary. Rosemary would drive them to Mifflinburg, where they could get a bus to somewhere, anywhere.

She took a breath. She had time. Pete operated on brute force, not brainpower.

Still, sooner or later it would occur to him to start asking around. People, even English people, knew the Beilers.

She couldn't go out on the street. He'd see her for sure if she did that. Wheeling, she hurried to the back of the store.

"Is there a rear door I can use? Please, it's important."

Maybe it was the quaver in her voice that convinced him. The pharmacist gave her an odd look, but he led her back through the pharmacy shelves to a door that opened onto the alley.

With a quick look in both directions she slipped out, murmuring her thanks. The alley was empty, and she scurried along toward the hardware store, thoughts tumbling even faster than her rushing feet.

Samuel would help her. She just had to get to Samuel. Did Pete know he was looking for an Amish family? Maybe, maybe not, but she couldn't take a risk that he might. Jannie had known.

Oh, Jannie, did you tell him? I trusted you to keep my secret.

Only another block to the hardware store, but now her luck ran out. The alley ended abruptly at a fenced-in lot. She had no choice but to go back to Main Street.

She stopped at the corner, taking advantage of the cover provided by some passing shoppers to peer down the street. Pete was still sitting on the bench, a block down.

She had to get to Samuel. She'd have to pray Pete didn't know he was looking for someone in Amish dress. She waited for the next passersby and then slipped onto the sidewalk just ahead of them, hoping they screened her from view. Her stomach twisted, and she held her breath, waiting for the sound of running feet, of Pete shouting her name.

Nothing. And there was the hardware store, with its hitching rail along the side for Amish buggies. Samuel stood next to his buggy, lifting a box in.

She couldn't contain herself any longer. She rushed to him, grabbed his arm. "We have to go. Now!"

The surprise on his face gave way to a startled comprehension. Without a word, he grasped her arm and helped her up to the buggy seat. He released the line and swung himself up, clucking to the horse to back him away from the rail.

"Not by way of the square," she said, urgency filling her voice. "We can't go that way."

He nodded, turning in the opposite direction, and in a moment they were heading down the side street, away from danger.

Samuel kept his tension in check as they wound through several back streets to get clear of town. Obviously something had happened in the few minutes they'd been apart—something that had frightened Anna badly. The baby's birth father. What else could it be?

He turned onto the road that led home. Anna kept swiveling, staring behind them, her hand up to shield her face.

If she wouldn't break the silence, he would.

"Is anyone following us?"

She turned around, hands grasping the seat as if to force the buggy to go faster. "It doesn't look like it. I can't see anyone."

He waited, but she didn't go on. Apparently he'd have to pry the words out of her.

"What is wrong? Was it him . . . Pete?"

She nodded, fingers tightening on the seat until her knuckles were white. "I was about to come out of the pharmacy when I saw him crossing the street to the square." Her voice quavered. "If I'd walked out a minute sooner, I'd have walked right into him."

"But you didn't." Samuel put his hand over hers where it gripped the seat. Her tension was so strong that her skin seemed to spark. "God was watching out for you."

She bit her lip. "I hope so."

"I know it," he said, hoping that gave her strength.

there are plenty of English who know where the Beiler family lives."

"Anna . . ."

"It's over, Samuel." Her voice was filled with anguish. "I don't have a choice. Gracie and I have to leave. We can lose ourselves in some big city where he'll never find us."

Never. Now, when he was about to lose her, he knew how much he loved her.

"Don't, Anna. You can't just leave." *I love you.* "We'll take care of you and Gracie."

"I can't stay." Her fear was so strong it was like a third person sitting on the buggy seat between them. "I have to keep my daughter safe."

Samuel fought to keep his feelings in check. It wouldn't do, when she was terrified for her child, to put the burden of his love on her.

"Anna, I understand that you must protect Gracie. But this man—surely he will listen to reason. He has no right to the baby, and he's not able to take care of her. Why would he want to take her away from people who love her?"

Anna stared at him, her face bleak. "Did you never run into someone like him when

"I couldn't go out the front of the store He'd have seen me. He sat down on a bench in the square where he could watch the whole area. The pharmacist let me go out the back way."

Samuel considered. "So he doesn't know exactly where you are."

"If he knew that . . ." She sucked in a breath. "If he knew that, it would already be too late."

He tried to think it through, tried to put himself in the mind of the man. He couldn't do it. It was too great a stretch.

"All right, then. If all he knows is that you're from this area, then he's just guessing that you're here. He can't be sure you'd come home, because you didn't tell anyone. You can lie low until he gets tired and goes away again."

She was already shaking her head. "I can't. He's bound to ask around. Sooner or later, he'll find someone who knows me."

"Amish are ser gut at playing dumb in the face of nosy questions. No one will give you away."

Her mouth twisted. "I wish I could believe that. But even if no Amish would tell, you were out in the world? Someone with such a skewed view of reality that they were lost to good reason and common sense?"

"If that's the case, I wonder that the baby means anything at all to him."

"He's not thinking straight." Her lips pressed together as if to hold back the pain. "Liz had it right. She says Pete always wants most what he can't have. Right now, that's Gracie."

"But if we all talk to him . . ."

"Don't, Samuel." All her pent-up grief seemed to fill the word. "This does no good at all. If Pete finds me, he's going to try to take Gracie. If he does . . . if he does, it's not just that I'll never see her again. I'm afraid that if he takes her, she won't survive."

Her voice shook on the final word, and Samuel's heart seemed to tremble in his chest.

"Anna, listen to me. You must tell your daad and Bishop Mose."

"No, they—"

"When they understand what is at stake, they'll help. They'll even go to the police, little though they'll like it. I'm certain-sure of that."

She threw up her hands in a gesture of helplessness. "Maybe you're right. I hope so. But don't you see? It might be too late. Pete isn't counting on the law to get Gracie back. He's going to grab her and run."

"We won't let that happen." He had to make her believe that, and she was already shaking her head.

"Pete is the kind of man who settles conflict with his fists. He's dangerous, and I've put all of you in danger by hiding here. All I can do is get out of his way. Once he sees I'm gone and no one knows where I went, he'll leave the rest of you alone."

It stabbed him to the heart that she thought she had to protect them.

"Anna, you must trust in the people who love you. Trust in God to deliver us from this evil."

But he saw in her eyes that she had gone far away from him already. She shook her head again.

His heart was breaking for her. Knowing what it would cost, still he had to say what he would do. "You must tell them. If you don't, I will."

She turned on him then. "You have no right to interfere."

"I love you, Anna. I believe that gives me the right to take care of you and Gracie."

Pain drew her skin tight against the bone. "If you do that, I will never forgive you. Never."

The instant Samuel stopped at the house, Anna jumped down from the buggy. She couldn't say anything—there was nothing to say.

Samuel had said he loved her. That was a separate pain that she couldn't begin to deal with now, so she closed it away. Now all she could do was get Gracie someplace safe.

She hurried into the house, registering that Samuel had driven off toward his barn. She had until he'd dealt with his horse and buggy and come back to the shop before he'd tell Daadi. By then, she had to be gone.

No time to pack their clothes—she could only stuff as much as possible into Gracie's diaper bag.

She barreled into the kitchen. Myra, coming in from the living room, gave her a startled look.

"Anna, I didn't realize you were back. Is something wrong?"

"No, nothing." *Everything.* But she couldn't tell Myra. She couldn't burden Myra with her troubles, and she certainly couldn't say she was leaving. "Is Gracie napping?"

"Ja, they both are." Myra smiled. "She was a little lamb while you were gone."

Myra always thought that. She was as gentle and loving with Gracie as she was with her own Sarah.

"I'll go take a peek at her." Anna hurried up the stairs, not letting herself think about all that Gracie would lose by leaving here. There were too many things she couldn't think about now.

She slipped into the children's bedroom. Sarah slept as intently as she did everything, her arm around her rag doll.

In the crib, Gracie lay on her stomach, thumb in her mouth, eyelashes forming perfect crescents on her rosy cheeks. She stirred a little as Anna pulled out the diaper bag and began to fill it.

She would take the essentials. There was no time for more. Pete could be on his way here right now. Her vivid imagination gave her too clear a picture of him rushing down the country road in a fast car, sweeping into the house, snatching Gracie. Disappearing with her.

Law-abiding people were always at a disadvantage when it came to defending themselves against the people who didn't go by the community's rules. The Amish were among the most law-abiding people anywhere, and so maybe the most vulnerable.

Anna swept the room with a quick glance to be sure she hadn't missed anything crucial, and then touched Gracie's cheek lightly.

"Komm, Gracie. We have to go now."

The child's eyelids fluttered. She looked at Anna and gave a sleepy smile. "Mammi," she murmured.

Anna's heart clenched. She lifted Gracie into her arms and took the blanket that lay over the end of the crib. She might need that tonight. Who knew where she'd be by then?

God knew. Samuel's voice echoed in her mind. *Trust God, Anna. Trust the people who love you.*

She couldn't. Not because she doubted their love, but because they had no idea what they were up against. Confronted with Pete, Daadi would make allowances for him, thinking him a father who surely had some right to his daughter, no matter what papers he'd signed.

Samuel, a little wiser in the ways of the world, would still try to reason with Pete. He wouldn't fight back—that would violate his most deeply held beliefs.

Hoisting the diaper bag to her shoulder, Anna took a last look around the bedroom. They had been happy here. They'd been safe and loved. But the safety had disappeared now, and she couldn't believe that love alone would keep them safe.

Myra stood at the bottom of the stairs. She watched as Anna came down, frowning a little. "Anna, what is this? Where are you going?"

She forced herself to smile, hoping she could look and sound natural. It hurt to deceive Myra, who was as dear to her as a sister.

"I need to run over to Rosemary's for a bit." That part of it was true enough. "I thought I'd take Gracie along. May I use your horse and buggy?"

"Ja, of course." Myra didn't lose her puzzled look, but she agreed without hesitation. "We'll talk later then, ain't so?"

Anna nodded. Later. Later, maybe, she could write to Myra, try to explain. Try to tell her how much she regretted this step.

She hurried away before she could say more. The image of Pete rushing down the road filled her mind.

She sped toward the barn. Thank heaven no one was in sight. No one stopped to ask her what she was doing or where she was going.

By the time she reached the barn, panic had a grip on her throat. *Run, run.* The words pounded in her mind. Run, just as she'd run when she left Chicago. Just as she'd run when she left here the first time.

Myra's mare poked her head over her stall door and whickered a welcome. Anna set Gracie down in the pen that was sometimes used for young animals, clean and empty now. The baby would be safe there while Anna harnessed the horse.

Go to Rosemary's. That was the first step. Rosemary would lend her English clothes, surely, and drive her to Mifflinburg. Once there, she could get a bus to Harrisburg, maybe change there and go on to Baltimore.

Baltimore was a big enough city for one woman and a small child to get lost in.

She had to hurry. Samuel could be telling Daad even now. Pete could be driving up the lane.

The mare, maybe affected by Anna's fear, began dancing, her hooves thudding against the wooden floor. Perhaps even Betsy knew Anna was crying inside at the thought of leaving.

"Hush, now, Betsy. Steady." The mare quieted at her voice, tossing her head a bit.

The barn door scraped. Anna spun toward the sound, and her breath caught. Pete stood there, fists clenched, eyes dark.

"Where is my baby? Where is she?"

CHAPTER TWENTY

Samuel had told them, and Anna would never forgive him. He walked out of the shop, giving Elias and Joseph the space they needed to discuss what they would do.

As for him—well, he already knew what he had lost, didn't he? He'd had no choice. All Anna could think was to run, as she had run before.

God had used her running then to bring her home again, where she belonged. Surely He couldn't mean for her to leave again.

He walked away from the shop and stopped in the yard, not sure what to do.

Maybe he ought to try talking to Anna again. He half-turned toward the house, but his eye was caught by the glitter of sunlight reflecting off something metal.

A car, parked up the rutted track that led from the road to the barn. The barn door, standing open. An icy hand seemed to grip his heart. Anna—

He began to run, his heart thudding. The man she feared must be there. Had he followed them after all? Anna and Gracie were in danger.

He reached the barn door, thrusting it wider as he went in. The man who stood facing Anna didn't even seem to notice.

"Give me that baby!" He punctuated the words with a violent gesture of his clenched fist.

Anna stood between the stalls, and beyond her Samuel spotted Gracie pulling herself up on the small pen. Anna held Myra's buggy horse by the halter. The mare shifted nervously at the unusual sounds.

"Anna. Are you all right?"

She looked at Samuel, her eyes wide and dark.

He took a step toward her, his gaze focused on hers as he spoke in the dialect the stranger wouldn't know. "Listen to me. Chase Betsy toward him, and then run and get the baby. Try to get over here to me."

She gave a faint nod.

"What're you saying?" Pete swiveled toward him, and any hope Samuel had of reasoning with the man vanished. Pete's thin face was distorted with anger, his eyes wild and dangerous.

Samuel held out a hand, as he would to a skittish horse, automatically trying to calm him. But all his attention was on Anna.

"Anna, schnell."

Anna let go of the halter and slapped Betsy's rump, giving a wordless shout. Betty's hooves scrabbled on the wooden floor, and she lunged toward the open door, baring her teeth at the unaccustomed treatment.

Samuel held his ground, knowing the mare was too smart to run into him. Pete shied away like a frightened animal himself, throwing up his hands to shield his face.

Anna snatched Gracie into her arms and whirled, but there wasn't time. She couldn't make it to the door before Pete recovered.

The distraction let Samuel move. He put himself between Anna and the stranger.

"Watch for a chance to run. It will be all right." *Please, God, let that be true.*

"Talk English, I said!" Pete took a step toward him and seemed to gain some marginal control of himself. "Found yourself a boyfriend, Annie? He can't help you. You just walk over here and give me that baby."

Samuel kept his gaze fixed on the man as he would on a copperhead in the woods. From the corner of his eye he could see the shake of her head.

"Gracie is my daughter, Pete." Her voice was calm, even reasonable, but Samuel heard the terror beneath the words. "You know that. You signed the papers. You told Jannie you didn't want anything to do with a baby. Remember?"

"Yeah, well, I changed my mind. She's my kid. I want her."

"The law says Gracie is my daughter." The edge of desperation was more noticeable.

"I don't see any law around. Just farm boy here." Pete jerked his head toward Samuel. "You think you could hide from me in that costume, Annie? You always thought you were smarter than everybody. Always telling Jannie she could do better'n me. Well, I found you, didn't I?"

"How did you do that? I covered my tracks pretty well."

Samuel knew what Anna was doing—stalling for time, trying to keep him talking. But time for what? Who would come to help? He should have gone for someone instead of racing in here.

"Your friend at the restaurant kept chasing me away. I went back one night, figuring I'd bust up his office. Then I saw his file cabinets. Guess whose job application form was in there. Yours, with the name of some bakery where you worked before, right here in the middle of nowhere."

Anna's lips pressed together. She'd said her friends wouldn't give her away, but she obviously hadn't thought of that application. She seemed to take a breath, as if to rally herself. "So you came here. I saw you in town."

Pete grinned. "I saw you, too. Didn't want to start a fuss out in public, so I just thought I'd follow along at a safe distance. See, the guy at the gas station already told me where the Beilers lived, so I didn't have to get too close." His face darkened suddenly. "Enough of that. Give me the baby."

"Why? You don't love her. You don't even know her."

"She's mine. I'm taking her." He flexed his fists. "You think farm boy here is going to stop me?"

"I will not fight you." Samuel said the words slowly in English. "But I will not let you take Gracie."

Pete didn't respond. Maybe his words hadn't even penetrated. Instead, he charged toward Anna.

Samuel stepped between them. He could not hit the man, but he could put his body between Anna and danger, and he would.

Pete jerked back, anger flaring in his face. Then he swung.

Samuel made no effort to deflect the blow. Planting his feet, he took it, hands at his sides, like being hit full in the stomach by a horse's kick.

"You think I'll back off because you won't fight? You're wrong." Pete swung again, this time catching Samuel on the jaw, snapping his head back.

"Stop it!" Anguish colored Anna's voice. "He won't hit you because it is against our faith. Please, Pete. Give Gracie a chance to have a decent life. That's what Jannie wanted for her."

"*My* kid," Pete muttered, shaking his head. "Mine." He feinted, trying to get around Samuel. Samuel stepped into his path again. How long? How long could he do this?

Pete charged him, his fists connecting viciously. Samuel's head spun, and he staggered back a step.

Had to stay on his feet. Had to. If he didn't, there'd be nothing protecting Anna and the baby. Couldn't let go, couldn't . . .

His feet went out from under him. He struggled, trying to get up. Pete kicked him, sending him back down again.

Red haze threatened to envelop him. He fought it, hearing Anna cry out. Blinking, he tried to focus, saw Pete grab Gracie and send Anna to the floor with a blow.

Gracie gave a frightened scream. Samuel struggled to get his knees under him, push himself up. Pete was going. He was heading toward the door with Gracie . . .

"Stop!" Elias's voice sounded like a clap of thunder. "Stop now!"

Anna had never heard anything more welcome than her father's voice. She rolled to her side, pushing herself up, trying to clear her head. Daadi was there. Daadi would make it right.

In an instant, sense came rushing in. What could Daadi do? Pete would not let one old man stop him.

"Daadi, don't . . ."

"You think you can stop me, old man? You want to fight?"

"I will not fight you," Daadi said evenly. "But I will not let you take my grandchild."

"We also."

Joseph was there, clinging to the door to stay upright until Myra slid her arm around him. Matthew pressed close to Daadi's side, his young face filled with determination. The four of them filled the doorway. Her people.

"You can't stop me."

But for the first time, she heard doubt in

Pete's voice. She forced herself onto her knees.

"Pete, stop and think. You don't want to do this. You can't take care of a baby. What kind of life will you give her? How can you travel and hang out with your friends when you have to watch a baby?"

Pete shook his head, his face twisting. "Tell her to quit the screaming. I can't think with all this screaming going on."

"She won't stop just because I say so. She needs comforting. She needs her mother. Please, give her to me, Pete."

"No!" His face contorted. "I'll take care of her. She's my kid."

"How will you care for her?" Daadi's voice was stern. "You have beaten an innocent man who would not raise a hand against you. You have hit a woman who loves the child. Is that how you will take care of her?"

"I wouldn't hurt the kid. Just make her stop crying." Pete's voice rose. He shook Gracie. Her crying lifted to a frightened shriek.

A fresh jolt of terror went through Anna. "Is that what you told Jannie? That you wouldn't hurt her?" Her heart was beating so hard that it drummed in her ears. Was he hearing any of this? "How long do you think it will be before you strike out at Gracie?"

"I wouldn't."

But she thought there was hesitation in his tone, and her heart leaped with hope.

"A father wants what is best for his children," Daadi said. "No matter how much it hurts him, he does what is best for them."

He didn't press. He just stood there, looking at Pete, his face grave. Waiting.

Please, God. Please, God.

Pete's expression hardened, as if he'd made a decision. He strode toward the four who stood in the doorway, and her heart seemed to stop.

He thrust Gracie into Daadi's arms. Gracie buried her face in her grossdaadi's shoulder, her shrieks fading away into sobs as he cradled her in his arms.

Joseph and Myra moved back, clearing a path. Without a word, Pete walked away.

A sob shook Anna. She managed to crawl the few feet to Samuel even as the others hurried toward them.

"Samuel! Are you all right?" Stupid. Of

course he wasn't all right. He had let Pete beat him. For her and Gracie.

His smile was the slightest twitch of his lips. "We are all right now." Then his eyes glazed, and he slumped into her arms.

Anna bent over Gracie's crib. She winced a little as the bar brushed her ribs. Once again, she had Pete to thank for a set of bruises, but this was the last time.

Oddly enough, she had no doubts about that. God had delivered them today. He wouldn't let them down in the days and years to come.

She stroked Gracie's hair, crooning to her. Gracie's eyes drifted closed as sleep claimed her. Anna lingered, reluctant to leave the room. Though she didn't doubt God's care, it might take a while before she felt easy when Gracie was out of her sight.

She kissed her fingertips and touched them lightly to Gracie's forehead. "Sleep well, my sweet girl," she whispered.

She tiptoed from the room. Judging by the sounds coming from downstairs, most of the family was still here. They'd begun arriving within an hour of Pete's departure, summoned by that mysterious Amish grapevine that seemed to work better than any telephone. Even Bishop Mose had heard and had come.

Anna started down the stairs, listening to the hum of voices in the kitchen. The women were there, it seemed, while the men had taken over the front porch.

Bishop Mose saying thanksgiving had, she thought, short-circuited all the wondering and questioning. The right reaction to such unprecedented events, his attitude seemed to say, was to praise God for His deliverance.

She reached the bottom of the stairs and hesitated. She wanted, no, needed, to see Samuel. To assure herself that he was all right.

He'd refused to let the paramedics take him to the hospital, insisting that his bruises would heal and nothing was broken. Maybe so, but the need to see for herself drove her to find him. A glance through the window told her he wasn't on the porch with the other men.

She went back to the kitchen, to be greeted by the smiling faces and loving voices of the women. Rosemary, who'd arrived with a message from Liz moments after Pete had left, had gone home finally, saying she'd call Liz back.

Everyone else was here, waiting. Leah, sitting on the bench with little Rachel asleep in her lap and her stepdaughter leaning against her shoulder. Myra, her face filled with a peace Anna hadn't seen there in what seemed a long time. Barbara, cutting slabs of apple walnut cake that Esther was passing around.

Her people, Anna thought again, as she'd thought when they'd put themselves between Gracie and danger. Not saints, just ordinary people who loved her. Her family.

"Did she go to sleep all right, poor lamb?" Barbara asked. "She wasn't still upset, was she?"

"No, she is fine." Anna hesitated, feeling as if she should say something to them, something of how she felt, of how dear they were to her.

"Ser gut," Leah said softly, her face communicating she knew exactly what Anna was thinking. "Everything is gut now."

Anna nodded, sure that if she did try to speak, she would burst into tears.

"Samuel insisted on going out to check

on the horses," Myra said, her voice casual. "If you wanted to go out for a breath of air, you might tell him there's cake and coffee ready anytime he wants."

Anna's heart filled. "Ja. I will." She went quickly out the back door.

They would talk about her and Samuel once she'd gone, but that didn't bother her as it once had. She understood now that it was all in love.

Their voices faded as she walked out into the cool evening. She stepped off the porch and paused. Would Samuel have gone over to his barn?

But there he was, leaning on the fence, watching the young colt grazing in the ring. Like a bird heading for its nest, she went to him.

He shifted toward her as she walked across the grass and joined him at the fence. His face was so battered that she grew in a shaken breath at the sight, but his eyes were peaceful.

"How are you?" She touched his hand where it lay on the rail, and he clasped hers instantly.

"I am well." He smiled. "Contented, I think, is the right word. Do you know what

I realized today, when I was lying on the barn floor?"

"That you should never have gotten involved in my troubles?"

"No. Never that." Gentle humor edged the words. "I realized how foolish I'd been, with all my worries about whether I would make the same mistakes my father did." He turned to face her, clasping her hand in both of his. "I knew then that I was ready to die for you and Gracie. If I would die for you, how can I doubt that I would live for you, always?"

He'd stolen her breath away. "Are you so sure of me?" she said when she could finally speak. "I have a bad history of running away when things are difficult."

"I'm not worried." His eyes were tranquil. "You will not run anymore. I love you, Anna, but I won't rush you. Take as much time as you want to answer."

She realized the answer didn't require any time at all. It was already there, in her heart. She'd come home in desperation, but it was God leading her to the place where she needed to be. The only place where she could be the person she really was in her heart.

She smiled, looking at him. "November is not so far off," she said. "If Bishop Mose thinks I'm ready to be baptized into the church, we can be married then. I have a feeling I would like to follow tradition in that."

"Anna Beiler, following tradition," Samuel said. "Think of that. Are you sure?"

"I'm sure." She lifted her face for his kiss. "The prodigal is home to stay."

EPILOGUE

Anna took the black prayer kapp from her head and set it carefully on top of the bureau. She picked up the white one that sat waiting and placed it on her head.

The act seemed almost as solemn as the vows she and Samuel had taken moments earlier before Bishop Mose and the gathered community. She and Samuel were husband and wife. In a moment she'd meet him to go back downstairs to take part in the wedding meal—their first appearance together as a married couple.

"Anna, do you need any help?" Leah paused in the bedroom doorway, smiling at her. "You are a bride, little sister. I am so happy to see this day."

"Denke." Anna blinked back the tears that sprang to her eyes. "I wish Mammi—"

Leah came quickly to hug her. "I know she would be very happy. She always liked Samuel so much."

"She did, didn't she?" Even when Samuel had been just Joseph's friend, Mammi seemed to have a soft spot in her heart for him. Now he was her daughter's husband. Leah was right; Mammi would be pleased.

"The food is ready to start serving." Myra came in, her eyes growing moist as she looked at Anna. "But first I had to come and see my sister."

"Twice your sister," Anna said, her heart filling with love.

Myra was rounder now, though it didn't show so much when she wore the cape, as she did today in honor of the occasion. She and Joseph had moved past the difficult adjustment they'd had to make into a state of serenity about the baby. The shadows were gone from Myra's eyes, and she seemed to look ahead with joy.

"Your friend from the city didn't know what to think of the wedding." Myra's eyes twinkled. "She asked if you were forbidden to wear a bridal gown because of the baby. I told her this is your bridal gown, but I don't think she understood."

Anna smoothed her hand down the skirt of the deep blue dress she wore, made by her own hands with a little help from Myra. And the white apron, which would be kept to be put on over her dress when she was buried. She wouldn't tell Liz that—it would be too much culture shock.

"No, Liz wouldn't understand, but I think she is happy for me." Liz had gotten over her initial surprise at learning Anna was Amish. She'd probably been a little hurt, too, that Anna had kept that from her, but she seemed to understand. And she had traveled all the way from Chicago to sit on a backless bench in a barn for three hours to see her friend married.

"Rosemary has taken her in hand," Leah said. "She'll explain it all."

Anna nodded. Rosemary had proved to be a staunch friend to the Amish. She'd begun volunteering at the medical clinic, filling her days with work that was valuable to the whole community.

"I have gut friends and family. I owe

you all so much . . ." She couldn't find the words.

"Ach, enough," Leah said. "There's no talk of owing among family."

"Besides, your groom is here, waiting to take you downstairs." Myra gave her a little shove toward the bedroom door.

There in the hallway, Samuel stood waiting, holding Gracie in his arms. He'd been solemn for the ceremony, but now his lips curved with pleasure at the sight of her.

She went to him quickly. "I thought Elizabeth was watching the little ones."

"Ach, how could our Gracie not sit with us at the eck table for our wedding?" Samuel cuddled her close. "She is our daughter, so she must share the joy of this day."

"Until she starts to fuss at being still for so long," Anna said, but her heart was touched by his gesture.

No, not a gesture. Samuel really did feel that way. He had been willing to lay down his life for Gracie. No one could love more than that.

She reached toward him, and Samuel drew her immediately into the loving circle of his arm for a warm, strong hug.

"So," he said, dropping a kiss lightly on

her lips, "are you ready to go downstairs and greet our friends as husband and wife, Anna Fisher?"

"I am." She said the words like a vow. She linked her arm with Samuel's, and they started down the stairs toward the waiting crowd.

Below, she saw the happy faces of those who waited for them—the dear, familiar faces of all who loved and supported them. Her family, her church, her friends. They would stand by this new family through all the years ahead, God willing, and she would be forever grateful that God had brought her home.

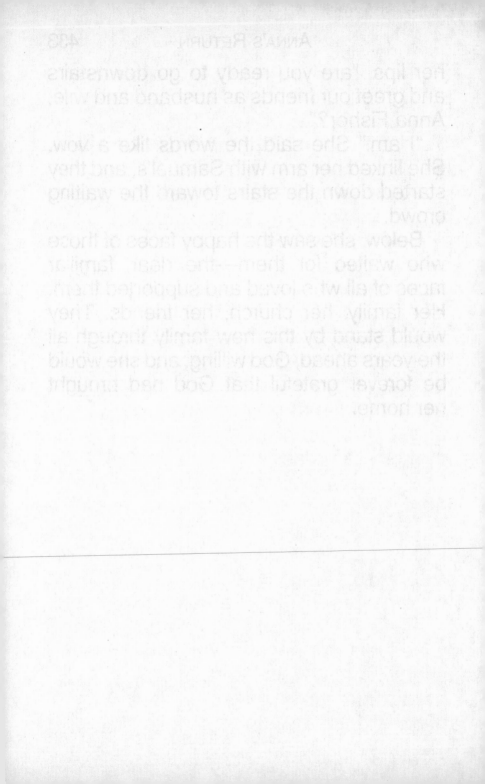

blaid. bashful

boppli. baby

bruder. brother

bu. boy

buwe. boys

daadi. daddy

Da Herr sei mit du. The Lord be with you.

denke. thanks (or *danki*)

Englischer. one who is not Plain

ferhoodled. upset; distracted

ferleicht. perhaps

frau. wife

fress. eat

gross. big

grossdaadi. grandfather

grossdaadi haus. An addition to the farmhouse, built for the grandparents to live in once they've "retired" from actively running the farm.

grossmutter. grandmother

gut. good

hatt. hard; difficult

haus. house

hinnersich. backward

ich. I

ja. yes

kapp. Prayer covering, worn in obedience to the Biblical injunction that women

GLOSSARY OF PENNSYLVANIA DUTCH
WORDS AND PHRASES

ach. oh; used as an exclamation
agasinish. stubborn; self-willed
ain't so. A phrase commonly used at the
end of a sentence to invite agreement.
alter. old man
anymore. Used as a substitute for "nowa-
days."
Ausbund. Amish hymnal. Used in the
worship services, it contains traditional
hymns, words only, to be sung without
accompaniment. Many of the hymns
date from the sixteenth century.
befuddled. mixed up
blabbermaul. talkative one

should pray with their heads covered. Kapps are made of Swiss organdy and are white. (In some Amish communities, unmarried girls thirteen and older wear black kapps during worship service.)

kinder. kids (or *kinner*)

komm. come

komm schnell. come quick

Leit. the people; the Amish

lippy. sassy

maidal. old maid; spinster

mamm. mother

meddaagesse. lunch

mind. remember

onkel. uncle

Ordnung. The agreed-upon rules by which the Amish community lives. When new practices become an issue, they are discussed at length among the leadership. The decision for or against innovation is generally made on the basis of maintaining the home and family as separate from the world. For instance, a telephone might be necessary in a shop in order to conduct business but would be banned from the home because it would intrude on family time.

Pennsylvania Dutch. The language is actually German in origin and is primarily a spoken language. Most Amish write in English, which results in many variations in spelling when the dialect is put into writing! The language probably originated in the south of Germany but is common also among the Swiss Mennonite and French Huguenot immigrants to Pennsylvania. The language was brought to America prior to the Revolution and is still in use today. High German is used for Scripture and church documents, while English is the language of commerce.

rumspringa. Running-around time. The late teen years when Amish youth taste some aspects of the outside world before deciding to be baptized into the church.

schnickelfritz. mischievous child

ser gut. very good

tastes like more. delicious

Was ist letz? What's the matter?

Wie bist du heit. how are you; said in greeting

wilkom. welcome

Wo bist du? Where are you?

RECIPES

Chicken Potpie

For noodles: Mix together 1 tablespoon butter, $1/2$ teaspoon salt, and 2 cups flour. Add 2 beaten eggs and 2 tablespoons milk. Mix together until a firm dough forms, then turn onto a floured board and roll out in a thin layer. Let stand for 30 minutes. Cut into 2-inch squares.

2 potatoes
2 onions, sliced thin

3 cups cooked chicken, cut into bite-sized pieces
2 cups hot chicken stock
salt
pepper
parsley, chopped

Slice potatoes ¼-inch thick. Line the bottom of a heavy kettle with potato slices. Add a layer of noodles, then a layer of onions, and sprinkle with salt, pepper, and parsley. Add a layer of chicken. Repeat all layers, including potatoes, using up all the ingredients. Pour boiling chicken stock over all. Cover tightly and simmer on the stove top for 20 to 30 minutes, until potatoes are tender.

Funnel Cakes

3 eggs
2 cups milk
¾ cup sugar
3–4 cups flour
½ teaspoon salt
2 teaspoons baking powder
vegetable oil
confectioners' sugar

Beat eggs in a small mixing bowl, then add milk and sugar. In a separate large bowl, sift together half the flour with the salt and baking powder. Add the milk and egg mixture. Beat batter until it is smooth. Add only as much more flour as is needed to make a batter just thin enough to run through a funnel. To a large, heavy skillet add vegetable oil until it is two inches deep. Heat oil until hot. Drop dough through the funnel into hot oil, twisting the funnel as the batter falls to make swirled shapes, each one seven to eight inches round. Cook until the bottom is light brown, then turn and cook the other side until it is also light brown. Remove with a slotted spoon and drain on paper or linen towels. While still warm but not hot, dust with confectioners' sugar.

End-of-the-Garden Relish

12 large green peppers
12 sweet red peppers
12 large onions
1 small head cauliflower
1 stalk celery
3 cups sugar

3 tablespoons salt
2 tablespoons mustard seed
1 quart apple cider vinegar

Substitute cucumbers or other types of peppers as desired. Core and remove seeds from peppers. Remove ends and outside layers from onions and the ends from the celery. Remove stem and any leaves from cauliflower. Chop the vegetables to a fine dice and combine them in a large stockpot. Add the sugar, salt, mustard seed, and apple cider vinegar (white vinegar can also be used). Cook over high heat for about 15 minutes. While still boiling, ladle into hot, sterilized canning jars and cap.

Dear Reader,

I'm so glad you decided to pick up this book, and I hope you enjoyed it. I appreciated having the opportunity to tell the story of Anna and her growth since she was first introduced in Leah's Choice, *and also to visit Pleasant Valley again.*

I would love to hear your thoughts about my book. If you'd care to write to me, I'd be happy to reply with a signed bookmark or bookplate and my brochure of Pennsylvania Dutch recipes. You can find me on the Web at www.martaperry.com, e-mail me at marta@martaperry.com, or write to me in care of Berkley Publicity Department, Penguin Group (USA) Inc., 375 Hudson Street, New York, NY 10014.

**Blessings,
Marta Perry**

An Excerpt from

LEAH'S CHOICE

Pleasant Valley
BOOK ONE

by Marta Perry

Knowing your proper place was a basic tenet of Amish life. Leah Beiler smiled as she watched her class of thirty-five scholars living out that belief. The number was up by three with the addition of the Glick children just today, and they were all in their assigned seats. Thirty-five heads bent over the work she'd set for her first- to eighth-graders, and not a whisper disturbed the stillness of the one-room school.

Despite the quiet, ten years of teaching had given Leah an extra sense where her scholars were concerned. Excitement rippled through the room, even though no head lifted for a furtive look at the battery clock on her desk. The prospect of a picnic lunch to welcome the newcomers had everyone, including, she had to admit, the teacher, excited. It would be a welcome break in the usual routine, with the Christmas program now in the distant past and their end-of-school-year events not yet begun.

The April weather had cooperated today, bathing Pleasant Valley, Pennsylvania, in sunshine rather than showers. Through the window, she could see the horses and buggies lined up outside that told her the scholars' mothers had arrived with food for the picnic.

She clapped her hands, amused at the alacrity with which pencils were put down. "It's time for our picnic lunch now, scholars. We'll eat first, and then there will be time to play. You may go outside."

It wasn't necessary to add that they should go in an orderly manner. Order was another precept of Amish life, ingrained since birth. Pencils were in their grooves on the desktops and books were closed before the children stood, murmuring quietly among themselves, and filed toward the door.

Leah followed her scholars between the rows of wood and wrought-iron desks, and out the door at the rear of the classroom that led onto a small porch and then to the schoolyard.

The white school building, looking like every other Amish school she'd ever seen, stood in a grove of trees, its narrow dirt lane leading out to the main road, a good half mile away. The Esch farm lay to their east and the Brand farm to the west, so that the schoolhouse seemed to nestle in their protective, encircling arms.

A trestle table had been set up under the oak tree that sheltered the yard. Her volunteer mothers and grandmothers, probably also happy with the break in routine, had spread it with a bountiful lunch—sandwich fixings of cheese, chicken, cold meat and bread, an array of salads, bowls of fruit, and jars of milk and lemonade. Trays of cupcakes and brownies were covered, reminding the children that dessert came last.

Rachel Brand, Leah's special friend since

girlhood, hurried over, apron fluttering, to thrust a well-filled plate into her hands. "Leah, I fixed a plate for you already, ja. If you waited for everyone else to be served, you might miss my macaroni salad."

"Never," she said, her pleasure at the day's treat increased by the presence of the friend who was as dear to her as a sister. "It's wonderful kind of you, Rachel, but we should be seeing to our guest of honor first."

Daniel Glick, the newcomer, stood out in the group, the only adult male in a bevy of women and children. If that bothered him, he didn't show it. He was accepting a heaping plate from Leah's mother, bending over her with courteous attention.

"Your mamm is taking good care of him," Rachel said. "And if she wasn't, someone else would jump at the chance, for sure. A widower just come from Lancaster to join our community—you know every woman in Pleasant Valley will be thinking to match him up with a daughter or sister, they will."

"They'd do better not to matchmake. Daniel Glick looks well able to decide for himself if he needs a wife."

Daniel's firm jaw and the determined set

to his broad shoulders under the plain work shirt he wore suggested a man who knew what he wanted and who wouldn't be easily deflected from his course. He was probably a gut hand at avoiding any unwanted matchmaking.

Rachel, her blue eyes dancing with mischief as if they were ten again, nudged her. "You'd best tell that to your mamm, then. I expect she's already inviting him to supper so he can get to know you."

"Me?" Her voice squeaked a bit, so she was glad that she and Rachel stood a little apart from the others. "Rachel, that's foolish. Everyone has known for years that I'm a maidal."

"Years," Rachel scoffed, her rosy cheeks growing rounder with amusement.

Rachel did still look like the girl she'd once been, her kapp strings flying as they'd chased each other in a game in this same schoolyard. Leah couldn't remember a time when Rachel hadn't been part of her life. They'd shared enough joy and sorrow to bond them forever.

"I know very well how old you are, Leah Beiler," Rachel continued, "because we were born within a month of each other.

And you are only an old maid if you want to be."

Leah crinkled her nose. "A maidal," she said firmly. "And I'm a schoolteacher with a love of learning besides, which frightens men off."

Rachel's smile slid away suddenly, and her smooth brow furrowed. "Leah, it would break my heart if I thought you meant to stay single all your life because of Johnny."

The name startled her, and it was all she could do to keep dismay from showing on her face. When Johnny Kile left Pleasant Valley, fence-jumping to the English world like too many young men, he'd left behind his family, including his twin sister, Rachel, who'd loved him dearly.

And he'd left Leah, the girl he'd said he'd loved. The girl he'd planned to marry that November, once the harvest season was over.

Many of those young men who left came back, penitent and ready to rejoin the community, after a brief time in the English world. But not Johnny.

She had to speak, or Rachel would think this more serious than it was. Close as they were, she didn't want Rachel to know how Johnny's loss had grieved her. It would only hurt Rachel, to no good end.

"No, of course that's not why. Johnny and I were no more than boy-and-girl sweethearts, you know that."

Rachel's hand closed over hers in a brief, warm grip. "You loved him. That's what I know."

"It was a long time ago," she said firmly, shutting away bittersweet memories.

An Excerpt from

RACHEL'S GARDEN

Pleasant Valley

BOOK TWO

by Marta Perry

A flicker of movement from the lane beyond the kitchen window of the old farmhouse caught Rachel Brand's eye as she leaned against the sink, washing up the bowl she'd used to make a batch of snickerdoodles. A buggy—ja, it must be Leah Glick, already bringing home Rachel's two older kinder from the birthday party for their teacher.

Quickly she set the bowl down and splashed cold water on her eyes. It wouldn't do to let her young ones suspect that their mamm had been crying while she baked. Smoothing her hair back under her kapp and arranging a smile on her lips, she went to the back door.

But the visitor was not Leah. It was a man alone, driving the buggy.

Shock shattered her curiosity when she recognized the strong face under the brim of the black Amish hat. Gideon Zook. Her fingers clenched, wrinkling the fabric of her dark apron. What did he want from her?

She stood motionless for a moment, her left hand tight on the door frame. Then she grabbed the black wool shawl that hung by the door, threw it around her shoulders, and stepped outside.

The cold air sent a shiver through her. It was mid-March already, but winter had not released its grip on Pleasant Valley, Pennsylvania. The snowdrops she had planted last fall quivered against the back step, their white cups a mute testimony that spring would come eventually. Everything else was as brown and barren as her heart felt these days.

A fierce longing for spring swept through her as she crossed the still-hard ground. If she could be in the midst of growing things,

planting and nurturing her beloved garden—
ach, there she might find the peace she
longed for.

Everything was too quiet on the farm
now. Even the barn was empty, the dairy
cows already moved to the far field, taken
care of by her young brother-in-law Wil-
liam in the early morning hours.

The Belgian draft horses Ezra had been
so pleased to be able to buy were spending the winter at the farm of his oldest
brother, Isaac. Only Dolly, six-year-old Joseph's pet goat, bleated forlornly from her
pen, protesting his absence.

Gideon had tethered his horse to the
hitching post. Removing something from
his buggy, he began pacing across the
lawn, as if he measured something.

Then he saw her. He stopped, waiting.
His hat was pushed back, and he lifted his
face slightly, as if in appreciation of the
watery sunshine. But Gideon's broad shoulders were stiff under his black jacket, his
eyes wary, and his mouth set above his
beard.

Reluctance slowed her steps. Perhaps
Gideon felt that same reluctance. Aside

from the formal words of condolence he'd spoken to her once he was well enough to be out again after the accident, she and Gideon had managed to avoid talking to each other for months. That was no easy thing in a tight-knit Amish community.

She forced a smile. "Gideon, wilkom. I didn't expect to be seeing you today."

What are you doing here? That was what she really wanted to say.

"Rachel." He inclined his head slightly, studying her face as if trying to read her feelings.

His own face gave little away—all strong planes and straight lines, like the wood he worked with in his carpentry business. Lines of tension radiated from his brown eyes, making him look older than the thirty-two she knew him to be. His work-hardened hands tightened on the objects he grasped—small wooden stakes, sharpened to points.

He cleared his throat, as if not sure what to say to her now that they were face-to-face. "How are you? And the young ones?"

"I'm well." Except that her heart twisted

with pain at the sight of him, at the reminder he brought of all she had lost. "The
kinder also. Mary is napping, and Leah
Glick took Joseph and Becky to a birthday
luncheon the scholars are having for Mary
Yoder."

"Gut, gut."

He moved a step closer to her, and she
realized that his left leg was still stiff—a
daily reminder for him, probably, of the accident.

For an instant the scene she'd imagined
so many times flashed yet again through
her mind, stealing her breath away. She
seemed to see Ezra, high in the rafters of
a barn, Gideon below him, the old timbers
creaking, then breaking, Ezra falling as
the barn collapsed like a house of cards . . .

She gasped a strangled breath, like a
fish struggling on the bank of the pond.
Revulsion wrung her stomach, and she
slammed the door shut on her imagination.

She could not let herself think about
that, not now. It was not Gideon's fault
that she couldn't see him without imagining the accident that had taken Ezra away

from them. She had to talk to him sensi-
bly, had to find out what had brought him
here. And how she could get him to go
away again.